Tattered Wings

SUSAN KEENE

Published by Stray Dog Press, LLC

ISBN-13: 978-0-9898831-0-8

DEDICATION

To Molly and Diane, with love.

Other Publications by Susan Keene

Finding Lizzy Smith (Kate Nash 1)
Who's Roxy Watkins? (Kate Nash 2)
The Twisted Mind of Cletus Compton

Acknowledgments

Thanks to Ozarks Romance Authors and Sleuths Ink members for all of your support. You inspired me to get this book finished.

A special thanks to Susie Knust for editing, to Kylie Douglas for the cover art, and to Sharon Kizziah-Holmes for putting it all together.

Chapter One

Ian Michaels only had one foot in the back door when Maggie stepped into his office.

"Ian, I'm glad you're here. There's a girl in the waiting room. She says she must see you."

"Who is she?"

"She's the sister of the Johnston kid who supposedly killed all of those people."

"Why does she want to see me?"

"She didn't say. When I drove up this morning she was sitting on the steps. I told her it would be best to have an appointment, but she wouldn't leave."

"Strange." Ian shed his overcoat.

The phone rang and Maggie reached over the desk to answer it. "Ian Michael's office, may I help you?" There was a pause before she spoke again. "Yes, I'll tell him. One moment please." She pushed the mute button and looked up at her boss. "It's the district attorney's office. Tom Waters wants to speak to you."

The lawyer shrugged his shoulders. His practice

1

was almost exclusively divorce oriented with a few corporate accounts and wills for old friends and neighbors. None of his clients warranted a call from the district attorney. Taking the phone from his secretary, he pushed the button to activate the sound. "This is Ian Michaels. How can I help you, Tom?"

"I'm calling about the Johnston boy."

"Why me?"

"In his initial interview he told me you were his attorney."

"This is the first I've heard about it. I don't handle criminal cases."

"I didn't think so, but the kid had your business card. He gave it to me himself."

"If it weren't for him having my card, I'd say I was a random pick. I don't want any part of it, truthfully, I haven't followed the case. Isn't he just a kid, fifteen or sixteen?"

"He's sixteen."

"What do his parents say?"

"They're not in the picture. Because he's a minor, we tried to get them down here. I finally sent a patrol car for his father and we hauled him to the station. He sat in on the interview. All he did was say over and over he had done all he could. I think he's relieved the kid's in jail."

"My suggestion is that you get him a public defender. Isn't that standard in a case like this?"

"I would think you would want to see him if only to find out where he got your card. So, his parents haven't contacted you?"

"No, but his sister is camped out in my waiting

room. She told my secretary she couldn't leave without seeing me."

"Well, let me know what you decide to do," Tom continued. "He's a strange little bastard."

"I want no part of this. I don't intend to see him or his sister. Get him a public defender."

Ian set the phone in its cradle and turned toward Maggie. "Tell the girl we're too busy to see her today."

Maggie stood rooted to her spot. "Don't you have the slightest curiosity about her?"

"Not really."

"She's awfully upset."

The phone rang again. Maggie turned on her heel and walked toward the door leading to the waiting room and her desk. "I'll answer that from out here."

Ian pushed away from his desk turning his chair toward the window. The panoramic view of Forest Park below always made him feel better. He was beginning to relax his way into the day when his secretary came back into the room.

"Yes, Maggie?" He had a feeling about what was coming next.

"Ian, please see the girl. She isn't going to leave and what we're going to end up with is a nasty scene if we've got to have her removed. It's only a couple of minutes out of our day. Your first appointment isn't due for over an hour."

Turning to face his secretary he heaved a heavy sigh and stood. Taking his time, he stretched each muscle in his neck and back until some of the tightness was gone. Maybe he was overreacting.

3

What could it hurt if he saw her?

He was suddenly tired as he followed Maggie to where the girl was waiting.

A slow sweep of the outer office showed nothing had changed. Everything was as he wanted it- but for the girl. She sat tucked into a massive chair at the far side of the room, near the exit.

There she was, crumpled like a rag doll. Her clothes were neat and clean. She wore skinny jeans and a crop top and looked like a thousand other teenage girls he had passed on the street.

Maggie was at her desk, busy with the computer. Ian looked at her and back to the girl. "So you're still here?" he said.

The girl didn't answer him. All he got was a slight nod of her elfish head.

"Bring Miss Johnston into my office," Ian said in a voice that cut the unnerving quiet in the room.

Maggie jumped to her feet. "Yes sir." Ian could feel her hot stare on his back. He was out of the room before her words reached him.

He looked up as his secretary and the girl walked into the room. He saw Maggie give the child a smile.

How could someone so small and insignificant looking, so young, be the cause of so much uneasiness in a grown man?

"You've been waiting a long time, Miss Johnston," he said in his most businesslike voice.

"How's it you think I can help you?"

"I've come about my brother." She wiped her hands on her jeans, and then massaged her temples.

"What about him?"

4

She glanced over to Maggie and then back to him before she spoke. At five feet six inches Maggie's tall lean slender body looked huge next to the child. The kid sat ramrod straight with a poise well beyond her age, quite different from the waif he had encountered in the waiting room. Ian watched as Maggie nodded at the girl and gave her another smile.

"My brother wants you to come to the jail and talk to him."

"Why me?" Huge tears began rolling down the teenager's cheek, staining her already tired and worried looking face. He hated to see a woman cry.

"I don't know. I'm only doing what he asked me to do."

"Don't cry," he said, acknowledging her tears. "Maggie, would you get our guest a tissue?"

It wasn't in his nature to make the girl suffer, but he didn't want to encourage her, either. He overcame the urge to relax and lean back in his chair. "Let me explain my position. I'm not the kind of lawyer your brother needs. He seeks an attorney who handles crime. I don't do that. You'll have to explain that to him."

"Mr. Michaels. You don't know Kenny. He'll haunt you, make your life miserable, until he gets his way."

Ian slammed his hand on the desk with much more force than he intended. "Do not threaten me, young lady."

"I'm not threatening you. I just want you to understand." Her hands trembled as her voice quivered in a bizarre unison. She hesitated before she continued. "Kenny is – well – different. He's got no one to help him- only me – and I don't want to. Our parents are divorced, our mother doesn't live here. Our step-mother won't lift a finger to help. She wants it known he's not hers and she's not responsible for what he did. My dad, well, he does what needs to be done to keep peace in the family. I think he's seen Kenny once because the cops came and got him." She was talking so fast, Ian couldn't stop her until she paused.

"I understand he's your brother, but your family's best course of action is to contact the public defender's office. They'll appoint someone to represent Kenny." He stood to indicate the interview was over.

The girl looked at Ian but remained seated. "Kenny doesn't want a public defender. He wants you." He could see she had no intention of leaving now. He saw fear in her eyes. After taking a deep breath, Ian glanced toward Maggie. She'd been watching the entire exchange as if it was a tennis match. He wondered why she seemed to be rooting for the girl.

Ian was still standing. Tension hung like stale air in the room. A man beaten at his own game, he looked down at the tiny girl as if for the first time. He let his body fall back into the familiar seat behind him.

"What's your name?"

"Amber."

"How old are you?"

"Seventeen."

"All right Amber, I'll speak to your brother. I'm

only going to find out what's going on, and how I became a part of it. I'm not consenting to defend him."

Amber all but melted in her chair. The expression in her eyes was what he imagined he would see in the eyes of a convict getting a stay of execution ten seconds before the switch was thrown. "I'll drop by the jail tomorrow."

"Oh, Mr. Michaels, thank you, thank you, and thank you." For a minute Ian thought the teen was going to come over the desk and hug him. Instead she backed out of the room, tripping over things as she went. She mumbled to herself as she left the office.

Maggie and Ian sat in silence. Ian turned his chair toward the window.

Why was the girl so afraid?

"Maggie," he said.

"Yes, Ian?"

"Can you get me the papers with the accounts of all the murder and mayhem the boy's supposed to be a part of? And call your buddy over at the court house. Find out what they're saying. Not the official stuff, I want to know what they really think." He glanced at his watch. "How does the rest of the day look?"

"Mark Robertson will be here at eleven and we've got Mrs. Schneider and her will at two. At four- thirty David Marshall's coming by to sign his custody papers and go over the terms of visitation.

All in all we have a light day."

"Thanks." He remained staring out the window.

"Was there anything else?" He was lost in

thought and had forgotten she was still sitting there. "You can go. Let me know when Mark gets here."

Ian heard the door close softly behind her as she went back to her office. He stood and ran his hand from his collar to his waist to straighten his tie and leaned on the window sill. He could see Amber running down the street and he shook his head.

"Mark Robertson's here."

"Send him in."

He was never fond of Mondays.

Chapter Two

Amber left the lawyer's office in a dead run. When she got outside she kept running, knocking into everyone and everything in her path. The pounding of her heart hammered in her ears. She wanted to stop, but she was out of control. She tripped and a man behind her almost knocked her down. He tried to steady her. She wrenched away and took refuge next to an old brick office building. Tears streamed down her cheeks as she laid her hot face against its cool facade. It felt moist and soothing. Her hands still shook and her eyes blurred from the cold and wind.

The sky was turning gray and the wind picked up. As she stood there, trying to get her bearings, the wind increased from blowing to howling.

She was miles away from home, not knowing what to do next. The house she shared with her family was in the next county.

Her dad and step-mother, Shauna, would assume she was at school and would then go to her part-time job. This was her senior year. She wanted to make as much money as she could to get as far away from all of them as possible. Even so, she sometimes felt she would never escape; she knew her memories would follow her wherever she went.

She couldn't go home. It was the lesser of two evils: going home to face Shauna with where she had been and what she had done, or finding someplace to pass the time.

Amber grimaced at her own pathetic joke. There was no choice. She would go home at her regular time and pray Shauna never found out she went to the lawyer's office.

After wandering the streets for what seemed like hours, Amber stopped at a movie theater halfway down the block. Halfway down which block, she wasn't sure. Fumbling through her purse she pulled out the money to pay the admission and went inside out of the cold.

She took a seat near the back of the auditorium. She tried to get interested in the film playing but it was no use. Laying her purse on her lap, she examined her hands. Her fingers were blue and aching from the bitter cold.

It troubled her to be so afraid of Kenny. It didn't seem possible to be out of his reach. Her first memories of Kenny, in fact all of her memories of him, were thoughts of pain, suffering and humiliation.

As close as she could recall, it started when she was six and he was five. Was it her fault he was in jail today? Could she have done anything to change him? She didn't know. It was like all of the horror he perpetrated came so naturally to him. All of the pain and hatefulness and deceit came out of him as easily as laughter escaped from the rest of the children she knew.

It all began playing out on the movie screen; she looked up to watch it.

There she was, playing with a toy train, happy and singing, when her little brother came into the room. Kenny demanded the train. Amber ignored him and kept playing. Simple sibling rivalry, yet it grew into something more. Kenny stormed off like any other petulant child only to come back with a hammer smashing it into her hand, over and over again in a rage, until her screams summoned help and he was forced to stop.

Her hand ached now as she relived it.

There was Daddy, running toward her screams. She smiled at the tenderness with which he comforted her. All but two bones in her hand were broken. Her brother's explanation of the accident rang in her ears as though the movie was real. "Daddy the train wouldn't work. I was fixing it and Amber put her hand down." Tears ran down his cheeks as he explained. Even at her age she knew they were faked. He was proud of what he'd done.

After his heartfelt apology, Kenny turned his attention to Amber with a stare she would never forget. It was superiority, hate, contempt, and evil, all rolled into one flat-eyed hateful glare. It was a look she would see many times in her young life.

Could she have stopped him then? Kenny, after all, wasn't yet six years old.

Thank God he was gone. With him out of the house she could sleep- well-sometimes.

Other times she awoke and sat bolt upright in cold sweat thinking about Kenny and the last time he made his way back to haunt her. She was still chilled yet clammy with emotion. She tried again to watch the film playing in front of her, but the story of her childhood was still on the screen.

Kenny invaded her entire mind. He always had. Most things she did in life were with him in mind. Don't upset him. Don't get in his way. Stay away from home as much as possible. Don't talk more than necessary. It didn't help that Kenny, although a typical skinny teenage boy, was almost twice her size.

Her mind insisted on reliving the past.

...It was the first day in the new house. Shauna and their father had married the week before. Their new mother had two children of her own and the three of them were out shopping, leaving Kenny, Amber and their dad at home. The entire blended family had worked on the house for weeks. It was freshly painted and scrubbed. The yard, however, was a mess. A large porch ran the entire length of the back of the house. Shauna called it a veranda and talked about how and when they would use it. There were three separate sets of stairs off the porch leading to the back yard. It was quite pretty except it was ill kept and weeds overtook everything. It was almost impossible to see the steps.

Kenny was eight years old. His father showed him the finer points of using a sickle to cut the weeds to get them short enough to mow, and then he walked off to find the lawnmower. Amber stood on the porch watching the high grass fall with every purposeful swipe.

Kenny stopped cutting. Bending over he came up with a shiny piece of metal.

There was genuine excitement in his voice when he called to Amber. He said he had found a real treasure. Without thinking she jumped down into the yard to join him. Kenny grabbed the sickle as fast as he had thrown it down. With both hands and all of his power, he took a giant swipe in her direction. She didn't feel anything at first, standing there, looking down, not quite knowing what happened. Then she saw the blood and heard Kenny screaming for their dad to come.

"Daddy, Daddy!" he lied. "I was cutting and then, suddenly, there was Amber. I cut her, didn't I? Oh, I'm so sorry. Daddy, will she be okay?"

Her dad picked her up in his huge arms "Kenny, get the car keys and meet us in the driveway." Laying his young daughter in the back seat of his old Toyota, he wrapped her leg and set Kenny next to her holding pressure on it until they arrived at the emergency room. Oh, he held pressure on it alright. Once in a while when she dared open her eyes, Kenny would give her his hateful flat eyed glare followed by a smirk.

It took sixty-four stitches to close the wound.

Amber lay in the stark white emergency room pale and frightened. Kenny appeared so shaken by the incident he was allowed to hold her hand while they stitched her leg. She looked for an opportunity to tell how it really happened. With any mention of the *how* of the accident, Kenny would squeeze her hand with all of his might and fix his icy stare on her.

Her fear of him was overpowering.

She spent most the summer sitting out of the usual fun things. No swimming or bike riding-but lots of time to reflect on what had happened and devising plans to stay away from her younger brother at all times.

She never told a soul what he did.

When she realized Kenny could and would kill her without a second thought, her fear became paralyzing.

Dead pets showed up all over the neighborhood and no one could figure what was happening to them. Amber knew. How stupid could they be? It was obvious, even to a child, these animals were brutally murdered.

She knew something drove Kenny because he never let up.

Amber's solution was simple and straightforward. Every night she got on her knees and prayed Kenny would have an accident or contact a fatal disease and die.

It never happened.

There were minor abuses and major abuses.

"Here, Amber." Kenny said handing her a hot dog for lunch. "Shauna asked me to bring you this."

He handed her the sandwich, loaded, the way she liked. Later she found out the rest of the kids had had peanut butter and jelly for lunch while she ate a rancid hot dog out of the neighbor's trash. Kenny had doctored it up-just for her.

When Amber turned thirteen she thought things would change. She and Kenny no longer went to the same school. Never before had she realized how pleasant a simple school day could be. She made friends and spent as much time away from home as possible. For the first time she was happy and relaxed. She savored every minute away from Kenny. Her personality blossomed. Quick smiles and spontaneous laughter were now a part of her daily life and she loved it. Maybe there was hope after all.

When Kenny turned thirteen, his interest in her changed. He became obsessed with sex and thus-with her.

She shook herself out of the past. Even sitting in the warm theater she shuddered as more horrendous memories surfaced, and she wasn't able to stop them.

The movie played on.

New tortures began right before Christmas, the year she turned fourteen. By this time, there was another child in the house. Shauna and their father had a little girl of their own. All five of the children were invited to a party across town put on by a local church. Shauna was big on church. They were being picked up by the church van at seven.

There was a lot of hurrying and scurrying around trying to get all of them clean, dressed and ready at the same time. About ten minutes before they were ready to leave, Kenny took her aside and said he was staying home. She was to make sure no one noticed his absence or she would be sorry. If any of the younger kids asked about him, she was to shut them up and get them into the van. There was mass confusion as they were leaving. The vehicle was full of happy chattering children. Kenny walked out the door with them and slipped away. No one missed him.

As Amber and the children were leaving, she saw Kenny sneaking into the walkout basement where he hid near the sliding glass doors.

The next night Kenny forced Amber into his room. She tried to close her eyes and ears to him but she knew little about sex and voyeurism. She listened to his story with a mixture of horror, curiosity and embarrassment.

It seemed after they all left for the party, Shauna and Bob locked the house and went downstairs to the family room. Bob woke up the smoldering fire in the fireplace and joined his wife on the couch. They began talking, laughing, and enjoying their night at home alone. As the fire died to an amber glow, and the bottle of wine they shared was empty, they began to make love.

They had no reason to believe they were not alone so they made no effort to hide their nakedness or what they were doing. Kenny sat near the door, hidden and quiet, watching everything.

He described it detail by detail, sight and sound to his sister.

When the newness of his escapade wore off, he told her of new ways he found to amuse and arouse himself. Any money she could earn he would steal and use to buy books. He made Amber use her lunch money to help him. The books were full of ugly and perverted pictures.

Kenny made Amber do the things in the pictures.

The first time he asked, she refused. The next morning as she dressed for school she found a razor blade sharp edge up inside her shoe. It was all she could do to get through the day. That evening, she sat down to tend her wound only to get cut by more razor blades booby trapped to her bed. They cut her worse than the one in her shoe. Not knowing how to explain what happened and wanting to avoid another confrontation with Kenny, she tended the wounds herself.

Three days later, Amber got blood poisoning and spent five days in the hospital. She never refused Kenny again.

Even now, she could not stand for a boy to touch her. She was a popular girl. Boys were attracted to her and she enjoyed them- in a group. As soon as she was alone with one, she would freeze. The thought of one of them touching her made her stomach churn. She would picture Kenny holding her head between his legs and shouting horrible obscenities if she didn't meet his expectations.

Bile rose to her throat. She had to swallow hard to keep from vomiting.

Amber wasn't sure what had happened. She thanked God every day; however, for whatever was taking Kenny's attention away from her and onto someone else. One day, out of the blue, Kenny began a personal vendetta against Shauna. After he started his hateful reign of terror on his step-mother, he bestowed only token punishments on

Amber to keep her in line and afraid enough not to tell anyone about the past.

Life for Amber became livable again.

She glanced up at the movie screen. The film was still playing, or perhaps it was a different one. She didn't know. Standing, she buttoned her coat, slung her purse on her shoulder and walked out into the cold dark night.

On the way home she prayed the day would never come when Kenny was again free. The thought of seeing him sent a cold chill to her bones. She was at home and in bed for several hours before she felt warm and safe. She couldn't, however, shake a feeling of impending doom.

Chapter Three

Ian woke refreshed. As he showered and shaved he thought of nothing in particular. Then, like a bomb exploding, the debris of yesterday hit him hard. Remembering the task before him he put both hands on the bathroom vanity and looked into his own eyes. Why did the boy pick me?

The eyes stared back at him but provided no answer. He had a ritual he used when he was upset. It calmed him. Looking into the mirror, he gazed past his eyes and tried to connect with the one behind his eyes. For several minutes he stayed in that position. The tension in him faded as things went out of focus.

Pulling himself away from the mesmerizing stare, he strolled into the bedroom and looked down at the bed where his wife lay sleeping.

"Heather," he whispered, leaning down to kiss one of her partially exposed breasts. "Are you awake?"

She didn't answer. She raised a willowy arm and ran her finger tips up his arm resting her hand on the back of his neck. Twisting his hair around her fingers she pulled him toward her. Not bothering to open her eyes, she made a peaceful purring sound in his ear. Ian perched on the edge of the bed and kissed her lips. They were warm and inviting.

"Come back to bed," she breathed.

"I can't." He answered with regret. This time he kissed her on the cheek indicating their minds were not running in the same direction. His wife, of twenty years, pushed him away, opening her eyes for the first time. Ian watched as she searched his face as if to read his mind. There was no doubt that his unrest was apparent on his face.

"Ian, what's wrong?"

"Nothing I can't handle. Especially if I know you'll be waiting right here when I get home."

He patted the bed as he talked, trying to reassure himself as much as her.

Heather pulled the pale orange coverlet higher onto her shoulders and sat up. "Ian, I'm serious. What's going on?"

Ian moved away. Crossing the massive bedroom, in giant steps, he sat in a chair on the other side. Resting his elbows on his knees, he put his thumbs together near his face. From this vantage point, he looked over his fingertips toward his wife.

At forty-two Heather was as beautiful as she was at twenty, when they met. Her body was slim and firm. Her eyes sparkled and dimmed with her moods. He liked the way her blond hair circled her face and made a curly halo, giving her a perpetually soft aura.

"Ian," she said, and he flinched. "You were preoccupied last evening. I didn't want to say anything in front of the children, but now; I want to know what's distracting you."

"It's about the Johnston boy, the kid in the papers, the one who apparently killed six people."

Once he began talking it was a though he knew how he felt about everything. He wasn't sure what had changed. "I've decided to see the boy this afternoon." Ian proceeded to tell his wife in the minutest detail all of the events of the previous day.

"Will you defend him?" she asked when he finished.

"I don't know. I find it both intriguing and sick."

"It's your decision Ian, I won't interfere. What if it was Timothy?"

It would be difficult to picture Tim, his seventeen year old son, a murderer.

Tim was quiet and studious. He spent all of his extra time running cross country. Tim had his faults, but he was the kind of kid any parent would be proud of. Of course, he knew, it wasn't what she meant. Heather was referring to the fact that Kenny's parents didn't appear willing to help him. There had been no word from them except for the brief time his father was forced to be present when Kenny was charged.

The television showed reporters going to the Johnston's suburban home to interview them. They lived in a middle class neighborhood only about seven miles from his. The house they showed on the news was big and well kept. No one answered the door to reporters. Bob Johnston, Kenny's dad, supposedly hadn't shown up for work since the day of Kenny's arrest. Shauna Johnston, who had a beauty shop in the home, hadn't had a customer either. The younger children weren't in school. The house was dark. No one came or went. They were either holed up there like they committed the crimes themselves or they had moved somewhere else.

Ian knew the situation would be difficult for the family under any circumstances. It was, in this case, because everyone seemed to agree on one point- Kenny was guilty. No one disputed it.

It was like the day Ian went home after school and found his own father dead in bed.

He knew it would happen. The only thing he didn't know was when. Did the Johnston family know they lived with a walking time bomb?

They continued to discuss the pros and cons of the situation. There was the fee. He didn't know if there was anyone willing to foot the bill. From the looks of the house and cars the family drove and the clothes Amber wore, he was sure they could afford a lawyer. But, money wasn't the motivator in this case. For some reason he didn't care one way or the other about it. Why does a sixteen year old decide to go on a murderous spree? Finding the answer to that question was his motivation.

As they talked, Heather added a comment now and then. She said she believed he should take the case. After two hours of bantering with his wife and fighting with himself while Heather sat listening, the decision was made. He would take the case and defend the boy, if only to ease his own mind. But, like all decisions that don't turn out well, he would later spend hours going over whatever possessed him to make the choice he did.

Ian crossed the room and kissed his wife one last time before he headed to the downstairs den. There were several phone calls to make. His first phone call was to the St. Peter's Justice Center, only to find out Kenny was being held at the St. Charles County jail. His next call was to the jail. He knew he could call Maggie and have her do all of this yet, he felt the need to do something. His neat little world was becoming complicated. Ian was sure the decisions made upstairs would make it even more convoluted. He was okay with it.

After identifying himself as Attorney for the Defense, he requested copies of the arrest records and any pertinent statements along with the original probable cause warrants be sent by messenger to his office. Next, he called Tom Waters and made an appointment with him for the following day. If Tom had any remarks or thoughts about Ian's change of heart, he didn't voice them. His last call was to his own office on the private line. Maggie answered on the first ring. He was quiet and easy with her. He asked her to call the Johnston home, then call Jim Martin. Jim was a private investigator Ian had known for years. He told her to have Jim drop by the office. There was important and tedious leg work to be done, and Jim was the guy to do it. He was detail oriented, correct in his findings and stayed calm and detached no matter what. His last request was for Maggie to call St. Louis University and find a couple of law students to prepare histories and briefs as he knew the information he would need to dig through would be voluminous. This story had dominated the two major newspapers The Post-Dispatch in St. Louis and the Journal in St. Charles County, for many weeks. Going through everything would be a daunting task.

Hanging up the phone after his call to Maggie, he realized Heather was watching him from the doorway.

"What'll you do with your other clients?" she asked.

"Most of it is routine. I can do it with my eyes closed." It struck him odd to give such an answer. It never occurred to him before. Maybe it was the subconscious truth. Maybe he wanted to do this because he was bored with his practice? He shrugged off the thought for another time. Pushing himself away from the desk he forced a big over eager smile toward his wife. "Come on, I'm starving!" he added and playfully pushed Heather toward the kitchen.

The smell of bacon floated down the hall. He had walked down this hall hundreds of times over the years but never quite looked at it as he did today. Picture after picture of his boys, Timothy, Daniel and Benjamin from birth to the present, lined the walls on both sides. Happy scenes with Ian and Heather, snapshots of the kids alone and together were portrayed in numerous activities. It brought back memories of happy times with Heather and the kids. This huge collage depicted the fun and active childhoods of their three boys, and Ian again wondered about Kenny and his life as a toddler. He would find out soon enough. Right now the aroma of good food was drawing him closer to the kitchen. He heard his stomach growl. Ian quickened his pace to help ward off a feeling of dread rising in him.

Ian's favorite meal was breakfast. Rosemary, the housekeeper, made sure his favorites were fresh and hot. Today there was bacon and eggs over easy with Rosemary's warm, sweet homemade raisin bread. She had the massive oak sideboard, in the dining room, covered with cantaloupe, fresh pineapple and orange slices. Rosemary sat a heaping plate of food in front of him. He ate like a starving man, but noticed Heather had only one egg, no bread and a large helping of fresh fruit. He guessed Heather was watching her figure, as always. Ian was blessed to never have to worry about his weight. He ate when he was hungry and didn't worry about exercising unless it was something fun he wanted to do anyway. Handball in the park was one of his favorite pastimes. He kept clothes at the office in case the occasion arose he could grab a game in the middle of the day.

Heather and Ian ate in silence. He had wanted to keep the mood light. His efforts were wasted. He fought the urge to pick up the morning paper knowing it would be full of stories about the murders.

As it was, Heather's vivid blue eyes gave away her angst although he could see she was trying to be her always positive self. Ian shook his head. Boy, they were a great pair. Most of their life together had been spent skirting the issues between them. This morning when they talked was a rare moment, yet easier for them than most because it was about someone else. Ian had handled enough divorces and broken marriages to understand it was discussing intimate subjects that made couples stronger. It was a skill they both lacked.

He wanted to be honest. He knew Heather tried. It was too late now. Ian realized it as he glanced at his wife. Years and years of polite conversation and routine gestures were piled one on top of the other. The wall around their relationship was far too high to climb over or tear down. The gap was becoming too wide to cross.

When Ian finished his plate he took it into the kitchen and set it in the sink. Rosemary told him, as she did every morning, he didn't have to do it. He leaned down as he did each time she cooked for him, and thanked her for being such a wonderful cook. The little round lady smiled her biggest smile back at him and in her thick Russian accent protested his compliments, grinning even wider. Ian gave her a peck on the cheek and told her to enjoy her day. He put his hand up to the collar of his crisp blue dress shirt and ran it down to his waist to straighten his tie before walking back into the dining room where Heather was getting up from the table.

"You aren't sorry, are you?" he asked slipping into a dark blue tweed jacket.

"No." She walked him down the hall where he stopped at the closet to retrieve his overcoat.

Then without a coat on herself, she walked him all the way to his car in spite of the brisk morning air.

"Ian, what if he's guilty?" she breathed the

words.

"I guess I didn't make myself clear," he answered, as if he was explaining something to a child who didn't get the concept. "Of course he's guilty," brushing her cheek with his hand he added, "He might not be responsible. I don't know yet. I would like to hold on to my belief there is no good reason to kill, yet he maimed small children. We'll see." He got into the car as they finished their conversation. "Don't expect me until you see me," then he was gone.

Ian drove in the direction of his office, then changed his mind. It was time to meet the boy. Swinging the car around on Highway K was a dangerous thing to do but he pulled it off and headed down Highway 94 toward St. Charles. In his twenty years of practice he had only been to the jail once, when one of his client's wives had her husband arrested for abuse, in the middle of their divorce proceedings. Ian stood looking at the building.

The jail was across from St. Joseph's Hospital and in the middle of the block. Not where one would expect to see a jail. St. Charles was a Missouri river town. It was known for its historical downtown, antique shops, old houses, Lindenwood University, with its gorgeous campus of tree lined sidewalks, hundred year old buildings, and manicured grounds. The famous Katy Trail supported a trail head in the historic old downtown giving rise to micro-breweries and fine restaurants. It was a neat place and didn't want or need the publicity the entire area was getting from the murders. St. Charles was a people and tourist town, geared to please even the pickiest person. It was six miles from St.

Peter's where the murders took place, and about twenty-four miles from the city of St. Louis. So the story was getting much more attention than it would have if it had been farther away.

The jail could house three hundred prisoners. None had caused as much notoriety as Kenny Johnston.

The entire building seemed to echo his hollow footsteps as he walked down the massive hallway to a desk at the far end. He was aware of the security cameras and a guard waiting to run him through a scanner before he could talk to the officer at the desk. It was a fortress. After emptying his pockets and stepping into the machine, he was allowed to speak to the man in charge. He was sitting behind a desk on an elevated platform giving his otherwise unimpressive looks an air of authority. Were it not for his place and position he could have been easily overlooked. The buttons on his perma- wrinkle shirt were about to burst from the girth of his beer belly.

"My name's Ian Michaels," he relayed to the Sergeant passing one of his cards to the man at the same time. "My client Kenneth Johnston is being held here. I'd like to see him."

Some men he hadn't bothered to notice sprang to their feet, rushing in his direction. Thank goodness they were on the other side of the security gate and were forced to stop. Each one of them shouted the name of a newspaper or news source. This thing had gone national. In a most unprofessional manner they began shouting out questions. They could get no closer than twenty feet from him, so they were making quite a bit of ruckus with their loud voices. And they didn't want answers because they didn't pause long enough for him to respond to their constant and inappropriate queries.

Ian took a long deep breath and walked back closer to the x-ray booth, yet far enough away so he didn't feel threatened. It was nice knowing they could come no closer than they were. "Gentlemen, Gentlemen, please!" he raised his voice to shout over them. "I can't answer your questions. I haven't yet spoken with my client. If you'll call my office and leave your name with my assistant, I'll see that you get a statement before the end of the day." He dismissed them by turning his back and walking toward the man at the desk. After showing the proper identification, he was led on past the desk. Behind him he heard a series of grunts and grumbles as the reporters retook their seats. Ian was taken into a large stark white room. It was furnished with a huge old conference table and three chairs. Noticing the third chair, he wished Maggie was with him. He scanned the room-not much to see. It was the most uninviting room he'd ever been in. The once expensive oak table was marred from years of scratches and carvings. Walking around it he ran his fingertips over the markings.

They meant nothing to him yet he knew it was the legacies of the many people who passed through here either showing defiance, or a mark to immortalize their life. As he rounded the table he looked toward the only light. It came from a small window up high where no one could climb out if the two-inch round bars placed about six inches apart weren't enough to hold them. The sun shined through it creating a pinstripe pattern on the table making each flaw appear more prominent. It all made for a hypnotic effect. He was forced to close his eyes for a brief moment, to stop the dizziness it created.

He forced himself back to the business at hand. Opening his briefcase he took out a yellow legal pad and a mechanical pencil. Ian always preferred a pencil to a pen, using a pen only when necessary. He sat down in the small straight back chair with no cushion and tapped his pencil on the notepad as he waited.

During the ten minutes it took for the guards to arrive with Kenny he grew bored and turned his attention to the table top once again. What stories must lie beneath the worn initials and symbols it bore. He was tracing one pattern of particular interest when the door opened.

There before him stood a child.

Ian pushed back his chair and stood up walking toward the guards and the boy. Kenny was shackled and bound with a chain around his waist securing his hands and another around his ankles giving him only enough length to shuffle his feet along. It didn't seem possible, to Ian, this kid could have done all of the gruesome things in the stories he had read. The guards almost carried him to the table and chained him to one of the massive legs with one restraint and to the chair with another. They nodded to Ian and backed out of the room.

As they were leaving Ian asked, "Is that necessary?" his throat drier than he thought it should be.

"Orders," the jailer answered. "Be right outside if you need us." The closing of the door echoed in the cavernous cold, sparse room.

Ian was left facing the closed door. Turning himself and his attention toward Kenny, he noticed the kid's facial features were more those of a twelve year old. His face was smooth with no sign of whiskers to mar his baby face. He was short and skinny and broad shouldered. He looked like he belonged on a football field or in a wrestling competition. The boy looked out of place chained to a table in a jail, locked up, perhaps forever.

Crowning the boy's head was a mass of light brown hair. It circled his already round rosy cheeked face giving him a feminine look despite his build. All in all he was nice looking and scrubbed. Were it not for the light gray lifeless eyes gazing out into space, Ian may have even laughed at the thought of this boy, sitting across from him, being a murderer. As it was, eerie, mean, transparent eyes that showed what Kenny really was. They were unsettling and seemed to make the room a few degrees cooler.

The eyes of a maniac. Insane was the word Ian would later use when he described the boy to others. Kenny sat in a sort of catatonic state he knew was prevalent in the worst of cases. The bright sun shining into the room didn't do a thing to curb the chill in the air.

"You Michaels?" the boy asked, his dead dull eyes resting their gaze somewhere above Ian's head, refusing to look him in the eye.

Ian was shocked at the kid's voice. It was the voice of an old whiskey- throated drunk.

"I'm Mr. Michaels," Ian replied emphasizing the Mr. "If you don't know who I am, how's you had one of my business cards?"

"I got it from Tim, at school."

"Timothy gave you one of my cards. Why would he do that?"

"'cause I asked him for it- in English class." He spoke in fragmented sentences. Words put together enough to communicate. Ian wondered if he was sedated. It had not occurred to him Kenny would go to the same school as his own kids.

"Did you think you'd need a lawyer?" Ian pursued.

"Don't matter now-she's dead."

"Who's dead?"

"Mother."

"I'm sorry to hear that. How'd she die?"

"She was killed- murdered- I guess."

Ian's mind raced back to yesterday. Hadn't Amber said their mother lived in another state? Had she died during the night? Ian was getting weird-ed out. Minute by minute he wanted to bolt and run rather than sit and talk or try to talk to Kenny. A foreboding feeling of doom began to fill the room. The air got thicker and more uncomfortable. Ian felt it might overtake him.

Reaching up to his neck, he loosened his tie and unbuttoned his collar. It didn't help.

Now they were engaged in silence. Ian didn't know what they were talking about anyway. He knew he had no control over the interview. Was it an interview? Or was he in the middle of a lesson in abnormal behavior?

Ian's thoughts were interrupted by a hysterical laugh. Kenny was trying to get up from the table. When he couldn't he threw his head back and began laughing even harder at some private piteous joke.

Ian tried to remain calm. The sweat beaded on his forehead as he tried to relax.

Kenny's eyes began to flash. They lost what little tint they once held and were now a ghostly white reflecting the lack of color in the room. Ian's skin began to prickle as he watched the drama unfold. He remained in his chair for as long as he could. Coming to the end of his rope and not knowing how to stop the shrill laughter encapsulating the room, Ian got up. He leaned over the table and slapped Kenny across the face with enough force to regain his attention. In a low authoritative tone, Ian told Kenny to straighten up.

Bull shit! Ian thought.

Kenny changed. He seemed to notice his surroundings for the first time. He made a quick scan of the room as if to orientate himself. When his eyes fell on Ian, he seemed a bit startled to see he wasn't alone. His manner, attitude and look were not the same. His eyes were now a deep royal blue. His pupils were large and round. They stayed dilated even though his pupils should have been small since he was facing the bright sun shining into the room from the window.

It was as though one Kenny had left the room and another took his place. Ian sat. He said nothing. Silent moments dragged by. He was beginning to think maybe he had slapped the boy too hard. It was an unorthodox thing to do in the first place.

This was an unorthodox situation.

Ian ventured a question. "I didn't know your mother was deceased. Did it happen recently?"

"My mother isn't dead," Kenny answered in clear English. "She lives in Oklahoma City." The voice was the same and Ian again wondered if the kid had a sore throat but decided not to ask.

"Only a moment ago, you told me she was dead, never mind." Ian rethought. It was better not to go back. Kenny was responding. No telling for how long. Ian wanted to take advantage of it. "Kenny. Do you know why you're in jail?"

"Yes."

"Tell me about it."

"There isn't anything to tell."

"Surely there's something you'd like to say. Did you do all the things they say you did?"

Ian didn't come right out and ask him if he murdered those people. He didn't know what would send the kid into orbit again and he didn't want to take the chance. Realizing he was sitting on the edge of his chair, Ian tried to sit back and go with whatever happened next.

"I'm not sure."

"What's that mean? You're not sure?"

"Well, sometimes I picture bodies and places and screams, but I don't know if they're real or if I'm dreaming."

"Why would they be dreams?"

"I dream a lot."

"Did you dream your mother died?" Ian pressed on.

"I'm not sure."

Ian stopped. His own apprehension was growing. He might be asking questions too fast.

He might be asking the wrong questions. He didn't know what he'd do if he pushed Kenny back into the other self he had seen earlier.

Kenny was sitting in his chair with his head bowed. He began to click the steel cuffs together to a beat only he seemed to hear. The sound echoed off the walls, and it was driving Ian crazy.

"Are you a Doctor?" Kenny stared above Ian's head.

"No, I'm your attorney."

"Yeah, that's right, I remember." But the words came without conviction.

Again they sat across from one another in a restless quiet, save the clicking of the handcuffs. Ian could think of nothing else to say or do. Kenny didn't seem to mind the silence. In his own way, he was confused too, and sat with his mind in neutral.

What had he planned to learn with his visit here? Was Kenny in a dream world? He wasn't sure what he thought when he came, but now he had one bit of truth. He planned to keep it fresh in his mind at all times. He was leaving the jail knowing whether Kenny was found guilty or innocent, the boy was hopeless. There would be no turning this kid around.

The attorney wasn't sure how he felt about all of

this. The choking sensation he felt earlier was overtaking him once again. The mesmerizing sound of the handcuff music was like a tribal ritual.

He had to fight hard to keep from passing out.

"Well, Kenny, we'll talk later," he forced himself to say. Reaching over the table he put both of his hands over Kenny's to stop the clanging. "Is there anything you need?"

"They won't let me have my belt." he muttered

Sounded reasonable to Ian, but he swallowed his comment.

The room was now emptier than before without the sound of the handcuffs metal symphony. Ian intended for the interview to end here. He stood up and walked around the table to where the boy sat. For a long moment he stood behind the boy's chair. Reaching down, he patted Kenny on the back, called for the guard and walked out of the building the way he had come.

Grief overwhelmed Ian. It was a strange emotion to be sure, but he couldn't control it.

His many years of practice taught him to look straight in a person's eyes. Now he wished he could blank out what he had seen. Ian Michaels knew, no matter how old he got or how many people he met in his lifetime, Kenny's eyes would be the ones standing out forever in his memory.

As he got into his car, he realized for the first time in his life:

Things didn't look better in the light of day.

Chapter Four

It was a long drive from the St. Charles county jail to Ian's office. During the drive he slipped into a sort of euphoric daze. It could have been considered a deep state of concentration, but if it was, he had not one thought in his head to prove it. He was in the office parking garage before he realized it. He sat for a moment trying to visualize the landmarks he passed between the two points. The I-70 Bridge between St. Charles County and St. Louis County required the utmost concentration. There was never a time, day or night, it wasn't a busy thoroughfare.

Kingshighway, his favorite way to go to the office with its tree lined divider and diverse scenery. Forest Park itself with the aviary built for the 1904 World's Fair. All the things he smiled about on the drive he made twice a day. He always went blocks out of his way to see them. He must have obeyed the traffic signals and speed limits. He remembered none of it, nor could he remember any thought or reaction he must have had during the drive.

The feeling was ominous. He now knew what distracted driving meant, shaking his head as one shakes a toy whose battery has run down. Ian got out of the car and turned his attention toward his office. It was familiar and safe. Once inside he was confident the events of the morning would slip into place.

Delmar Boulevard was a gorgeous street. One side of it supported massive homes with ornate trimmings and circle drives. The other side was Forest Park with its well-kept lawns and eclectic scenery. At the corner of Delmar and Skinker sat his office, high atop the only office building on the street. Behind it on Skinker used to be his favorite eating spot, Taleyna's. After years of issues with the safety of the patrons due to parking problems and dark alleys, the restaurant moved. It was a loss he still felt. His building had underground parking for the tenants and clients. There was one office on each of the ten floors. Some fifteen years ago, Ian was fortunate enough to be able to buy the entire building. Pride of ownership swelled up in him every time he saw it.

What little ground he acquired with the building he had had paved, with the exception of two small flower beds, one on each side of the above-ground entrance. He was responsible for the way it looked, inside and out. Ian was satisfied. It created the look and image he wanted.

The entranceway was filled with plants and recessed lighting to help them grow and thrive.

Vicky, the plant lady, attended them once a week. They were spectacular. Ian smiled as he admired it all on his way up to his tenth-floor office. There was a back elevator for the people who worked in the building and a front elevator for visitors. Now he took the back elevator and walked down his private hallway to the office where he could enter through a small kitchen off the hall and avoid any and all people who might be in his waiting room.

Ian didn't use the back way often. He enjoyed the feeling he got every time he walked in the front reception area. He liked the combination of the smell of fresh flowers and leather and the informal atmosphere he worked so hard to create. But this morning he didn't know what might be waiting for him. He didn't want to be caught off guard by reporters, or anyone else for that matter.

He was looking forward to seeing Maggie. He had had little time to think about her since this whirlwind began. He liked the relationship they shared. They worked well together. She was his good friend, and an excellent secretary.

She was also exquisite.

Ian, if given the right set of circumstances, could sit just to watch Maggie move. She didn't actually walk, she floated. It was a way of moving one didn't see often off the movie screen. To

Maggie it was natural. She also had a way of putting people at ease. Ian felt she was responsible for a lot of the growth and success of his practice. For example, if a man called the office, she handled him with a calm friendliness and a gentle intelligent manner. After one conversation with Maggie he was sure he had picked the right lawyer for his particular situation and knew he would be comfortable when he visited the office. And, just as important, she treated a woman with equal respect.

Ian loved Heather. He was no longer in love with her. Their life flowed on through the ups and downs of raising a family. The respect was there, they made love enough to keep some closeness. But the passion was a thing of the past. It had died over the course of many years and he didn't think either one of them could put a finger on the day it burned out.

His relationship with Maggie, he told himself, was business, friendship and otherwise physical, but it wasn't. Ian wasn't a philanderer. He loved both of them, yet he was in love with Maggie. Heather was the mother of his children; Maggie was his link to his youth.

There was little Ian didn't like about Maggie. She was the right height and build, a sharp dresser with impeccable taste and grooming. Thinking of her always made him smile. There was no one in the world that smelled as good to him as Maggie did. She was blessed with emerald green eyes one could get lost in and long auburn hair she liked to let flow down her back. Her hair was all the same length with no bangs to mar the beauty of her flawless face. She was thirty-two now; he, forty-three. It really wasn't much of a difference he rationalized, when he allowed himself to think about her. She asked for nothing and he was comfortable in the relationship. Although she said she had never married, a fact he found surprising, he sensed she could have had anyone she wanted.

Maggie replaced Jo Ellen, Ian's previous secretary who retired. She came with an excellent recommendation from the Dean of the Law School at St. Louis University. She wasn't what he had in mind for an assistant. After the interview he had balked at her age and lack of experience. But the dean had assured him Maggie could handle it. What an understatement.

No one lied to Maggie. Men tried to charm her when she was charming them right into her confidence and into telling the truth. Men adored her, women admired her, including his wife. Heather was one of the reasons he hired Maggie in the first place. His wife was intrigued by the girl who gave no past employment, no previous address, no answers whatsoever, yet somehow got the recommendation of the dean of one of the most prestigious universities in the United States.

Maggie was one of the most stunning girls one would ever see outside of the movies or on the stage. The most captivating thing about her was she seemed unaware of her looks. One had to wonder how she could help but notice her own beauty when she looked in the mirror or saw it reflected in the eyes of others.

If Heather ever suspected her husband of having an affair with his secretary she never let on. She had opened the doors of her home and heart to Maggie years ago.

Ian stuck his head out into the reception room and exchanged a warm genuine smile and hello to Maggie - since he had come in through the back. He felt safe for the first time all day.

Before he sat down at his massive cherry desk he took a moment or two to look out the window and admire the day and see what was happening in the park. He loved it. Today, more than ever, he was thankful for what he had. The park was like a new painting every minute of every day. Sometimes it was hustle and bustle and flurries of activity. Other times it was quiet and non-moving.

After several minutes he took a deep breath and turned his attention to his agenda for the day.

In any other room his desk would look gaudy but here it was perfect. His office, unlike the waiting room was filled with pictures and drawings of St. Louis and the surrounding area. They were grouped into different geographic locations. The Arch, the old luxury boat, Admiral, where his high school prom had been held, and the statues at Keener Plaza, as well as Union Station. And so it was all the way around the room. It would be easy to tour the entire bi-state area by exploring the walls of Ian's office.

Like every other room in this building, it was huge. He had it set up in different groupings, the plush couch and two chairs with matching tables and soft lighting near the door where he met with clients for the first time. It gave the allusion of being in someone's living room. The setting put nervous men and women, whose lives were falling apart, a feeling of hominess. It was very effective. On the other side of his desk were two soft brown leather chairs where he did business for business' sake.

Ian took off his coat, loosened his tie and

prepared to work. The digital clock on his desk flashed four-forty-seven. Using the intercom, he asked Maggie to join him. She came in smiling and took her usual seat to his right. When she had come to work for him he had taken her to an office furniture store where they picked out the perfect chair for her to sit in as they worked.

"Did you take care of everything?" he asked.

"Yes, but before we get started, Heather's called twice. She's very upset but didn't say why. Should I get her for you?"

"Yeah, but dial from out front. After I talk to her we can get to this." He pointed to the stack of papers and literature she had been gathering since his call earlier in the day.

Maggie left the room and within minutes had Heather on the phone. She was frantic.

It was all beginning. All of the negative feelings and thoughts Ian had yesterday about publicity and lack of privacy were becoming realities today.

The press corps had not taken Ian at his word. Instead of waiting for a statement or coming to the office to speak to him, they went to his house. Heather, being naive and every bit a gracious lady, had opened the door to them. They began hammering her with questions. They asked general questions, personal questions, and rude questions. Finally she ordered them out of the house and off the grounds. They were still tormenting her by hanging around on the sidewalk and in the street. Rosemary was even questioned as she tried to walk to her car. She acted as though she didn't understand much English, pushed through the crowd, got in her car and left.

These folks were dedicated to keeping this story front page stuff straight through the trial. It was the most sensational crime ever committed in this area. Also it involved children. Everyone knew it would be dealt with as soon as possible because of the children involved, any angle to sell papers. Interesting, Ian thought, how the human mind worked. A dozen people could be killed in a spectacular accident and in a week no one except loved ones could quite remember the details. Let one child get into harm's way and people would remember it for years. People did and always would take a special interest in anything involving children. In this case there were children who appeared to have been slaughtered.

It was news.

Heather was reacting as he had expected under the circumstances. Twenty plus news people sticking microphones in her face and flashes from cameras exploding in her eyes. Yet the picture she was painting was too much even for a concerned husband. It took all of his control and concentration to keep his voice low and level as he talked to her.

Anyone listening in on their conversation would have pictured a poor hysterical woman held captive in her own home by reporters at every conceivable exit. Newsmen being lowered onto the roof from helicopters, and poor Heather herself, strapped to an uncomfortable straight back chair with one bare light bulb swinging above her head while she cried for mercy. She kept telling him she was 'afraid for the children'.

Damn! Damn! Damn!

The children could be of some concern, but he doubted they were in any danger. Timothy, sixteen, would be the one they would single out. He and Kenny went to the same school and shared a class together. It would take some stretching to link them. How about: YOUNG KILLER AND ATTORNEY'S SON SHARE HISTORY NOTES?

He was becoming cynical after only one day. Not good.

The other two boys, Ben and Daniel went to a different school and he couldn't think of a way to bring them into this unless one of Kenny's younger siblings went to school with them, he didn't know.

Children were off limits in something like this. If someone was angry with Ian for taking the case, he should take it out on Ian.

In spite of the way his mind was tracking, Ian talked to his wife, reassuring her. He apologized for worrying her by not telling her he was going to the jail. He assured her from now, on until this ordeal was over, he would make sure she could get hold of him any time she felt the need.

He sympathized with her about the rudeness of the news crews and promised to call a press conference as soon as he could. He even offered to have Timothy pick up the other two boys at their school. Timothy was driving to school this year and wouldn't mind. The other boys were in a car pool with some of the neighborhood mothers. Thank goodness this wasn't Heather's week to drive.

As best he could, he impressed on her she wasn't alone. The public was up in arms against the boy. They were crying for any and all information they could get. He likened it to the long traffic jams on the freeway caused by rubbernecking motorists and their morbid curiosity. Publicity was part of it.

He should have made it clearer to her this morning, which now seemed days ago. Instead he skirted around it, powder puffed it, so to speak, he should have made it sound as horrible as possible and then anything short of the scenario he created would have been a blessing.

He tried to lighten the conversation by asking about dinner. Knowing he wouldn't make it home at a reasonable hour he suggested she order a pizza from Stephanina's in O'Fallon and spend a family night with her boys. They were great company. His last suggestion was almost an order. He told her to take the phone off the hook and after dinner to draw herself a hot bath and soak in it while listening to some soothing music. Ian reminded her how relaxing she always found it. Things would look better in twenty minutes, he reassured her, and he would call the police about backing the press further from the house. Tomorrow, he assured her, there would be other aspects of the case to occupy them and she wouldn't be bothered again.

As Ian hung up the phone, he swung his chair toward the window. All of his fears from yesterday were slapping him in the face. His beautiful people and fun-filled park gave him no comfort now. He gazed out the window as usual but now every face seemed to turn to stare up at him with cold dead eyes. Trying to shake his mood he turned his chair back toward the desk. A moment later the hair began to rise on the back of his neck. He felt the cold fish eyes resting on his back. He got up and shut the drapes.

Never! Never before had he closed the drapes. He almost did once during a severe lighting storm. Maggie had been with him in the office and she had a deep seated childhood fear of lighting. Instead of closing the drapes he had helped with her fear. Before the storm was over, they had stood together at the window and watched the storm rage in the distance.

He stood again and with every bit of mental power and reserve he could muster he pulled on the cord. The thick rosy- colored drapes pleated themselves away from each other. The realization hit him at that moment. Nothing was going to help him face his own fears.

Should he have trusted his first gut reaction about all of this? Yes, was the answer. He should have listened to himself. More emotion had past though his soul in the last twenty-four hours than had affected him in his entire life. They were foreboding and ominous feelings of hopelessness and doom. The people were murdered, children and adults with their lives cut short by a young insane boy. God only knew what had driven the kid. It was too late for any of them. The only daylight the boy was likely to see again was what he could see from his cell or his time in a prison exercise yard.

These feelings wouldn't go away. Instead they became sharper. Now they wanted to consume him. They included sadness for a thousand children over a thousand years. He knew he would go on.

Something drove a child to act as this one did. He knew he couldn't save Kenny but maybe he could bring to light something in all this sadness to help others from going down a similar path. Something kept a father from stepping forward to stand beside his son in need. Ian, for the first time, felt a purpose. He intended to find out and bring to light whatever those things were. With a determination he didn't possess before, he rang for Maggie to come back into his office.

***

Maggie came back with pen and paper in hand. She was prepared to get to work although it was now after five and they should have been ending their day, not beginning it. This time Maggie stood near the door until he addressed her. Ian saw her questioning look and uncommon hesitancy.

There was a new side to Ian she was seeing for the first time. The gentleness and naivety she found so attractive in him was absent from his eyes. It was gentleness she called his 'attitude of life'. It was his most adoring quality. It was what drove him to see some good in every person in every situation. He tried to reconcile each divorce minded person who walked through the door. If he couldn't accomplish it, then he helped them move on. She had thought he realized the bad was there but he had always taken the time to dig out the good and place it on top so people could see it again or at least recognize it was there. Perhaps he thought they had forgotten there was any good, which is easy to do when the bad is standing up on its hind legs and looking you straight in the eye. Maggie felt a chill as she watched him now. He seemed to be digging the biggest hole he had ever dug. The difference being he was coming up with only more dirt this time.

"Where do we stand?" he asked her.

"Everything you asked for is here. Jim will be here when he can-sometime this evening.

He was in the middle of something. The dean is sending over two of the best students they have. He had a couple in mind who would excel at the job." She paused to consult her notes. "I ran into a snag with Mrs. Johnston. She did answer the phone. I woke her. The father wasn't there. She let me know in no uncertain terms she isn't Kenny's mother. She is very verbal. She says she has done all she intends to do for the boy. She called him an 'ungrateful brat'. After much avoidance on her part and much persuasion on mine, I got her to agree to have Kenny's dad call here in the morning. Truthfully, after talking to her, well, it was much more than I thought I would get."

Maggie had walked over and sat down as she talked. Again Ian saw her watching him, keeping eye contact, or trying to. He said nothing, and turned his chair to face the window. It was a habit he knew she was well used to.

When he wanted to think, he faced the outside. He began to speak without facing her, something he knew he had never done before. Perhaps he was talking more to himself than to her.

"I went to see the boy today," he said in a low monotone. "He's sick, mentally ill. I wish I knew

49

what to do. I really don't know much about criminal law and I know even less about mental illness. Other than having a doctor evaluate him I'm afraid I don't know what else I can do for him." Ian stopped talking. Maggie had moved up next to his chair and was kneeling down next to him. A heavy sigh escape from deep within him, his shoulders sagged. It left the comical impression that someone had let all of the air out of him. She said nothing and remained quiet and still. After a long pause, Ian began speaking again. "We need to find out all we can about the boy. Was he born with a problem? Was he a problem at school? Was he a problem at home, or for his siblings? Did he maim small animals? I want to know about his mother. Why does his father have custody? That's unusual," He muttered the last as a sort of statement/ question. "What kind of person is his dad, and his step-mother, how did she treat him? There has got to be a reason for this. But you know what, Maggie? No matter what we do or what we dig up, this boy's a tragedy. He made a tragedy of six families, no seven families because his own was destroyed also. I think if we find out the why, the what- happens next will take care of itself."

The lawyer looked at his assistant now, sensing her nearness. He looked deep into those green eyes looking at him with concern, but he said nothing more. Maggie seemed to be melting under his intense stare, yet she also didn't speak or make a move toward him. He knew he needed to look away now. To make the decision for her about what was the best course of action between them, right here and right now. He noticed beads of perspiration breaking out on her forehead. Someone needed to break this spell.

Now.

Ian and Maggie had always maintained a professional relationship at the office.

There were too many variables, too many people roaming in and out, too many chances to be overheard and lessen their credibility. Now it was annoying him. Couldn't she see he needed encouragement? Why did she kneel beside him and hold his eyes with hers as she did if she didn't feel she could come the last few inches toward him? He needed her now more than ever.

Heather wasn't going to be of any emotional help to him. He didn't expect her too. She was now taking the role of the mother lion whose cubs were being threatened. He would have to minimize everything to her because it was how they began, Ian and his perfect wife whom he always protected.

Ian considered his affair with Maggie a tiny ripple of transgression in a great sea of immorality. At this moment, he felt it was necessary. The longer their eyes held, the more his need for her filled his entire being. Never before had he allowed his personal needs to interfere with his work or his family. Now he wanted Maggie to replace all of it, if only for a few minutes.

Theirs started out as a relationship revolving around business trips and Heather's visits to her family. It had become so much more. They were good, close, easy friends. The sex was great and the closeness became stronger and stronger over the last seven years. At this moment Ian would give all he had if only Maggie would smile and come to him across the great distance of jagged unspoken rules and barriers.

If Maggie ever felt neglected she never let it show. When he allowed himself to think about it, which until now was seldom, he felt Maggie was pleased with the arrangement. Maybe her being content was what was keeping her where she remained right now. She didn't seem to want a more binding commitment. Right this minute it was driving him crazy. His prior selfishness was hitting him smack in the face and he wasn't pleased with himself. All he could think about himself at this moment was 'what a selfish son-of-a-bitch' he had been all these years.

Facts about her and their relationship were slapping him in the face one right after the other.

Maggie never talked about herself or her past. He had never pushed the issue. She would answer his questions with lighthearted jokes and he knew he had let it go. Now he realized he had let her stay distant to protect himself. He had done it to make their situation seem less wrong in his own mind.

Ian, noticing something he could not read in her eyes, broke the spell. "How about getting some dinner? It is well after seven and I'm starving." She bowed her head and moved away from him as he talked.

Ian couldn't believe it. Poof. The moment was gone. Glancing over at the clock he answered. "Okay but let's eat here." He smiled at her trying to bring back what they had only an instant before. It was much too late. He wouldn't push her. "Order a little more in case Jim shows up while we're eating. I also want to go over the arrest records before he gets here. Do you know where they are in this mess?"

Maggie walked over and found the courthouse documents, put them on the top of the stack and went off to order dinner from her desk where she kept the phone numbers of their favorite places. Tonight she picked Tortillaria on Euclid in the popular Central West End. It was only about two miles from the office and even though they didn't officially deliver, they would bring it to them without charging too much more.

With all the stress in the office this was a good choice. They were famous for their fish tacos, homemade salsa and chips. All of their ingredients came from the Soulard Market. On top of all the stress, they didn't need any processed food to make them sluggish. The restaurant agreed to bring it up to the office within forty-five minutes.

Maggie came back into the office. Instead of sitting in a chair, she perched on the edge of Ian's desk. He put his hand on her knee. Maggie smiled down at him, allowing herself to look at him. She leaned over toward him and gave him a gentle kiss. He felt her relax. When he started to remove his hand from her knee and use it to pull her close, she stopped him dead by placing her hand over his. She moved away from him.

"I want to help you, Ian, but I can't unless you tell me everything."

"Like what?" He was already standing to come

toward her and she smiled.

Maggie took a deep breath and stood a little straighter and with a lower, louder voice, she asked. "Like what's bothering you, and what's bothering Heather? Like what the boy said and is that what has you so upset? Like what you're thinking right now?" She laughed. "Okay, forget the last one," she added over her shoulder as she ran to open the door for the delivery man.

As they ate he opened up to her. He didn't sugarcoat anything. There was no need with her. She was strong and capable. He told her every detail, every feeling, every fear. They were sitting side -by -side on the couch finishing up their food and conversation when the telephone rang. Maggie grabbed a napkin to wipe her hands as she got up to answer it. It was Jim Martin. He was going to be held up for another hour or so.

Ian glanced at his watch. He still had time to get to the library to pick up some books he wanted to look at on child development and abnormal child psychology so he could talk to the doctor who would examine Kenny. Maggie picked up the trash from dinner and put the office back in order and went back to the outer office to finish up some correspondence she hadn't had time for earlier and to check the telephone messages on the recorder. Only the private line was left open when this ordeal began.

It would actually be morning before they could do much more about Kenny's case. They still didn't have all of the newspapers starting with the account of the first murder almost six months ago.

Ian felt the public spin on all of it was important and that came from the newspapers. They had the court documents and probable cause statements but when all of it went down, Kenny wasn't represented by an attorney. Who knew if it made a difference? They didn't. The coroner's report weren't at the office yet. They were an afterthought. No one thought about them until Jim mentioned them in his initial conversation with Ian. They would be at the office by ten am tomorrow along with the physical evidence papers. They also needed school records. Ian was sure there must be a witness or two out there also. No one could do all of this without someone seeing something.

Ian had always been convinced the only way the perfect crime could be committed was if it were carried out in a dark closet by oneself on a three hundred acre estate with no one around. Then he felt it would still be iffy that no one saw or heard anything

Maggie had the completed list of what they needed. With any luck it would all be at their fingertips by noon tomorrow.

There was one plain and glaring fact facing them at every turn. The State of Missouri must have an air tight case against the boy. Everyone involved with the case knew Ian was involved yet no one called asking to meet about a plea. No one wanted to discuss anything. There must be evidence he didn't know about yet.

Chapter Five

Maggie finished her work before Ian returned from the library. Her head was pounding at her temples. She opened her desk drawer looking for the ibuprofen bottle she kept there. It was nowhere to be found. The more she searched the worse her headache became. She was beginning to get sick at her stomach. Knowing there were aspirin in Ian's desk she went in his office to get them. She sat in his chair and opened the top drawer. What she saw made her smile.

The paper on the desk was all Ian. He doodled when he talked on the phone. While he was talking to Heather earlier he had bordered a page with tulips. Toward the middle of the page were several pairs of eyes. After what he had told her earlier about Kenny and his dead eyes, she knew what it all meant. She sat looking at the drawings so hard they went out of focus.

Maggie's mind wandered back to the first time she met Ian. So much time had passed since the first time she saw him and the moment today when they could neither one let go of the other with their eyes.

He was a quiet man. At first she feared him. He said little to her other than to tell her what he needed her to do. It was as though he had made up his mind to dislike her before he knew her. The fear and shyness she felt when she was around him gave way to respect. She liked the way he handled and treated people. Rather than take their money for the divorce proceeding, he would try to get them to first consult a marriage counselor. Only when all possibilities were exhausted did he go on with the proceedings. He treated the partner who wasn't his client with the utmost respect. He didn't sling dirt. Ian's philosophy was one where he considered each person to be worthy. To him they were just two people who didn't like one another. He knew with different people they would be different also. It was a fine line and Ian walked it without causing more damage than needed. He was even gentler when children were involved.

Ian handled his business accounts with the same honesty. There was such a demand for his services he could have headed a large firm with three or four partners. For some reason, only he knew, he kept his practice small and handled all of it himself with the help of a few trusted people he had known most of his life.

The respect Maggie had for Ian soon turned to infatuation. He took her everywhere he went. She took notes when he handled a big oil merger in Houston and again when he settled an estate in Chicago for an old college buddy. He became her good friend. They laughed together and had hours of compatible silence on road trips. She was included at holiday dinners with his family.

When they traveled they frequented the best restaurants and drank the best wines. They sometimes laughed so hard they cried. If their meetings were over soon enough, they went to plays and movies. During all the time they spent together he never seemed to notice her for herself. He never mentioned a new dress or hairdo, always smiling at her and somehow making it his nod of approval. Ian didn't complain if he was on the golf course with one of his out- of- town clients and she spent her time at a day spa. In some ways he was super attentive. He never forgot her birthday, or what she liked and didn't like at the venues where they dined. He remembered her favorite wine and salad dressing, always the perfect companion.

The more time Maggie spent with Ian, the more she wanted him. He, on the other hand, remained a gentleman. It infuriated her. She sometimes wondered if he had a problem. Was he the devoted husband who wouldn't stray? Years of being the go-between with messages from Heather to Ian and those going the other direction, she knew the closeness wasn't there. His marriage wasn't ideal. Maybe he was the sort of husband who wouldn't stray under any circumstances. If so, Heather was the luckiest woman on earth and didn't know it.

Maggie didn't picture herself as a home wrecker. And she wasn't naive. She was in love with Ian and wanted to do something about it, plain and simple.

She made sure she was the best secretary and companion any person could want. She began to watch for any sign he thought of her as anything more than his confidante and companion. There were no signs. There were no lingering glances, no pauses at her door. There was never a time when his hand stayed on hers for a moment too long on those occasions when they were forced to touch.

As time passed, it became more and more difficult for Maggie to bear the distance between them.

She knew he was married. She knew her longing for him was wrong. There wasn't a thing she could do about any of it. No matter what she did, his face, his actions and his smell filled her very being.

Maggie decided to make Ian notice her.

She planned it for his birthday. She made sure his day at the office was quiet and uneventful.

She took hours to pick out the perfect gift. She chose an exquisite tie tack. Ian had a cute habit of running his hand from the top of this tie to the bottom several times a day. He wore no tiepin at all. Whenever he was working and his tie bugged him he would stick it inside his shirt between the buttons. Maggie figured he had been caught many times with his tie stuffed in his shirt. His habit was one he developed to save embarrassment. Why he didn't conform to wearing something to keep his tie in place escaped her. She kind of smiled to herself as to whether it was an appropriate gift for him. Before he arrived she sat it on her desk in plain view. He smiled as he past her desk. It wasn't unusual for her to buy him a little something on special occasions. Today there was an electric shock beating where her heart was supposed to be. She was giddy and jumpy with a wheel turning in her stomach causing her angst. But she was a determined lady.

A few times she wished she had made more appointments for the day. There wasn't enough work to keep her mind off Ian, her feelings for him, or her past. They were all a part of her life and were all in constant conflict.

Around one o'clock she stood up, straightened her dress, took a deep breath, picked up the box and walked into his office. With all the natural tone she could muster she ordered him to stand in the center of the room. Struggling, she kept the same playful tone she always used as they joked around. She fought her own stiff and animated movements. What if this backfired? Should she leave it alone and let things remain the same? He was, after all, her best friend. Ian obliged, standing there smiling. "Close your eyes," she ordered. He kidded with her as she ran her hand from his neck to his waist, following his tie, as was his habit. Then putting the new tie tack right where it belonged. "Now don't open your eyes." She warned as she took a step backward watching him stand there so innocent.

Then before she lost her nerve she stepped closer to him. As their bodies met he opened his eyes. She tipped her head toward him and kissed him. It was a passionate searching kiss. An instant later she felt his arms around her, caressing her as he returned her feelings.

It was glorious.

She was certain she had done the right thing. Yet, as suddenly as he held her, he now let her go. He pushed her away. Holding her at arm's length,

Ian had searched her face and eyes with an unreadable look on his face. Maggie stood before him not breathing, afraid to break the spell holding him.

Damn. What was happening? She could not read his look at all.

As she was resigning herself to the fact she had done the wrong thing and ruined all they had built over the years, he pulled her to him. For what seemed like a lifetime he had held her so close she could feel his breath on her lips. He whispered, "You are so lovely." His lips brushed her with some of the words. "Thank you." he finished before he let her go.

Maggie's knees began to buckle. My god, what had she done? She ran from his office, grabbed her purse and coat. Out the door she flew not thinking about anything but her humiliation.

Over and over she played the scene in her mind. How could she have been so dumb, so stupid, and so wrong? Every word, every gesture, and every feeling would be embedded in her mind forever. She was torn between the passion she felt for the way he held her and the hate she felt for him letting her go as he did. That night she fell into an exhausted fitful sleep.

Morning came too soon. With it came a headache, a horrible feeling in the pit of her stomach and remorse she couldn't get a handle on. Maggie debated as to whether she should go to the office or not. How could she face him? Her mind settled on a plain and simple fact. What could she lose that she had not already lost?

She need not have worried. He treated her the same way he had before the incident. In a way, it made it worse. Did she mean so little to him? Was he so cold he could just go on? Maggie decided the answer was to go on as he did, ignoring and pretending all was the same as before. Days turned into weeks. Weeks turned into months. Not once did Ian mention what she began to think of as her 'transgression'. Was he so pure of heart? Whenever she found her mind wandering to thoughts of him, she would force herself on to another subject. The times she felt herself watching him, she made herself turn away. Maggie never saw the tie tack again. He continued to use his hand to keep his tie in place. She felt he had been wrong on all levels.

Spring came. The flowers in Forest Park peeked through melting snow. Everywhere there was bustling activity. People were thrilled to get out of their winter cocoons. They walked in the park every chance they got. Maggie began joining the lunch crowd every day, breathing in the fresh smells of spring and watching the park crews plant annuals in the common spaces as they did each year. The memory of her debacle with Ian faded and they were back to business as usual. Ian was busier than usual, making settlements and appearing in court.

Each Easter, Ian took his family to New England to visit Heather's Mother. He looked forward to it and whistled his way around the office as they finished what needed attended to and moved forward those cases able to be put aside for ten days until he returned. Ian loved the East. He used the time to walk the Atlantic coast line, reconnect with his boys and spend some time with his wife. He always came back relaxed and tanned.

About ten minutes before Ian was to leave the office, they received a frantic telephone call from the wife of his close friend and college chum, Dan Collins. It seems Dan was playing tennis with one of the members of their club when he shouted across the net he didn't feel well. Twenty seconds later he died of a pulmonary embolism. Ian canceled his trip, sent Heather and the boys on and stayed to console and advise his old friend's wife.

Heather and Maggie chatted now and then, yet when Heather called as she was leaving to ask Maggie to look after Ian while his family was gone, she felt a pang of guilt. It was the first time she had thought about the birthday incident in a long time.

Maggie realized, although there wasn't anything between them, her guilt arose from the knowledge of how much she wished there were. Her face was scarlet and she was glad they were talking on the phone and not in person. She promised to try to make him stop working at a reasonable hour and see he ate while she was gone.

The two women shared a sincere affection for one another, a mutual admiration one holds for another whom she believes to be of equal station and ability. Maggie was once the wronged woman in a triangle. She should know better than to instigate such a situation. She knew she didn't want to force someone else into the situation she had been in. She was unable to deal with or define her own motivation with Ian. She guessed it was love. She closed her mind to the pain.

The first week rocketed by. Late Friday they were polishing up a case for a Tuesday court date. Ian had stayed pretty close to Dan's widow, Marcy, during the funeral and was handling the probate of his will. He was exhausted from staying strong for Marcy and dealing with his own loss of a dear old friend. Ian talked of flying to New England to meet his family for the last few days they were at Heather's mom's to renew himself with a few solitary walks on the beach. On her side, Maggie was plain tired of writing, filing, typing. They had ridden a roller coaster of emotions all week. She too would relish a few days alone.

When they finished it was after ten. It was a brisk spring night, yet after the long cold St. Louis winter it seemed delightful. Ian suggested they have a late dinner before they went off in opposite directions. Maggie refused, saying she was too tired to eat and was going home to put on some comfortable clothes before heading for a walk around the University City Loop where she lived. She was aggravated because since her conversation with Heather almost a week ago she felt guilty and shunned at the same time. It wasn't a good place for her to be. Maggie was finding it more and more difficult to be around Ian if they were not busy. She knew the problem was hers and hers alone, but knowing and accepting were miles apart.

Before they got out of the office, the spring night gave way to a pop-up thunderstorm. They were famous in the Midwest. St. Louis was second only to Tulsa for its severity in the spring.

Out of nowhere a storm blew up with cloud to

ground lightning and thunder she felt could rival the sound of any war zone during a battle. Maggie made several false starts to her car which she left on the upper level of the parking lot anticipating a short fresh aired walk to clear her head as she left the office. Each time she headed for the car, her unnatural fear of lightning forced her back into the safety of the foyer. Her heart was pounding and her palms were sweating as she made her decision to go back up to the office and wait out the storm where she could close the drapes, muffle the sound of the thunder and block out the intense lightning flashes.

She was back in the office with all of the heavy drapes drawn. She backed away from the last curtain with an audible sigh as she backed into Ian. She didn't realize he was still in the office. He must have been in the office when she entered, but in her panic and fear didn't look around for him or notice he was there until he walked up and touched her. Maggie jumped and gave a little shriek at the same time.

"Hey, it's only me." He had rested both hands on her waist as she had begun to back into him. He didn't make any move to remove them. A warm flush began in her toes, lingered in her groin and then proceeded to her face where is became a hot volcanic pulse. Warmth or no warmth she would never embarrass herself with him again. She remained frozen, afraid to move.

"I'll bring the car up. You could use a drink." Before she could answer, he was gone. A moment later she forced herself to take the elevator back down to the lobby. Ian had his car as close to the front door as was possible. He had the passenger door open. All she had to do was make a twenty yard dash to get in. Maggie took a deep breath, waited until a bolt of lightning flashed somewhere to her left, and opened the main door. She covered the small distance as fast as she could but was still soaked by the torrential downpour before she could close the car door.

"Are you okay?" he asked looking at her ashen gray face.

Maggie only nodded. Her fear of lightning was such an all-consuming thing. As a child she had professional help to try to dispel her fear or at least get it under control. Her parents gave up after two years. Nothing anyone did seemed to help her.

Ian asked where she wanted to go. "Home, go home and get out of the storm." It was only sprinkling as he walked her to her apartment door." I have some wine if you'd like to take the chill off," she offered. They both stepped inside as soon as the door was unlatched.

"I have a better idea. You go get out of those wet clothes and I will put on some water for tea." It was both an offer and a suggestion.

She no longer wanted to be alone with him. Why did she let him come in? It was too frustrating for her and she was about to nix the tea idea when he rested one hand on each of her wet and tense shoulders, bending over to kiss her neck. Turning to face him she kept her arms by her sides.

She wanted to look in his eyes and be sure of what was happening. Ian slipped her soaking wet jacket off her trembling shoulders. It fell in a soggy wet heap on the floor. He began kissing the nape of her neck as he undressed her, fondling and caressing as he explored.

Maggie was panicked. Like a school girl she was lost but he guided her. He took her to places she never knew existed. No longer was the storm important. There was no Heather, no office, no past, only Ian.

She could not get close enough to him, be close enough to feel secure. They were good together, not only in their lovemaking, but in their likes and dislikes. It was all natural and spontaneous. They spent the entire weekend together, never discussing a serious issue or any of the complications sure to arise from their actions.

They were both embarrassed on Sunday night when he got ready to leave only to realize her car was still in the office parking lot.

From then on Ian made all of the advances. She never questioned or demanded anything of him. He was who and what Maggie wanted in her life. He was a safe physical attraction. She had it all sorted out in her mind. There would never be a stifling commitment with him. He had a wife, a family, a law practice and her. To Maggie it was the perfect relationship. She never told him anything about her previous experiences with men or about her marriage ending in divorce after four years because of a young husband with a drinking problem and a wandering eye. How she came home one day to share the exciting news of a new job to find him in bed with the neighbor. How she would always keep a part of her to herself. A part no one could have or touch so she would never have to face the hurt and humiliation she faced then.

Sometimes her past seemed long ago and far away when she was with Ian. She shrugged at her true deep feelings about men. She wanted sex. She enjoyed it. She wanted a personal relationship, one giving her mental and physical stimulation without commitment. Some of her feelings she couldn't understand herself so she stuffed them away. Did they matter at this point? She knew she was obsessed with Ian. Was it physical? No. It was his gentleness and his attitudes she liked and his whole being she wanted when they were together. Was it love?

Damn.

Maggie sat at her desk praying this situation with Kenny Johnston wouldn't change her relationship with Ian. "Please God, don't let him lean," she mumbled out loud, then pushed the thought to the back of her mind. Her thoughts were still jumbled when she look up toward a noise at the door.

In walked Ian with an armload of books and a schoolboy look in his eyes. "Sorry I took so long. I went by the house to make sure everything was okay and ran into some reporters. I couldn't get away from them. I hope I read well in the morning papers. They were relentless."

Maggie's reply was lost in Jim Martin's greeting as he appeared behind Ian in the doorway.

Jim was fifty-ish. He was one of those men who would always look young and could best be described as cute with an athletic build.

He was one of Maggie's favorite people. He was

casual in both manner and dress. She had dealt with him many times over the years under many different circumstances. Jim had played center field for UCLA in college and was picked up by the Angels. A baseball career didn't work out for him. He went on to have an illustrious career with the St. Louis Police Department but retired after having to shoot a young man who was in the midst of committing the robbery of a Fast Mart. About six months after the incident Jim opened Martin's Private Investigations.

He had told Maggie the two things he disliked most were suits and ties. He wore either a sweater or his shirt sleeves depending upon the weather. Jim would have made the perfect TV detective. He had blond sun bleached hair making what little gray he had almost impossible to detect. His polite manner and his police background, it was all pat. He had good repose with the legal community and the police force. Between the two venues Jim was always busy.

The men shook hands after Ian put the books on his desk. He walked over to Maggie and gave her his standard one-armed hug accompanied by his million dollar smile.

They settled their business and without unnecessary words.

Ian wanted Jim to track down Kenny's natural mother. Jim snacked on the tacos they had for him as they talked. Maggie gave Jim the pertinent information. Ian wanted to know how and where Kenny's mother lived. Jim wasn't to contact her at this point. He was to watch, dig and then report.

Maggie made reservations for the investigator to leave the next afternoon. It would give him ample time to finish his pending business and do any needed local legwork before leaving for Oklahoma City, the last known address for Kenny's mother.

After Jim left, they decided to call it a day.

Tomorrow they would have all the material they needed to start a complete investigation of Kenny and his family. As they were leaving the office, the phone rang. It was Judge William Massey's office. They were both astounded the call was so late, but decided the night clerk had not expected anyone to answer and had intended to leave a message. Ian was to attend a meeting at noon the following day to discuss the case and set a date for the preliminary hearing.

While Ian talked to the clerk, Maggie locked the doors and turned out the office lights.

"Can you spare a minute?" he called to her as she walked out of the door ahead of him. For the first time ever she wanted to resist him but his lips were on hers before she had the chance.

Ian was still something she wanted. Ian using her as a crutch to get him through this ordeal with Kenny Johnston, she didn't want. She was, after all of these years, unable to resist Ian and her reaction to him and as they stood in the dark doorway it was proved to her once again.

Chapter Six

Kenny's cell became his refuge. He felt safe there. Safety had eluded him his entire life, or as far back as he could remember. He knew there was a shadowy person in his distant memory that made him feel safe and secure, but the memory was old. It faded more each time he needed it for soothing. In his young mind he knew it would someday be gone and he would be more alone than ever.

Being confined in a five by seven foot space didn't bother him. Neither did the lack of the creature comforts society took for granted. Simple things like sheets, pictures, and a toilet seat, a pillow and a modicum of privacy. All of these things were missing yet not needed in the world Kenny's mind was furnishing for him.

He basked in the glory of his new freedom. It was a kind of freedom he never knew existed. He was living in the land of no responsibility. He didn't have to go to school. He had limited interaction with other people. He made no decisions. Nothing at all was demanded of him.

When he was first put in his cell, he used his time to think up clever answers for every question anyone might ask him, and a clever reason for every action he had taken. Life had taught Kenny one huge lesson. He learned he was smarter than those around him. He learned all he had to do was watch, then follow someone and in a day or two he was able to pick up on their habits and weaknesses. Then they were his. People were so unaware. Kenny was always aware. He knew who was where in his family. He knew to stay a little out of arm's reach when an adult was angry.

Kenny felt he was a survivor. He believed all unaware people had no right to stay safe. In his eyes, everyone was a potential victim because they didn't pay attention, listen or learn. This made everything bad they encountered in life their own fault. Kenny was fond of showing his superiority. Would people never learn the lessons he was forced to learn? Would they never learn to stay alert for a slap you didn't know was coming or being backhanded for chewing a carrot that crunched. He gave them every opportunity to notice him as he stalked them and learned their patterns.

At first all of his thoughts were on Ian Michaels, his attorney, and how he could watch and manipulate him into giving him the best possible defense. The problem was, every day the details of what happened during last year's cold hard winter became vaguer until they were reduced to flashes of shadowy figures, screams, fearful eyes and tormenting dreams.

Within the first week, Kenny was no longer able to orientate himself to his surroundings. He could no longer distinguish night from day, lunch from dinner or reality from fantasy. He seldom slept and when he did it was a fitful sleep filled with demons, a stark white behind his eyes or bright colors he could not erase. His appetite was gone. By the time he first met with his lawyer, he could no longer remember the story he had memorized for the occasion.

Amber was his only link to reality and she seemed to not want to be around him. He forced himself to smile when he saw her, the times he realized she was there. His moments of lucid sanity were slipping further and further apart. Soon there would be no more of them but he was too far into his own mind to realize it.

Amber brought newspapers and magazines in the beginning. Kenny decided he was spending too much time reading about himself to keep fact and fiction separated. It was all confusing him. Everything was confusing him. Breakfast was being served in the middle of the night. During the middle of the day they were turning the lights off and in the middle of the night they lit everything up again. They were trying to drive him crazy. It was the one thing he was sure of.

He lay staring at the ceiling trying to remember the meeting he had with his attorney. All he could recall was the sudden panic engulfing him as he walked toward the room where the meeting was to take place.

Now his mind wandered from place to place, subject to subject. It was impossible to think of any one thing. Kenny's ears began to ring. He closed his eyes as if it would stop the noise. It didn't help. Panic sat in and he clasped his hands over his ears so hard it left red marks. There was no relief. A great pressure was building in his head. It was going to explode. His brains were going to splatter all over the room. He shut his eyes even tighter. A spiral of color began to whirl before him. It was a giant spiral and seemed to go on forever leading into a deep hole filled with more noise and brighter colors.

GREEN. RED. BLACK.

It stopped.

It started again.

It stopped.

Kenny screamed.

The spiral faded as though his scream scared it away, but the colors remained. His entire being was red now. Standing in the eerie glow was a woman. The ringing in his ears was back as a buzzing sound. The buzzing of a million bumblebees was circling his head. Figures and shapes began moving far too fast for him to grasp. The woman was familiar. She had no face.

God, the awful noise!

A tiny figure appeared. It was nondescript and stood outside of the cold red color in his mind.

A wind was howling. Fear! The tiny image was afraid. Oh, it was a small boy. The boy needed to use the bathroom. There was a door in the red of his mind. The child pounded on it. He cried:

"Mama. Mama. Mama!" Over and over again.

Now there was silence and darkness as the little boy wet himself.

Green flashed like a strobe light in Kenny's tormented mind. A large figure soared at him.

No, wait. Two people were there. One of them was Amber. Kenny recognized her and smiled. He called out to her. She didn't respond and the world turned black behind his eyes.

He smiled and relaxed in the dark quiet.

Oh, no! Everything lit up again, in a putrid green. The noise of clanging cymbals took over. This was the most horrendous noise yet. He was puzzled. There was a scary indistinguishable greener figure in his mind. It was trying to overtake him. It was trying to be him. He could not stop it. The figure grew bigger and played with Amber. It was always crying for "Mama." He could feel his jaw move and hear the words come out of his mouth. He could not stop it. Sometimes Amber comforted the dark green phantom. Most of the time, however; the two of them were alone in a big cold impersonal place. It was a place where the little green figure was always afraid.

Kenny turned over on the modest cot putting the paper thin scratchy blanket over his head. It didn't do a thing to help. The sound was now ringing in his ears and becoming more demanding of his attention.

The green shadow screamed for its mama.

There was never an answer.

Never!

Kenny began to sob. Maybe he could sort this out if the noise would stop or if the green and sickening red hues would subside. It didn't happen. If the noise died down then the colors either flashed or the spiral returned. If the colors faded to black then the noise exploded in his mind and in his entire body.

Now a woman was pinning a tag on a little boy. Through the ever changing colors, and the debilitating sound of his own real screaming and sobbing he could not make out what was going on.

Then he saw *him*. "Daddy!"

Now the noise stopped. This time Kenny wasn't going to be fooled. He was sure it would come back. He used the much needed break to take a deep breath. He let out a deep sigh. Along with the sigh came a yell for help. No one had ever come when he cried out for help before, so he didn't expect it to happen now. It was a steam release valve to keep him from exploding into a million different pieces.

This time when the colors returned, Kenny no longer saw the shadow. He *was* the shadow, the phantom, the figure in the ever changing colors of his own sick and twisted mind.

Lambent lights, black, white, black, white, black. More noise. God, stop the noise.

Kenny was clinging to the woman with no face. She pushed him away, reared her head back and let out a vindictive laugh in his direction. Kenny hated her.

"Please, God, not green." he pleaded out loud. He wailed. "It is too cold." With the green color the sound in his head had its own beat.

Kenny lay still, afraid to move. He tried to hold his breath. He could not clear his mind no matter how hard he tried. With all of the sanity he had left he opened his eyes.

The noise stopped.

The colors disbursed.

Filled with an uncontrollable rage, he jumped from the cot and with both hands and legs, leaped for the bars on the door to his cell. With a new found super human strength he shook the door and tried to climb to the top like a monkey. The noise beckoned guards from down the hall but they didn't know what to do. One watched Kenny while another ran for a medic.

He ran around the tiny cubical as fast as he could. He smacked his leg into the stark toilet yet it didn't slow him down. Blood oozed from his leg. He rammed into the walls, beating them with his fists. He screamed, "Mama. Daddy. Hate. Love. Scared. Cold." The scene brought tears to the eyes of the guard watching. Kenny's head was bleeding from hitting it against the walls. His fists were raw.

The pain became so insufferable it was able to penetrate his mind even in its tormented state. He sprawled out on the concrete floor on his stomach trying to gain a little relief on the cold damp surface. The floor was dirty, cold and musty, yet somehow it soothed him. It felt good on against his battered and beat up body.

Alone and exhausted, Kenny laid his head on his bloody hands and fell asleep.

Chapter Seven

Judge William Massey had chosen this time for his meeting with Ian Michaels and Tom Waters for two reasons. First, he knew it would be an emotional gathering. Tom Waters was known for his short fuse. Ian Michaels knew little if anything about the criminal element. The D.A.'s office handled every type of horrendous crime one's imagination could dream up.

Some of the things they encountered were far more imaginable then the average citizen could comprehend. Michaels was a clean lawyer. He did all of his work in an expensive office. His clients were stressed, yet were normal people who didn't settle their problems with violence. This in itself set the stage for an unorthodox meeting. The judge wanted to control what he could, which was the time, place and pace of what was about to happen.

Second, he hated cases such as this. The sooner he could get this case opened and closed the happier he would be. The longer it all sat in limbo the more bias he felt building up inside him.

If things didn't proceed soon he felt he would have to recuse himself from the sheer tension alone.

Whenever children were murdered, the public commentary and publicity ran rampant. Parents were grieving. Friends and family were discussing their feelings with anyone who would listen.

With each passing day it became more and more difficult to see to it the Johnston kid got a fair trial, if indeed there was a trial. Even trying to turn a deaf ear to the news, it was impossible to wait until court to hear the details.

They were everywhere, all the time. These murders had taken on a life of their own. He prayed this meeting might be the end of it. No one wanted to take this to trial. The district attorney's office didn't want to make it any more sensational than it already was. They felt they had a slam dunk case and wanted to settle it now. Ian Michaels, according to the local gab line, didn't want to be involved either. He was an innocent bystander whose son involved him because he went to school with the young defendant.

Now, to further compound his stress and aggravation, Ian Michaels was already thirty minutes late. The magistrate wasn't only livid, but shocked. This was contrary to everything he had heard about Ian. Even though they had never met, this isn't what he expected. It took two of the variables out of the Judge's hands, time and pace.

Tom Waters, also angry, explained to Massey for the third time how Michaels had no apparent respect for the court and his schedule didn't allow him time to sit idly by waiting for rude people. It wasn't a good situation.

Ian and Maggie had begun early sorting through the tons of information they had compiled over the last two days. It was after noon when they realized the time. He had no excuse. He knew he had put himself at a disadvantage with both the judge and the assistant district attorney, yet there wasn't anything he could do at this point. Judge Massey wasn't the type of man to be kept waiting and Ian wasn't the kind of man who kept people waiting.

Anger and frustration radiated from Massey's face when Ian stumbled into the room.

He informed the group consisting of Ian, Tom Waters, a court clerk and a guard, that he was now due in court in exactly ten minutes. He addressed them all together as 'Gentlemen' yet he looked straight at Ian when he spoke.

Adding Judge Massey's displeasure to the clutter already spinning around in Ian's pounding head from trying to absorb, sort and file all of the information he got this morning, the counselor was on the defensive.

Ian fell into his seat as Tom Waters started the discussion. "As I see it, the punk should be held in maximum security until the preliminary. The State will charge him with six counts of capital murder and one charge of statutory rape. I don't think confinement presents a problem. He has been incarcerated for three weeks and no one has stepped forward to acknowledge him, much less ask for bail. Of course his lawyer could waive his right to a trial and we will put him away on the evidence we have. It will save a lot of time, money and emotion. Either way, the kid will never be free again."

The judge turned to face Ian. "Well, Counselor?"

When Ian didn't have his answer ready, Massey turned his attention back to the young D.A.

"If this goes to trial, are you charging him as an adult?" the judge asked.

Ian found his tongue at the last minute. He didn't want to get into the schematics of the trial. He didn't have any of those details worked out on paper or in his mind. Having Kenny be tried as an adult was something Ian had not even thought of. It once again reminded him of how little he knew about criminal law. He shook his head. He only knew what he had to know to pass the bar. What he did know about criminal law was the fact he wanted nothing to do with it.

Ian faked looking through some papers in his brief case and then said. "I didn't know about the rape charge. I didn't see it in the records or any statements. Why am I just now finding out about it?"

Tom gave him a coy smile and a chill went straight up his spine. "Few people know about it.

We didn't have to disclose until today. It has been tough on the girl's parents. We didn't want it in the news. Some facts are held back so we can see if the defendants in these cases know the facts. We don't want people confessing to things they didn't do. We have had several of those in this case already. It only muddies the waters. There are enough sick bastards out there wanting fame at any price without giving them all enough rope to hang themselves. Besides, it will be murder trying to find a jury anyway."

Ian wondered if there was a pun intended. If so, he didn't find the humor. "Which victim was raped?" he pursued.

"The last one, the little girl."

Now was as good a time as any to try out Tom's temper. He was notorious for losing it. Ian had listened to many a story over the last few years. He was about to see they were true. This might be criminal law, but in any contest, knowing your opponent was essential. It was sometimes the factor making the biggest impact on how a case was prepared.

"Tom, Judge," Ian said nodding to each as he spoke their name. "I would like to see the lad moved to the Juvenile Center."

Bingo!

"Lad, my ass! The prosecutor screamed, getting to his feet. "Absolutely not, he's right where he belongs. Shit! I have witnesses out my ass with enough physical evidence to see the little bastard fry. After he broke out of St. Joseph's and went on his rampage..." Tom stopped when he caught a glimpse of the defense lawyer's smile. "I want him where he is." Tom finished, while bowing his head, realizing how much information he had given up.

Well, Ian thought. 'I think I hit a nerve.'

Ian started to speak in Kenny's defense, but the judge silenced him. "Gentlemen, please, save your arguments for the courtroom. Tom, sit down." He nodded toward the prosecutor's empty chair. The D.A. sat down.

When the Judge spoke again, it was with quiet

and unquestionable authority. "I feel we have already overstepped our legal bounds by holding the boy this long without a formal charge.

The latest word from the jail is that Kenneth Johnston is no longer lucid. Mr. Michaels, it would be in the best interest of your client to get him evaluated as soon as possible. Ian nodded.

"I've set the preliminary hearing." the judge continued, "for eight am Thursday morning in room twelve. Until then the defendant will stay where he is, in solitary confinement at the St. Charles County Jail. I believe it's the safest place for him and the public. At the hearing we'll hash out everything else. Good luck, gentlemen." Massey added as he rose and walked out of the room.

It was best this way. Both the prosecutor and the defense attorney knew it would be fruitless to pursue the meeting further. They stood, shook hands and left the room together.

"How about grabbing a quick cup of coffee?" Tom Water's now spoke to Ian as if they were buddies instead of adversaries in what was unfolding as the most bizarre case in the area's criminal history.

It took a moment for the comment to sink into Ian's preoccupied mind. He was thinking Tom made a poor candidate for a case involving so many children with touchy, hurt and grieving parents. Tom, he felt, was too easily riled and, guilty or not guilty, there could be serious complications in Kenny's trial if Tom had one of his outbursts in the courtroom at the expense of someone's feelings.

This could turn into a circus.

"Sure, I could use a cup," Ian answered.

They walked out of the courthouse and across the street to a coffee shop frequented by lawyers, legal secretaries and courthouse staff of all kinds. He knew being seen having a cup of coffee with

Tom would be the gossip of the day. It didn't thrill him. Also, he hoped he would be spared the thousand questions Tom could ask about why he had taken Kenny's case. The answers to those questions were hard enough to rationalize to himself. He knew they would seem insane if they were ever allowed to hit the air.

The meeting with Judge Massey had not been a total loss. Ian felt he learned more than his learned colleague had intended. Now he had a new lead, St. Joseph's Hospital. It was a bit of knowledge he didn't have before. Oh, he would have found it, in due time, in the massive stack of papers arriving at the office. But now he could work on the information while other things worked their way to the surface. He felt as if he were reading a book, starting in the middle and reading back to the beginning and having figured out the ending. It was becoming more and more important to talk to the family. He needed to talk to Bob Johnston, Kenny's father.

Today was Tuesday. It gave Ian two days to compile enough information to plead his case with authority. Even though the hearing was a formality he would have to study day and night to maintain his credibility. The way he handled the hearing would lead to the way he handled the selection of the jury and carry on throughout the trial.

Glancing at Tom he noticed the guy radiated confidence. Shit. Why not? He had everything in his favor including a huge staff to do his research and grunt work. He could spend hours on any minute detail he found interesting or important.

Ian's goal was to steer the conversation away from the case.

Damn. He wasn't sure why he agreed to coffee in the first place. It was a lapse in judgment. The butterflies in the pit of his stomach kept reminding him, this was a bad idea. He was beginning to amaze himself with his own weird behavior.

After chugging his coffee and contributing little to the conversation, he glanced at his watch and begged off saying he hadn't realized the time and he had a meeting at the office in fifteen minutes. Shaking his head he trudged back to his car. The weight of the world rested on his shoulders and he could not shake his uncertain feelings. Once he got in the car, he felt safe and secure. The warmth of spring sunshine radiated through the windshield and melted the chill he felt to his core. He had to force himself to move. It was a wonderful, simple thing and it made him feel good, better than he did since this all began. Although it was a couple of days ago, it seemed much longer.

Two days wasn't much time to try to learn about sixteen years of a person's life. He was going to give it a try. It occurred to him he hadn't questioned Kenny's innocence or guilt. No one did.

It was about getting some public closure for the victims' families, and about finding something to do with Kenny for the rest of his natural life. Even before Ian met Kenny he knew he was guilty. There was something in the girl's eyes. She had not come to his office seeking help for her brother. She was seeking help for herself, protection, or something he couldn't put his finger on. It wasn't something a sister was doing because she loved and was concerned for her brother. It was so much more and he wanted to find out what her driving force was. Also, he didn't judge Kenny. What mattered to Ian was the why of it all. Did he wake up one morning and decide to murder people? What was the catalyst moving him from high school activities to homicide?

Why did someone so young harbor so much hate? And hate against strangers! He did know enough about criminals and crime to know most people were killed by someone they knew. There was no mention anywhere to make him think Kenny knew any of those he killed. Ian drove back to his office. The more he thought about the real facts the more hair prickled on the back of his neck. Once he even glanced in the rear view mirror for the sole purpose of seeing if he was alone.

Knowing he was, didn't make him feel one iota better.

The law students Ian hired were waiting for him. He spent a few minutes with each of them. Student number one was a good-looking kid with a dark tan and dishwater blond hair going every which way on his head. He hadn't combed it in the last week or so. The young man had a slow deliberate air about him. Intelligence radiated from his deep set blue eyes. His manners were impeccable and Ian thought it refreshing how he leaned forward and listened to every word, asking questions and taking notes as they talked. Ian knew the work he did would be neat and thorough, one less thing to stress about.

In about ten minutes the student, Mike Turner, was back at the table in the conference room, to the left of Ian's office, getting started. His task was to dig through every newspaper article beginning six months before Kenny's arrest. There were three major newspapers in the area, the St Louis Post Dispatch and the Journal newspapers, and the Sun. The Sun had Kenny and his exploits on the front page of every edition and had for months and months. He was interested in details in one paper that were omitted by another and each of their slants on the story. What was speculation and what was truth? Ian wanted a story board in chronological order. Mike began to get started but Ian was still standing behind him so he turned around again to give his new boss his complete attention. "Then read them again for detail. I'm interested in the discrepancies, if any. Note them. We've only got two days so make this easy for me." Ian gave the boy an easy pat on the back and turned his attention to the other student who had been sitting at the table waiting his turn.

These men were exact opposites in look and build. This guy was almost square. He was no more than five feet three and was about as wide. He looked a little like an unmade bed. Rumpled pants and a Washington University sweat shirt were stretched on his body with little room for him to maneuver. When Ian asked his name he gave a big white toothed smile. It would have put the tooth paste models on television to shame. It didn't fit. Oh, well, Ian smiled to himself when he realized the man had no neck. His head sat right on his shoulders. He had seen linebackers with the same trait. There was something about him Ian liked. He bet this kid was the more perceptive of the two.

"I want you to wade through these coroner's reports for me. Summarize them. They're always cluttered with whereas' and here-to-fores. Break them down for me. Put them in simple computer type language. I want to know how each victim was killed. I want to know the exact cause of death. I figure there are some three hundred plus pages here. Try to bring it down to three or four for me. Can you do it?"

The student, Jake Simpson, shook his head as a shy, grin took over his face. There were those teeth again. "Okay. Then let's get started. If you have any questions, Maggie will be here. Make yourselves comfortable. There are coffee and snacks in the back and Maggie will have some lunch brought in for you later." they both acknowledged.

The soon to be lawyer began gathering the data in his chubby little hands as Ian added. "By the way, on the table are some medical dictionaries. Put this report in layman's terms, whenever possible. Medical terminology isn't my strong suit."

"Sure, Mr. Michaels." Jake moved all of the materials he had gathered over to the couch at the end of the room under the window. By the time Ian left the room the two were hard at work.

Ian smiled as he stood at the door and took one

more look back at the work going on. It was his first smile since all of this began. He wasn't sure what he was doing, but at least he was doing something.

Ian and Maggie spent the rest of the afternoon working on the cases they had pending.

Ian spoke to his clients by phone, took care of details in custody battles and helped one of his restaurant owner friends interview a new chef. It was the high point of his week. For the first time in days, the tension was gone from his shoulders and neck and he could take a deep breath without thinking about it.

His break from Kenny's case didn't last very long. Soon he was done with the familiar tasks he liked. He was full from tasting the offerings of the chef and was now pouring over volumes of behavioral and child development material. He felt a deep longing. It was an unsettling stir. He felt it was a product of his desperation. He needed knowledge. He looked around his office. He had lots and lots of information. It was all around him. He had no knowledge. Knowledge, he knew, was acquired in many ways. A wise man gains knowledge from those who know more than he. One learns shoe shining from a shoe shine boy and preaching from a preacher. No one ever charmed a cobra from a book. One might learn the technique for snake charming but he would never entrance the snake with information and without the experience. It was a fine line Ian had never understood until right now.

He slammed one of the giant books down on his desk causing Maggie to jump "I'm going to the

Johnston house. Care to come along?"

"Do you think we should?" Maggie asked. "It's getting late."

"Well, he's their kid. Who knows what they're thinking. I've got to have some answers and I'm sure as hell not getting them this way. I think this is the perfect time. They won't expect us."

"Well, I don't intend to send you to face the lions alone."

Ian called his wife. Heather answered the phone on the fifth ring, just as he was preparing to hang up.

Had he not promised to let her know what was going on and where he was, he wouldn't have called her. He chastised himself for his fleeting thought about her being an extra added burden to him right at the moment.

She, on the other hand, was much better today. No one was hanging around the house, but she said the phone rang all of the time. It was either a friend wanting to know why Ian was defending such a person, or a stranger asking the same question. So far none of the calls Heather received had been anything she couldn't handle.

The morning papers were full of Ian. There were pictures of him from grade school, high school, college, and law school. There was a picture of him taken through a high power lens the day he visited Kenny at the jail. With the pictures was an almost true biography stating his achievements and speculating why he was involved with the case in the first place. All in all, it was pretty benign and designed to create more human interest in the case.

He supposed they were trying to keep the story alive because right now nothing was going on. Kenny was in solitary confinement at the jail. The trial had not started and the victims were all in their final resting places. How boring for the news makers.

Heather made it clear, she didn't like the notoriety. She was grateful the boys were not mentioned. She felt they were safe from all the hype for now. Ian assured her things would settle down for the after Thursday. All eyes would again be shifted toward Kenny and the whys and hows of the murders. Rubbernecking was all the same, whether it was an automobile accident or a murder trial. Human nature he guessed; each of us slowing down to take a look at what, for a stroke of luck, could have been us.

Ian said his customary "I love you." It was more habit than anything else. Since their relationship became serious all those years ago he had always ended their conversations the same way. It was a comment Maggie, who was now standing beside him, either didn't hear or chose to ignore.

***

It was a long ride to the subdivision where the Johnston's lived. They rode in a comfortable silence. Ian was busy making mental notes of the neighborhood hoping to pick up some clues to Kenny's personality and demeanor through his environment.

Maggie spent her quiet time studying Ian.

The first real communication the two shared came when they began trying to pin down the street and then the house itself. The neighborhood was upper middle class. The lawns were all mowed and landscaped. Each house was well maintained. They were all unique, not of the cookie cutter variety. The Johnston home stuck out because of a late model Suburban sitting in the driveway looking wounded with two flat tires. It crossed Ian's mind these flat tires could have something to do with public sentiment and Kenny. He shrugged off the thought since nothing else seemed disturbed.

The house was three stories. The garage was on ground level with stairs off to the left at the end of a well-manicured sidewalk. There was a large porch around the house and although they could not see the back of the house he had the impression it went all the way around, giving it an old southern plantation feel. They sat in the car while Ian studied his surroundings.

"Decent." he mumbled. "Very decent." He could now see a large above ground swimming pool in the backyard. The lawyer scrutinized, squinted and surveyed, looking for any clues reflecting the psyche of those who occupied the inside of those custom built walls. There wasn't a thing. The house could have belonged to anyone. Of course, he didn't think there would be a sign reading, mass murderer lives here.

It was dusk now, as Ian got out of his car. He went around to the passenger's side to retrieve Maggie, and escorted her to the front door with his hand resting on her slim waist.

She flushed with his light touch, he didn't know if it was him or the weather.

As they reached the door, two children, a boy and a girl came rushing out. The Johnston's were either no longer were hiding, or they never were, and it was erroneous reporting.

The two kids came close to knocking Maggie over, yet they kept going, oblivious to what was going on and without an apology. They were laughing and yelling with delight. To them, the couple was invisible. They left the front door wide open behind them.

Ian paused for a long moment and then stepped inside. "Mrs. Johnston?" He called. "Mrs. Johnston, is anybody home?"

No one answered. Maggie stepped in out of the chilling spring evening air. They were standing in an entrance foyer between the first and second floors. The house was as quite as a tomb. Ian stood trying to decide whether to wait, go in further or leave, when Amber came around the upstairs corner. Her eyes widened and her face paled when she saw them.

"Mr. Michaels? What are you doing here? Miss Dane?"

"I came to see your parents. Are they home?"

"No. Shauna is out and dad isn't home yet. He will be soon though. Any minute now." Ian could not read the look in the girl's eyes, but he sensed she was less than thrilled they were in the house.

Amber nodded. Ian gave her a reassuring and knowing look and she relaxed a little.

Ian stepped aside to let Maggie go ahead of him.

They climbed the few stairs to the main room and seated themselves. They chose seats away from one another. Ian sat where he could get the best view of the house. He sat Maggie so she could watch whoever came in the front door without being noticed. Amber had walked down to the same floor they were on and watched them with great interest until they were settled. Then without a word she turned on her heel and disappeared the way she had come.

Again, Ian took time to study his surroundings. The room in which they sat was neat and modern. The chair he occupied was expensive, as were the rest of the furnishings he could see from his vantage point.

A closer look revealed what he termed surface cleanliness. The center of the room had been vacuumed but the edges of the carpet were thick with dust. The stairs leading to the level where Amber had gone were the same way. All of the picture frames, lamp shades and knickknacks were dusty and webbed from lack of a good dusting.

He wished he could walk through the house looking into closets and opening drawers. His instincts told him the children were responsible for the cleaning chores.

Maggie sat in the same room, seeing the same sights but she seemed miles away. Her mind was stuck on Kenny. His environment seemed normal enough. Why, was he the way he was? She looked edgy and uncomfortable. When the door below her opened, she jumped.

A good looking man in work clothes was coming

in. From the looks of the uniform he wore he had put in a hard, dirty day. Even through the heavy layer of grime, Maggie saw a definite charm and gracefulness in the way he moved and looked. She felt corny as the thought crossed her mind, but if she were ever asked to describe the man standing unaware at the bottom of the stairs taking off his work boots. She would have to say he oozed with sex appeal. She flushed and smiled to herself.

As he took off his shoes Maggie and Ian studied him. He was about six feet tall, heavy built, and tanned. His face supported a full, trimmed beard. His beard was red and his hair was black. It was a strange combination yet it looked natural on him. It enhanced his dark green eyes. There was gentleness in the way he handled things. The way he closed the door, unlaced his boots and even as he touched his pocket as he reached for a cigarette. It was apparent in the way he walked.

He strolled up the stairs and down the hall like a cat. He didn't expect company so he didn't bother to look back over his shoulder into the living room. Both Maggie and Ian had ample time to study him as he moved around. Maggie blushed again wondering what conclusions Ian was drawing as he sat looking in the direction the man disappeared. They both knew they should have announced themselves long before now. They didn't.

Ian glanced over at Maggie with a look she could not read and then he stood up. She assumed he was going to follow the attractive stranger into the kitchen.

Before he could take a step, Amber rushed down

the stairs and went in the same direction as her father. They could hear a hushed conversation as they waited. The subdued tones came from the end of the hall. Not one word was audible. Several minutes later the man appeared and walked straight toward Ian, who was still standing.

"Ian Michaels." Ian said as the man came closer. He took the lawyer's outstretched hand. "Miss Dane, my assistant." he added looking toward Maggie.

Maggie blushed again as the man paused to smile at her showing perfect white teeth and his flashy green eyes.

"I'm Bob Johnston." the man replied in a deep voice matching his stature. He had looked down at his own hand before he took Ian's. Perhaps he thought his hand was too dirty to touch another.

"Please, sit down. Can I offer you something to drink? I think I've got ice tea."

"No. No think you." Ian stammered. This wasn't the person he expected to see or the treatment he thought they would receive. "I've come about your son."

"I know. I read the papers. Ken has created quite a stir."

Shit!

What the hell was the matter with people? Apathy was to be expected but in the boy's own father it was unforgivable. The entire family was wacko. Here the boy had killed, raped and terrorized yet his father acted as if he had taken a joy ride in someone's expensive car. How could he be so caviler, so disconnected, so dumb? Or was he in denial?

"Please sit down." Bob offered again. "How's Kenny?"

"Not well, I'm afraid. Word from the jail is he is no longer with us, so to speak." Ian answered between clenched jaws. "He's to be examined by a doctor today." Johnston's mood was no longer cordial. It now reflected anger and disgust. He dispensed with the pleasantries now and said in a flat matter of fact tone. "What is it you want, Mr. Michaels? I've got four hungry kids waiting for their dinner. Would you mind if we finish our conversation in the kitchen?" He didn't wait for an answer. He turned and walked off the way he had come.

Ian shook his head in disgust and shrugged his shoulders at Maggie who was sitting, trying to take everything in. Ian took a step toward Maggie and stopped. The look on her face was unreadable. There he stood, in the living room of a teenage Boston Strangler, trying to get some information and insight into Kenny and the informant had to cook.

He motioned to Maggie to follow him as he started down the mysterious hall everyone found so popular.

"Mr. Johnston." Ian began when he reached the kitchen. "I need to impress upon you the gravity of this situation. Your son's being charged on Thursday with murder and rape. In this state those charges are punishable by death. I need your help. Time's running out."

Ian wasn't finished with what he had to say, but

Bob stopped him. He quit getting things out of the refrigerator and turned toward Ian. There was a deep pain in his sea green eyes. They were now darker and cloudy. Ian had read him wrong. His face and posture said he was more than aware of the predicament.

"No Mr. Michaels. It's you who doesn't understand. I've have done everything humanly possible for my boy, Kenny. He's always refused my help, all of it. My discipline and my love were thrown back in my face. There isn't anything more I can do for him, absolutely nothing."

He turned his back to the attorney.

"Are you refusing to help?" Ian was grabbing at straws. He wanted to know more. He could tell it would take one wrong word and Bob Johnston would stop talking altogether.

Bob let out a big audible sigh as he pulled out a kitchen chair and dropped his big frame into it. His face lost all of its youthful charm. Even though his words were fiery, there wasn't so much as a dying ember in his eyes. "Listen, Mr. Lawyer, with your fancy suit and your private secretary. You couldn't possibly understand. Kenny has ruined two of my marriages with his behavior. This time I had no choice. It was either Kenny or my wife and the rest of my children. It's too late for Kenny "

Kenny's broken father continued after taking a shallow breath.

"When he started lying and stealing and having uncontrollable tantrums at Shauna, my wife, I sent him to a camp for troubled boys. Do you know what I got for my trouble? He tore the place up and had fights with the other campers. He nearly put one kid in the hospital. I was hit with a five hundred dollar out of court settlement because of his actions. The court demanded I get him professional help. I took him to a psychiatrist at St. Joseph's. They kept him. Kenny managed to get away twice. The first time they were able to get him back. You've been reading and are a part of the second escape."

Bob sat there, a deflated man, a man who appeared to once have high hopes squashed by his son's behavior. Something Ian could tell he would never understand. Ian wandered who Bob was grieving for, himself or his son. The realization hit him it would be difficult to separate the two.

"Now I'm ordered by the court to pay eight thousand dollars in medical bills because the insurance company won't pay. It's not only the money. It's the stigma to the other kids, the total destruction of this entire family. What in hell do you want from me?"

Ian was worn out both for himself and for the plight of the Johnston family. Was Kenny born a nut job or did something or someone take a boy prone to personality disorders and push him over the line?

"I want you to help me get to the truth." Ian answered. He tried to keep his voice steady and devoid of emotion. "Help me find out if Kenny's guilty. Give me some support. If his family doesn't stand next to him in court, or anywhere, for that matter, how can anyone else have any faith in his innocence?

Bob was crying now. "I believe the truth is

before us now. It's in every paper we've read, and in every face I see in the street. Kenny is crazy. Ever since he could reason, he's been different. He's always been cruel and spiteful. Now I know why. I guess I just never wanted to face it before.

I'm facing it now. There isn't a thing I can do. As soon as this is over we will try to move and change our names. There's no other way to escape this. It isn't fair for my other children to have to live with Kenny's sins. Please leave us alone. My legal obligations to Kenny will be met. I'll sign what needs to be signed and go where I need to go. But I won't sit and subject myself to the gory details of what my boy did. I can't and I won't."

Ian lowered his voice to show both sympathy and compassion. "But Bob, you can help me get to the real truth. If Kenny's insane, we can see he's put somewhere where he can never hurt another person. I must have your help and cooperation to do it. Surely you want that for your son?"

"Trust me." Kenny's father said it in a voice so soft Ian had to lean forward and strain to hear him. "Walk away yourself before he drags you down with him. Look at what he's done to your reputation already. It's best to let it all run its course. The truth, if there is any, can help no one. Please. Go away. Leave, now."

Bob Johnston never looked up again. Ian stood behind him for a long while. There wasn't anything left for him to say or do. He could feel the man's pain even if he didn't understand his logic.

He looked over at Maggie who was standing in the kitchen doorway with silent tears streaming down her cheeks.

Ian took a step closer to Bob and put his hand on the man's massive shoulder. Kenny's father was sobbing uncontrollably now. No one said another word. Ian wondered what he meant about the truth not being able to help anyone. He tried to shake it off as the ravings of a man trying to hold together what was left of his life.

After standing with his hand on the man's shoulder for a long minute, Ian and Maggie left the room. Bob didn't seem aware of them when they left.

On his way out the door Ian took one of his cards and laid it on top of the stair rail. Once he got outside he took a long deep breath of the damp, cool air to clear his head.

"Come on Ian." Maggie tugged at his sleeve. "I want to leave this place." A chill ran down her back causing her to make an odd sound and movement. It got Ian's attention and he began walking toward the car.

She pulled her coat around her as she waited for the heater to warm the damp car.

They again rode in silence. It wasn't, however; the same easy void as on the way over. This stillness hung heavy around them like a deep fog.

"You're shivering." Ian forced himself to say. "Come over here, closer to me."

Without answering, Maggie scooted toward him. It was warm in the car now yet Ian sensed her chill was coming from deep within, and not related to the weather.

Ian felt their moods plummet and he wanted to

stop it. "Are you hungry?" He asked with as much enthusiasm as he could muster.

"No." She answered, looking out the window. "But I could use a drink." she added.

"Good idea. There's bound to be a place around here somewhere." He turned onto a main street and stopped at the first nice place he saw.

Ian got out of the car and reached his hand back in to help Maggie slide out on his side. He closed the door and pinned her to it with his body. Resting both hands on the top of the car began moving up and down and sideways against her. Maggie responded. He knew she shared his need to be needed. She put her arms around him and buried her face in his coat.

Now Ian took his hands off the roof of the car and slipped them inside her coat so they were around her waist. They stood for several minutes, not thinking about Kenny or Bob or the weather.

They were building up to a crescendo. He brought one hand out of her coat and used it to lift her face up so he could look into her eyes. "I need you."

He looked like a lost puppy trying to get a prospective owner's attention. He kissed her. Then he stopped kissing her and pushed her away to arm's length where he studied her until she blushed. He drew her back to him and kissed her longer and harder. Each kiss they shared got deeper and more searching until he could stand it no longer. He stuffed her into the car.

There was no need for talk now. They drove back to the office without a word. The students were gone. It was quiet and dark. The only sound was their breathing and the beating of hearts.

He ushered her in though the side door and turned on a lamp near the desk. The thick shade spread an ambient light, a glow to light their lust.

Maggie felt a surprising shyness she'd never experienced before with Ian. She stood by the door unmoving and watching him. He was slipping out of his overcoat and loosening his tie in what seemed like one movement to her. "You are so far away," he breathed. "come to me."

"I feel strange." She admitted.

"Do you want me to take you home?" He asked walking toward her.

She answered "No."

He was kissing her now and her shyness was gone. For every kiss he had she had one to return. She didn't try to resist him. She craved his warmth. His body was shutting out the coldness of the world as she had seen it tonight. She wanted to feel safe and good again so she gave into it.

Alive, she needed to feel alive and attached.

She wanted to make love.

Ian was past her point. He wanted to have sex.

She led Ian to the couch on the far side of the room where she sat. He stood looking down at her like a timid school boy afraid to move until she took his hand and put it on her breast.

It was his okay and he took it.

Ian lifted her legs onto the couch so she was lying down. He knelt beside her. Undressing her as he went, he kissed every inch of her as he exposed her a little at a time. She in turn stripped his body naked in the same fashion.

They moved in unison from the couch to the floor and made love on the rug.

"I love you," rushed out of Maggie's mouth in a breathless exhale. She didn't mean to let it escape. She had never said it before but at this moment, she had never loved anyone more.

"You are beautiful." He whispered in her ear as he ran his fingertips down her body from her neck to her ankle stopping at her stomach to draw a little circle with his thumb.

Maggie turned over on her stomach. "I'm starving."

"Me too." He kissed her on the back.

Maggie got up and gathered her clothes as Ian watched. There was no shyness now. As she headed for the bathroom she took a glance over her shoulder and raised her foot and gave it a playful flick when it reached her knee.

"I'll give you five minutes, or I eat without you." He chided.

She smiled and struck up another seductive pose at the bathroom door an instant before she closed it.

Ian dressed and poured himself a drink. As he sat at his desk, lust and or love gave way to the present moment and the case. Bits of Kenny Johnston's life were scattered all over it. Picking up a pencil, he began taking notes. One was to find out about St. Joseph's where Kenny was held at one time. He would go there as well as find the camp Bob Johnston mentioned in their earlier conversation. He was almost sure it would turn out to be the Youth Needs Help Camp. It was State supported and fit the bill. When he finished Maggie was still in the bathroom so he called home.

Ian was talking to Heather when Maggie opened the door and slipped into the office. The feeling of love she held for him only moments before melted as she stood there.

Why was she jealous? Every rational thought fled her mind. All she could think of was how could the son-of-a-bitch make love to her and then call his wife and chat as if he had spent the evening bowling?

What kind of man was this who had such a hold over her mind and her body? Hell.

What she wanted from this relationship. What she had so carefully planned and orchestrated was backfiring before her eyes.

Her eyes caught the bottle of scotch sitting on the side board. She walked over and poured herself a drink.

Two days earlier she was worried he would lean on her.

By the time he hung up the telephone she had outward control of her emotions.

This evening had taught her two new emotions, love and jealousy.

Ian had caught a glimpse of the look on her face when she came back into the room. He also learned a new emotion, guilt.

Chapter Eight

Tuesday morning Ian contacted the Division of Family Services to see if they had any records on Kenny. Everyone had been talked to so many times; no one gave him trouble about subpoenas. They had an extensive file on Kenny. Complaints had been coming in from neighbors, teachers and the police for the past five years. Kenny's school truancy record was so extensive it had provoked a state investigation.

The conclusion was Kenny didn't fit into his family unit. When the determination was made, DFS came and removed Kenny from his home putting him in the Youth In Need Home and Camp. He was supposed to stay there with counseling and structure giving authorities a better handle on his problems to come up with a more permanent solution.

Ian called the director of the home. The state supported camp was on the edge of Cottleville, a rural suburb of St. Charles. The place was on about seventy-five acres and included a couple of bunk houses, a cafeteria, a school and several buildings which held a small hospital and staff. There was a shop building and a farm where the boys (it was all boys) could learn something productive. There were chickens, cows and sheep as well as some cats hanging around. They belonged to anyone willing to pet them. All in all it was a nice place and appeared to be run by people with the best interest of the kids incarcerated there at heart.

The Director of Youth in Need was a quiet, self-assured, reliable, unflappable guy named Alex Watkins. Alex had been with the home since its conception twenty years earlier. He agreed to speak to

Ian about Kenny's time was there. Mr. Watkins kept a detailed account of all the activities at the home and of all the incidents with the boys he could document. In Kenny's case he had done the same.

Alex said he had been over the material at least a hundred times since Kenny's arrest.

First with the police, then with the district attorney's office, then doctors hired by the district attorney's office, other state child welfare people and now he was going over it with Ian.

Ian could tell he knew the material well enough so he wouldn't have to look at his notes. He could also tell that the Director was using them anyway.

Kenny had been there for seven weeks. The reports involving the first six weeks were carbon copies of one another. They all stated Kenny was quiet and was non-responsive to the program. He wouldn't and didn't join into any activities, although with some prodding and guidance he would complete domestic and farm tasks. Most of the time, Kenny listened to music, and ignored everything else. He wouldn't even watch television with the other boys.

The seventh week was different. Kenny became argumentative and abusive. They increased his counseling sessions and put him on a small dose of an anxiety drug. Ian made a note of the drug in case his behavior could be a side effect. He doubted that it would to be the case. Kenny remained in an agitated state. On Wednesday, the notes read, his mood and demeanor were so different the house staff thought a search of his room was in order. Nothing out of the ordinary was found.

On the following evening Kenny attacked his roommate. "All we have's the boy's story."

Alex Watkins related. "Kenny refused to do or say anything in his own defense. According to Ben, the roommate, Kenny was listening to the radio and drumming on a night table along with the beat of the music. It was after eleven pm. Quiet hours are from ten at night to seven in the morning. Ben asked Kenny to turn off the radio, Kenny wouldn't. Ben got angry and shut the radio off himself. Kenny turned violent and cut him with a kitchen knife he'd sneaked into the room. Since it wasn't found in the room search, no one knew for sure how it got there.

I locked Kenny in my office until the police and his parents were notified. By the time they arrived he was gone. According to our by-laws, Kenny couldn't be allowed to stay at the camp any longer. He broke a cardinal rule and jeopardized one of the other resident's personal safety.

"Did you talk to his parents on that night?" Ian asked.

"Yes, they came here."

"Can you relate that interview to me?"

"Sure." I don't even need my notes. I remember Mrs. Johnston's comments verbatim. She said she wasn't surprised by Kenny's behavior. Her only surprise was it took Kenny so long to reveal his '\true self'. Right here in my office she gave her husband an ultimatum. Either he goes, or I go. Those were her exact words.

"What did Kenny's father have to say?" Ian perused.

"Very little, he was quiet and withdrawn He seemed embarrassed by Kenny's behavior and unsettled by that of his wife."

"Do you happen to know how long Kenny was on the loose before he was apprehended?"

"Oh, the police had him back here before I finished speaking with his parents. He couldn't stay here and his father didn't want him jailed so they agreed to sign him into St. Joseph's Hospital in the locked psychiatric ward."

After the proper courtesies were exchanged, the men hung up.

Ian sat looking at the notes he took during his talk with Watkins. Hour by hour, day by day this was turning into a case to be pleaded as an insanity defense. He sat tapping his pencil on the note pad in front of him. If he had a young girl or a small boy could he sit back and watch Kenny get what seemed like no punishment other than to be locked in a hospital facility for treatment? A chill ran down his back and the hair stood up on the back of his neck. No it wasn't something he could live with if he was one of the victim's families. This was a horrible situation, and it was getting worse by the minute.

Ian was about to call St. Joseph's Hospital when Maggie arrived. She made no mention of his being there before her although he could never remember a time when it happened before. She said she was at a loss. All of her little mechanical duties, the ones she had done for nearly a decade were all done for her this morning. The coffee was made. All of the lamps were turned on. The front offices drapes and the drapes in Ian's office were all open. The recorder was off the telephone. These were all things she did each morning. He had no way of knowing it was how she put her mind in the work mood. By the time she finished each day she was ready to work. Ian looked up to see Maggie standing , waiting for him to tell her what he needed done, as if it were her first day.

Aloof and professional Maggie asked "Was there something special you wanted me to do today?"

Before he could answer, one of the law students arrived with his assignment in hand. Ian laid out the next task for the young man. Search for cases of mental incapacity in murder cases involving young victims and young offenders. He was to spend his time at the St. Louis University and Washington Law libraries and bring back the findings. Time was running out so Ian told him to bring things, if he could find them, mirroring what they were working with. Ian shook his head. He doubted if there was anything out there like what they were working on.

Maggie wrote the student a check for the work he had previously done, going on the premise that most students were always broke.

Ian flipped through the large file Mike Turner had handed him. He took a deep breath

and wished he didn't have to read about the horrible deaths these six people suffered. He knew it would be gruesome and unsettling. It was written in outline form. Included was a picture of the murder victim before the crime and another at the crime scene in the position they were found. Ian began reading the report. Maggie pulled up a chair beside him and read over his shoulder.

Case #1 Mary Ann Rogers

Coroner's Notes: Well-nourished white female, age 32, multiple puncture wounds in her upper extremities, pharynx and upper thoracic region

Cause of death: Exsanguination

Case #2 Thomas Wayne Adams

Coroner's Notes: Extremely small 11 year old: Fractures of cervical spine, thoracic spine, both legs and both arms.

Cause of death

Beaten to death.

Case #3 James Wade Wallace

Coroner's notes: 9 year old well-nourished white male. Broken neck.

Hanged with belt.

Cause of death, strangulation

Case #4 Martha Jean West.

Age 29. Well- nourished. Hematoma on right side of brain.

Cause of death

Suffocation and head trauma

Case #5 Donna Ann Strapmeyer

Puncture wound to left anterior chest wall penetrating the aorta.

Cause of death.

Bled to death.

And the last was Andrea Sue Payne. Head crushed. Bones broken and lungs punctured, and

sexually assaulted. She was only six years old. Any one of her injuries could have killed her.

Ian sat staring at the pages before him. Words escaped him at the moment.

These were all violent deaths. They were mean and vicious. Were they random? Ian didn't think so. They were too violent to be random. The why of it swam around his brain as in a whirlpool. As it spun it made him sick at his stomach.

After a very long time, Maggie pried the reports from his hands. It took all of his waning energy to lift himself out of the chair. He felt like cement blocks were tied to each arm and foot with the biggest heaviest block tied to his breaking heart. It seemed the short walk to the bathroom took an hour. The vomit was in his throat.

"Are you all right?" Maggie was pouring coffee as she spoke.

"No, not really, I hate this. I wish we weren't a part of it."

"You sat and talked with the boy. Is he capable of doing these things?" she glanced down to the report as she asked.

Ian didn't answer. He closed the bathroom door. Alone, he leaned against the sink and sobbed into his hands. When he could cry no more, he splashed cold water onto his face. He wet a towel putting it on the back of his aching neck and clutched each end for security.

When he opened the door, he picked up the conversation as if he had never left the room.

"I hate to believe anyone's capable of killing anyone else. I saw enough in the service to know some people enjoy killing. You're certainly taking it calmly," he added.

"After the first case, I stopped reading," she said subdued. "I don't believe I have to know more than I do. I'm seriously afraid I'd never sleep again."

Ian was back in the office now. "I'm sorry I pushed the girl on you. I feel I got us into this," she added.

"I'm a grown man. It isn't your fault." He was still holding the towel so tight his knuckles were white. Walking toward the window, he stood before it, both feet planted, watching outside.

There were children going down a sliding board. Couples, young and old, walked hand in hand, whispering to one another, smiling. In front of each of them, Ian's mind placed a mutilated body and a tear-stained face.

"God help us all," he said aloud.

Ian never believed in destiny. Destiny was for underachievers. It was an excuse for those who never finished a novel or a song. It was for people who could never find the time to paint a picture or go back to college. They could always blame their lack of ambition or drive on destiny.

Now he wasn't so sure.

Why then was Ian Michaels standing there before a sunny window on a beautiful spring morning thinking of all of the grotesque facts spreading themselves before him? Why would a young man feel the need to do such horrendous things to another human being?

He remembered in 1966 Charles Whitman stood on top of the tower at the University of Houston and fired a high-powered rifle over and over again leaving sixteen dead and wounding thirty-one. Jared Loughtner went to a political rally outside a grocery store in Tucson shooting a congresswoman and killing six. Gary Gilmore was supposed to have killed the people he did because of horrendous treatment from his parents. He insisted on being executed after the death penalty was withdrawn by the Supreme Court and is one of the reasons it was reinstated. Francis Conley was a nineteen year old with a choir boy face who killed at will. The most recent was a young master's degree student who went to the showing of a Batman movie with only one motive: to see how many folks he could kill. Thank goodness his gun jammed. He left twelve dead and fifty-one injured. This wasn't something new. It was now up close and personal. he hated every minute of it.

Ian was an avid follower of the news yet he knew little about what motivated people to do these unthinkable things. Maybe he was being unfair. The world was filled with so many people, so many problems, so many causes, and each one important to one person or one group. It would be easier for all concerned to have Kenny declared insane. It wouldn't help anyone for all of this to be dragged through the courts.

Nothing would ever bring those people back. Nothing would ever bring a peaceful night's sleep to the parents of those children who had so many questions.

"I'm going to see Kenny," Ian blurted out into the silent room. "While I'm gone, try to reach Jim at his hotel. Find out what he knows about Kenny's Mother.

"After I see Kenny I'm going to St. Joseph's. Call them and tell them I'm coming. Don't ask for an appointment. Just tell them I'm coming." As he talked he was pulling himself together. In a matter of a few moments he looked fresh again.

He was at the jail in no time. It never failed with him. Whenever he was in a hurry to get somewhere it took forever, yet the times he acted on impulse, he was face to face with his decision long before he cared to be. Ian had no idea what he was going to say to Kenny. The report he had read at the office lay beside him. As he picked it up he shook his head.

Some things never change. The inside of a jail is one of those things. He went through security and as he approached the officer behind the desk, the man waved for him to sign in, then escorted him to the same room he waited in before. Kenny was brought in, he didn't wait long.

The guard escorting Kenny pulled out a chair and put the boy in it. He looked up at Ian. There was an unreadable sadness in the man's eyes. He motioned he would wait outside. There were no physical restraints on Kenny this time.

Ian stood on the other side of the table and examined the boy with his eyes. The differences he noticed were startling. Kenny's once rosy cheeks were scratched and covered with tear stains, dirt and dried blood. His hands, now folded on the table, had black and blue marks all over them. His knuckles were raw, bleeding and swollen. His once curly brown locks of hair were plastered to his head with sweat. His eyes were as dull and as fixed as those of a blind man.

Ian fell back into his chair. He sunk low down and stretched his legs under the table. What had happened?

"Kenny?" Ian asked.

Kenny didn't move or in any way acknowledge Ian's presence. Uncontrollable rage was building inside Ian. Again, he wanted to get up and run, to get out of there before he lost control. He ran his hand from his collar to his waist straightening his tie. The sad thing was he had no idea why he felt the way he did.

He had to stay.

"Kenny." This time he slammed his fist on the table with a loud booming noise. Kenny was unaffected. He tried another approach. "Kenny. Tomorrow is Wednesday. Thursday morning we must go to court. I'm going to ask you some questions. I want you to answer them as best you can." Ian's polite tone didn't faze the boy. Kenny sat in the chair as if in a trance and nothing could reach him. Maybe nothing could reach him.

Ian began to read the names of the murder

victims. He went through each slaying in gory detail. It was a grueling task. As he read he watched Kenny. The boy was in a different time warp. "Do you remember any of these people, Kenny?" He placed the pictures before Kenny's eyes so he was forced to look at them. One after another he held them up. Nothing happened. Ian was seething inside, but he wasn't sure why. Was it because this maniac was sitting there unknowing and unfeeling while the rest of the world was writhing in pain around him? Was this peaceful nothing going to be Kenny's punishment? Ian felt his heart would explode as his head began to spin. "Did you do these things, Kenny? Did you tie a plastic bag around Martha West's neck? Did you know she was pregnant, Kenny? Did you hit Andrea Payne with a stick until she didn't move or cry anymore?" With each question Ian's voice got louder. His anxiety mounted. "Kenny," he screamed. "Tell me about the Youth in Need House, Kenny. Tell me about the knife. Is that how it all started, Kenny? Did you like the way it felt when you cut that boy? How did you get out of St. Joseph's, Kenny?"

Ian stopped. It occurred to him maybe Kenny wasn't the only madman in the room.

The entire time he was badgering the boy, Kenny had not shown any sign of life other than his quiet breathing.

In slow deliberate moves Ian gathered his notes and photographs together stacking them on the corner of the table. He put his coat over his arm, picked up his things and walked out the door. Behind him stood the guard with a bewildered look on his face.

There, in the chair, still unmoving, sat Kenny. Whether he was in heaven or his own private hell was the mystery.

Ian stopped by the desk on his way out and told the officer he was sending two doctors over to examine Kenny. He was very much in control now. He was ashamed by his behavior with Kenny, yet no one knew what had taken place, and relieving his hostility and anger had helped him regain his objectivity. He was now much more aware. "How did Kenny get hurt?"

"Damned if I know what got into the boy." The big man shook his head. "It was the strangest thing I ever saw. A couple hours after you left, the kid went crazy. I got a disturbance call from the guard and I went back to help. That boy was runnin' and screamin' and kickin' and yellin' for 'bout an hour. We called the doc but by the time he got here the boy was quiet and layin' on the cot. Not twenty minutes after the doc left he started up again. Only this time he was writhin' on the floor like a snake and beatin' his head and fists against the cement. He was quiet after a bit and we put him back on the bunk. Doc came back and looked him over. Said there was no real damage to his body. He ain't said a word since. He just stays where ya put him."

"Does anyone else know about his condition?"

"Hell no, ain't nobody cares, really. You're the only one who comes now. His sister don't come no more."

"He has to appear in court Thursday morning. I'll send some clothes over for him. Try to get him cleaned up and dressed for me. And, if he should do or say anything, you know, snap out of it, call me will you?"

"Sure."

"Oh, another thing, don't mention this to anyone."

The big officer behind the high desk shrugged his massive shoulders. "It don't mean nothing to me."

"Thanks."

Chapter Nine

Ian walked outside into the warm spring sun. As he drove toward St. Joseph's Hospital his stomach churned. The momentary release of tension with Kenny had not lasted long. He felt he was approaching the entire problem backward. The investigation should have begun with Kenny's birth and gone forward. This way, the more he learned the more confused he became.

St. Joseph's looked like a large country estate. A high brick wall encircled the immense wooded grounds. The only break in the wall was created by an iron gate complete with elaborate scrolls and a small guard house. The guard house sat a few feet up the drive. There was room for one car to pull in the driveway without the gate being opened.

As Ian's car stopped, an armed guard appeared at the door of the little house. He wrote something down on a pad he held in his hand and then walked toward Ian through a smaller gate to the side of the big gate. Ian hadn't noticed it before. It was hardly big enough to accommodate the guy's large frame.

He asked Ian to state his business. Ian, in turn, presented the man with one of his cards and asked to see someone in charge. He was embarrassed not to have found out the name of the doctor he wanted to see. The guard took the card, mumbled something inaudible and pushed his too large frame back inside the way he came. Ian watched him waddle back to the guard shack. Although he was making forward progress, it appeared he was going side to side. His bulk swayed with him like a tidal wave as he moved.

Ian could see he was talking on the telephone once inside the guard house. A moment later the heavy metal gates opened and Ian was able to drive his car into the compound.

"Stay on this drive and go slow. Patients like to walk the grounds." He tapped the side of the car twice with the heel of his hand and motioned Ian forward.

Ian did as he was told. It was at least a mile to the front of the facility and he met no one on the way. At the door he was met by an efficient-looking woman dressed in street clothes and a short white lab coat. He had no idea who she was. She directed him to park his car in a lot to the left of the largest building in what seemed to be a giant medical complex made up of one big building surrounded by six or seven bungalows. He found it difficult to maneuver the car into the narrow space with her penetrating gaze in his rear view mirror.

Ian disliked this woman when he saw her. He had no reason he could put his finger on. After standing with her hands in her pockets and contemplating him for several moments, she walked toward him as he got out of the car. On closer inspection he saw she wasn't walking, she was strutting toward him with a gait stating she was someone to be reckoned with. Her short hair was out of a current fashion magazine as were the clothes she wore under her crisp white coat. The name tag she supported read doctor. Ian took a deep breath and extended his hand to her. "I'm Ian Michaels," he began.

"Yes, I know. I'm Marie Angerstein, Head of Psychiatry here. Even if you had not been announced I'd have known you, Mr. Michaels. Your picture greets me most mornings in the newspaper as I read it and have a cup of coffee. May I say your pictures don't do you justice?"

Ian flushed. Bold compliments from women were not something he was accustomed too.

"I've have been expecting you, Mr. Michaels." She had paused only long enough to take in his reaction to her earlier comment. "Kenny Johnston was under my care during his stay here."

In spite of himself, Ian smiled. Perhaps his first impression was wrong. After all, here was someone who was both refreshing and a rarity in his life as of late. Not only did she admit to knowing Kenny, she even admitted to treating him at her hospital. There was another reason for his smile. Dr. Angerstein spoke with a heavy European accent. Along with her demeanor it was reminiscent of so many old horror movies he had seen.

"Doctor, there are some things I need to know about Kenny."

"Of course, I'll help you if I can, Mr. Michaels." Her smile was provocative. "Shall we go to my office?"

Not waiting for his reply, she began to walk toward where she wanted to go. Ian followed.

There wasn't a soul around. It was dead-of-night quiet. Their footsteps echoed in the emptiness. Ian scanned his surroundings. They had entered the biggest of the buildings through a massive front door of oak and brass. Inside the polished floors of white marble reflected the wildlife and forest pictures hanging from the walls. The doors off the hallway were beautiful wooden masterpieces of craftsmanship. A flowing staircase loomed in front of them with a bank of elevators next to it almost hidden by the gorgeous railing following the wooden stairs to the top where it looked as if marble took over again.

They walked past the staircase and turned down another wide hallway with closed doors supporting room numbers and names he read as they strolled by. After a walk which carried them all the way down one hall and half way down the other, they settled in an understated office. The floors were random-width pine covered with area rugs in warm colors. There was a desk at the back of the room and Dr. Angerstein walked and sat behind it. All along the wall were floor-to-ceiling windows giving a wonderful view of the woods at the back of the compound. Her office supported inviting light and a nice picture to rest your eyes on anywhere you looked. It was remarkable in its calming effect. He was sure it wasn't a random feeling he had, but one orchestrated to make patients comfortable and relaxed. It all worked.

Ian looked toward Dr. Angerstein to find her studying him. For the second time, he flushed. He wasn't sure where to start. Kenny's personalities and behavior, past and present, were swimming around in his head.

"Maybe I can get us started, Mr. Michaels." She didn't wait to see his reaction, but went on. "Kenny Johnston is what we classify as a product of infantile insecurity." The lawyer sat and listened. Her voice with its calm resonance and accent was both authoritative and relaxing. "Ken's mother never wanted him. He didn't get the care or love he needed as an infant. Some cases are so severe the baby dies from lack of nurturing, love and cuddling. It's like the cases you hear about where children are found in cages or locked basements. He was deprived of the basic human contact a baby needs to thrive. I believe he was left to cry for hours in his own squalor. He was always hungry and always on edge with no way to soothe himself. Some children get over this. Most have one parent who tries.

"In most cases," she continued, "with love, understanding and therapy, it can be understood by the patient and they are able to cope. Some use stuffed animals, pets, a loving relationship with a sibling. There are any number of things to help one through the ordeal and healing process. Ken's wasn't correctable. Every human relationship he encountered as a small child was hurtful and abusive.

He went from a mother who hated him to a step-mother who abused him. She didn't try to understand him and only wanted his father. It's, at best, a tragic situation. Kenny's case has always been too harsh and too deep-seated to ever be reversible. So, he rebelled in several ways. Let me point out, some of his areas of rebellion are classic. Some aren't."

Ian sat dumbfounded. He didn't have anything to say. All he had to do was put Dr. Angerstein on the stand on Thursday and Kenny wouldn't be tried as an adult. He wouldn't be put to death. He would be locked up somewhere physically as his mind now was locked up mentally.

She continued. "First, he refused to be toilet trained. Even now he will revert to the toilet habits of an infant if overcome with stress. To further complicate things, his stepmother took his mental illness to be defiance. She couldn't handle him. Shauna was horrible to him." Dr. Marie Angerstein stopped and shook her head before she continued. Ian could tell she cared about her patients and tried to understand them as best she could. "Children need physical comfort, Mr. Michaels. Most mothers provide it out of a sense of love and instinct. Without it a child will become as deformed as the child who hasn't gotten the proper nutrition or sunlight or water. This lack of physical and physiological fulfillment stunted Ken's mental growth as a normal social person by our society's standards. He is a sociopath. There you have an abbreviated but clear synopsis of the determinants of Ken's behavior."

She gave an easy and complete lecture. Now Ian

sat trying to absorb what he had heard. This doctor knew her stuff. She seemed to take Ian's silence as a green light so she went on.

"The only stable force in Kenny's life is his father. The child is much too ill to realize it. His present mother, Shauna, tried to help Kenny in her own crude way, but she lacked the education and patience to do any good. When Ken became too much of a problem for her, she too pushed him out of her life. I'm not condemning her for it, you understand? I'm pointing it out for you to remember when you deal with her. The stories she tells are not pretty.

Ken's problems were too far advanced when Shauna came into the picture. At age six there would have been some hope but one or two years later he was a lost cause, much like a moth who has come close to the light so many times his wings are so tattered he can no longer fly.

"There are two roads ahead for Kenny now. He can be put into a permanent environment where he cannot hurt himself or others and will keep his stress to a minimum or he'll eventually become catatonic. Each time he goes into a catatonic state the longer it will last until one day he won't come back."

Again Ian had nothing to say. The room felt empty without Dr. Angerstein's thick accent filling every corner of it. When he did speak, his own voice sounded odd to him.

"Is Kenny capable of murder, rape and the other charges against him?"

"Most definitely. He probably knew what he was

doing at the time. I'm sure that in his mind he had a valid reason for each step he took. If given enough evidence and time I could tell you what motivated him in each instance. There are many people out there who came from normal families who have committed some terrible crimes, but judging from what I know about Ken, first hand, I can be sure when I say yes. Yes. I believe they're related."

"I know little about Kenny before two months ago. Could you fill me in on a few things?"

"Of course, ask your questions and I'll try to see if I can help you."

"What is Kenny's birth mother's name?"

"I have it somewhere," she answered looking through her notes for the first time. "Yes, here it is, Sarah Lee Johnston. Her new married name is Berle."

"Is she aware of Kenny's situation?"

"I doubt it. I hear she is reclusive and quite odd herself. She never did return a phone call or fill out any of the questionnaires about her son when we sent them. Actually, other than what Bob Johnston has said about her and what conclusions I have drawn from those conversations, I know nothing about her."

"What sort of mental testing and therapy did Kenny receive while he was here?"

Dr. Angerstein got up and went to a coffee maker sitting on a side board on the north wall of the room. The side of the room where there were no windows. She filled a cup she had picked up from her desk. Once there she picked up another mug supporting a St. Joseph's logo and held it out in Ian's direction, in effect, asking him if he wanted some coffee. She smiled her warm smile again and Ian raised his frame out to the chair and joined her and took the coffee, adding cream to it.

During the silence Ian walked around the room looking out the windows and reading the diplomas on the wall before ending up back in the same seat he vacated five minutes before, yet feeling much better for the slight diversion.

"No tests that have names," she continued as they sat back down. "Mostly I talked to him and observed. In most cases we don't actually administer any tests unless they are ordered by the court."

"In your opinion, is Kenny a sane and rational person?"

"No, no not at all." With her last statement she stood up. "I'm sorry, Mr. Michaels. I've got a patient who needs me. She can't be kept waiting any longer."

"I understand, just one more thing. Is there any way you can go over to the county jail and take a look at Kenny before Thursday morning?"

"Yes, of course," she said, taking time to jot a note on her desk pad.

There must have been a button or foot switch somewhere on the desk because before they finished speaking a young man, in all white, appeared out of nowhere. He escorted the lawyer all the way to his car. Then he stood in the driveway until Ian was out of his sight and in sight of the guard at the gate.

Ian drove around after leaving the hospital. If

this were a divorce case his next move would be automatic. As it was, he remained confused. He thought back to how it all began. There was the young frightened girl in his office, his immediate reaction to everything, his first conversation with the district attorney, and then Kenny himself.

In a few short days his life and attitudes had changed. Things were different now. He felt so aware. The question was no longer whether or not Kenny was guilty. Ian was becoming more obsessed with the why; even more than before. It was a question the court wouldn't take time to answer.

What drove someone to kill? Did the same motivation drive those who committed suicide? Was suicide less than murder? He had read it was healthier to be homicidal than suicidal. What a choice! What a troubling realization.

Why did it trouble him so? He didn't abuse his children nor was he an abused child. He could drop the case right now. No one would fault him for it. Hell. Nobody cared. To the district attorney's office it was another case to win to prove they were hard on crime and criminals. To the courts it was a case they needed to clear to get to all of the cases behind it. To the Johnstons it was an embarrassment and detriment to their family life. They needed it behind them so they could move out of the area and change their family name and try to salvage a life again. To the victims' families it was a chance to see the person who stole their loved one and ruined their lives. It was a chance for some closure, a closure they would never have because it was senseless and brutal and totally uncalled for. It was a lose, lose situation.

Five minutes testimony from Dr. Angerstein and Kenny would be declared insane and not stable enough to stand trial. The judge would make a ruling somewhere down the line to commit Kenny to a mental institution for the rest of his life. Ian felt uneasy and sick. It was a familiar feeling he remembered from childhood. He could not put his finger on what had caused it then, either.

He knew, if only for himself, he was going to follow through and try to find out Kenny's motivation.

Driving when he was upset always helped Ian. He knew he wouldn't be interrupted and he was warm and comfortable in his car. He drove out to one of the largest lakes in Bush Wildlife area and walked around it. He watched the sky and the trees and a father and son catching catfish. After about an hour, he took one last long deep breath of the crisp, clear, clean fresh air and thought how grateful he was for everything good in his life. He had managed to spend the entire day alone with his thoughts. It was beginning to get dark and he didn't want to be alone any longer.

Ian drove around so long after he left the lake, he wasn't sure where he was. He was forced to stop the car and get his bearings. At the first place he could get a signal on his cell phone, he called Heather at home. Doing his best to sound happy and carefree he told her he was ready for a night out. Could she be ready in a half hour? Heather agreed. He hoped she didn't notice the edge in his voice.

The Michaelses spent an enjoyable and much-needed evening together. They ate at a small but very good Chinese restaurant in O'Fallon. They were served by a young high school girl. If she knew who they were she didn't make it known to them. After egg drop soup, spicy chicken and vegetables along with sticky rice, a crab Rangoon and some green tea, Ian felt almost his old self again. He was relaxed, animated and happy. After dinner he suggested they go see a movie. They both laughed. Ian hated movies. Heather thought perhaps a play. No, he vetoed the plan. He wasn't dressed for it and there would be too many people they knew. He would end up getting dragged into a conversation about the case. It was the fastest way he knew to end a great evening.

They ended up at a movie anyway. It was supposed to be a comedy about an older couple who no longer connected in bed. It had its moments, but most of it was sad to him and he was uncomfortable for the people on the screen. Ian relaxed as he watched it. He would have rather fallen into a fantasy than the half-truths on the screen. All in all, he enjoyed it. He noticed Heather became more relaxed and talkative as the evening progressed. They needed some time alone and he knew it.

They ended their evening making love.

They tended to one another's needs as only two people who have known each other for years can do. He slept the rest of the night for the first time since all of this began.

In the morning Ian took a shower. He sang and didn't worry about it waking up Heather who had been sleeping soundly. He came out of the bathroom with only a towel wrapped around his lower half. Heather smiled

"You sound happy," she chided."

"I guess I am." He sat on the side of the bed and took her hand. "I think the worst of this is behind us."

"Do you really?" The tone of her voice made him want to look deep into her eyes. What he saw was something he could not put his finger on. He kissed her hand. He knew last night was superficial and didn't solve their problems yet he wasn't willing to let it go or negate it with a serious conversation. It would only serve to make their problems worse.

The look in her eyes wasn't something he chose to challenge.

Not here. Not now.

Chapter Ten

Wednesday may have started with singing in the shower but it went downhill from there. It turned out to be a most-nerve-wracking day.

There was no word from Jim in Oklahoma. Maggie had left numerous messages, Jim was out and either hadn't gotten or returned any of them.

Ian saw early on that Maggie was in-one-hell-of-a-bad mood.

They spent hour after hour going over the files on Kenny. Ian was looking for clues, anything that would give him insight into the boy's actions. Everything pointed to Dr. Angerstein being right on the button with her diagnosis. Witnesses put Kenny at each crime scene within minutes of the murders. His fingerprints were everywhere. There didn't seem to be any mystery about who committed the murders and the rape. Ian had the horrible feeling that something wasn't right, a sick sinking feeling from head to toe. It was all he could do not to check on his boys at school, his wife at home and scream at Maggie to get over it.

The pictures of the victims were lying on the conference table where he and Maggie were working. Ian thought a couple of the children looked familiar yet he knew they couldn't. He figured it was because he had seen their pictures in the newspapers and on television.

By afternoon any good thoughts Ian may have had at the beginning of the day were out the window. Maggie's mood worsened with each passing minute. He offered to take her to lunch. She snapped a flat refusal back at him. The pressures of the day were pounding down on him like a hot sun in the desert. When he reached his limit, he moaned piss on it under his breath and walked out.

Eating lunch didn't appeal to him. Getting out of the tense atmosphere of the office and into the fresh air seemed his only hope. There were not many people on the streets. Although it was spring, it was a cold crisp day. He had walked out without his coat. He refused to go back so he tucked his head toward his chest and against the wind and began strolling down Delmar Street. After about a half hour of mindless walking he found himself standing outside Dressels Public House. It wasn't a place he went often, yet today it fit the bill. Dressels supported a pub environment and catered to the local arts and literary crowd. He stepped inside. It was warm and inviting. He loved the wood, the art and the ambiance. He took a seat in the corner out of the flow of traffic and ordered a dark stout beer on draft.

Ian had not indulged in self- thought for a long

long time. Now he knew he had avoided it on purpose. He didn't want to have to think about Heather and Maggie, not together anyway. Not as in Ian and Heather and Ian and Maggie. He, up to this point, had gone to great lengths to keep them separate. He may not have done it on purpose, yet he did it all the same.

He viewed Heather as his loving wife. She was naive, charming, and beautiful, the mother of his children. They shared many a great moment together. For the second time in the last few days, when he thought about being in love with her he got an old familiar feeling he remembered from his childhood. It reinforced a feeling he had several times in the past years. He was no longer in love with Heather. He loved her for who and what she was and represented in his life. He respected her for being a great mother, in addition to everything else, Heather was the product of old money. She represented the perfect woman he had needed for the plan he manufactured as a young man. Heather was all the things he told himself were important as he had planned his life. Why didn't he recognize the shallowness of his motives at the time? The old feeling of lack, that followed him as a child, overwhelmed him now. It was as if a piece of glass was churning in the pit of his stomach always reminding him of the lack of security back then. The death of his mother had left him in the hands of a functional alcoholic who couldn't cope with horrible things life throws in your path as you try to plug along. He knew he was no longer in love with Heather, yet he loved her. Respect and friendship should be enough to carry their marriage through, but he knew she deserved more. Ian Michaels, the jerk, he admitted. Self-examination, he decided, was a trap. And this trap was about to clamp its jaws around him and he knew it.

Maggie was ten years his junior. She was young, beautiful and witty. Her almost fluid movements mesmerized him as he watched her. Sometimes he was sure he could make it his life's work. Was it lust or love? Was there a difference at this point? He thought of her as his secretary, close friend, and confidant, and now, he admitted for the first time, his mistress.

Funny how the mind works, he thought as he began sipping his second ultra-cold beer from a frosted mug. Five years of intimate weekends and long hours of pleasant conversation and it had never come to him in such a crude term. Now, today, because of something he might have seen in his wife's eyes and because Maggie wasn't her picture-perfect self, he put it all together.

Now what?

"Great timing, asshole," he mumbled loud enough so that the two ladies at the next table turned to look at him.

Life became more complicated with each passing moment. He could not say, I love my wife, or I love Maggie and go on with his day. He knew being self-indulgent over his cavalier lifestyle made him even worse, to himself and to anyone else, who he imagined might find out about him.

Ian stood and left a fifty dollar bill on the table because he didn't want to deal with a waitress. She was female and he was sure, at this point, all women could see right through him. They could see who and what he was. At this point he still had the decency to be ashamed of his actions.

After leaving the pub, he walked to the nearest bus stop and sat down. In spite of the cool weather he was flushed and his head was spinning.

Maggie was in such a wretched mood. Until now he hadn't allowed himself to know why. But, he realized, if she could go this long without realizing he was a cad, what else had she overlooked.

The three beers he had in less than an hour were having their effect. He couldn't get out of his own mind. He thought back over the past five years. Would his wife come to the same conclusion as he had? Did she ever suspect him of being unfaithful? Who was he being unfaithful to? This week he had made love to both of them. Damn. He hadn't realized what he had done, and he wasn't proud. He shook his head trying to shake all of the questions out and replace them with answers. It was no use. He wanted a real drink. He didn't need one; he still had a buzz from drinking the beer as fast as he did. Ian was never much of a drinker. He had wine with dinner and a drink at parties. Now he wanted a drink. He got up from the bus stop bench and headed back the way he came.

When he got to Duffs' he stopped. Duffs' had been around over forty years. It was a great place to eat before a show at the Fox Theater or a good quick lunch. Ian likened it to a pair of comfy jeans. Before taking his seat in the restaurant he stopped by the bar, ordered a double scotch, neat, and took it with him as he was seated at a small table in the northwest corner of the room where he could see everything.

Most of the lunch crowd was gone by the time he settled in his seat. He glanced around the room admiring its heavy wooden wainscot and hardwood floor. He was looking into the sun as he scanned the room so between the bright light and the dim interior of the room, he didn't see her at first.

Then he saw a silhouette, and it was Maggie.

"'Who's minding the store?" he asked trying to sound casual.

"'There is nothing to mind. Everything is set for tomorrow and the recorder's on the phone." He realized he wasn't the only one who had been drinking. She was using her polite business voice on him. It was the one he had heard so many times as she dealt with clients.

Saved by the bell, the waitress came to the table to take their order. Ian ordered a refill and Maggie chose a glass of Moscato d'asti.

The waitress left the area. There wasn't anything to save him now.

"Maggie, I owe you an apology," he tried to begin.

"Please, Ian," she looked around as she spoke. "Forget it. I'll be all right." He hated when someone played the martyr.

Conversation was suspended again as full glasses were set before them.

"It's rather difficult to ignore. You're not being your happy-go-lucky self. I should know why, but it's not apparent to me."

"Listen Ian, I don't want to have this conversation. I knew what I was doing when I got into this relationship, you didn't promise anything and I never wanted anything. Please. Let it be.

He reached for her hand but she moved it out of his reach.

"Ian," she pleaded, "Go home." She began crying and wasn't able to continue.

Ian didn't wait for her to regain her composure. Standing up, he took several bills out of his pocket and threw them on the table. Then he took her by the arm and helped her out of her chair.

She was crying even harder now. Every move he made was automatic. He escorted her back to the office parking lot by grasping her arm above the elbow and half shoving her. It was a long walk, about nine blocks. He didn't loosen his grip. They kept moving, he guiding and she crying.

In his mind there was neither rhyme nor reason to his own behavior. "I believe I know what the problem is. It's called the eternal triangle. God only knows why today it becomes a problem after all of these years. The truth is, it has become a problem and I'm going to give you a choice."

Maggie seemed to shrink away from him, as if she were afraid, buy it didn't deter him. "We can either go to your apartment and talk it over, or we can go to my house and include Heather."

Maggie snapped her head up and looked him straight in the eye. "You have got to be joking," she managed without a sob.

"Try me." He started the car and began speeding in the direction of his house. He felt Maggie's hot stare on him.

"Take me home."

He made a reckless U-turn in the middle of an intersection and raced toward her apartment. Once they were inside, and she had fixed them each a drink, he seemed to relax... to be the old Ian again.

"Let's begin again," he said, "I need to know what it is you want."

The wording seemed harsh yet it was delivered in a way neither harsh nor sarcastic. It came out of his mouth as an honest, direct question deserving an honest and direct answer. He waited for her to start talking. She seemed incapable.

Maggie's apartment was big. It had two bedrooms and two full baths plus a big eat- in kitchen and a private patio as well as a living room bigger than seen in most modern homes. It was on the bottom floor of a three story building. It was private and once inside it was easy to forget it wasn't a single family home.

The place was decorated in earth tones with lots of live plants in front of the big windows. There were bold color accent pillows on the overstuffed couch and chair. No television in the living room made any piece of furniture she was sitting on the focal point. No matter what time of day or night Ian had dropped by, it was always clean and neat as was its occupant.

"I don't know," she answered as she slipped her shoes off by the door and sat on the couch with her feet tucked under her body as if she were cold, scared, or trying to get away from the situation. Ian, on the other hand, paced.

"Surely you have some idea." His voice rose again and as he walked over to stand above her, he backed off less he intimidate her into further silence.

Not looking at him she managed to say, "I think I love you."

"So this is a new revelation for you, and it's become a problem?" he pursued trying to keep his voice low and thoughtful, trying to hide the irritation he was holding at bay.

"Because I only realized it yesterday," she confessed.

Why he had expected something different, he wasn't sure. All he was sure of at the precise moment was that he was badgering her for answers he didn't have himself. Again he felt ashamed.

"Why does it make you unhappy?"

"Unhappy isn't the word that applies here. Jealous is more like it."

"Why, after all of these years?" he kept going. He didn't want to but he couldn't help it.

Ian sat next to her on the couch now and they were face to face. "I don't know, please, don't cross examine me. I swore years ago no man could ever touch my heart again."

"What do you mean, again?" He almost touched her arm, but thought better of it.

What a fool he'd been. Of course there was someone before him. A beautiful young woman like Maggie wouldn't sign herself away to celibacy. Once again he was slapped in the face with his ego and conceit. Not once had he tried to find out about her life before him, content to think she was born fifteen minutes before they met. It all came into focus. Maybe once in a while he needed to sit down and think about his shortcomings. Shit. She was running away when she came here. How selfish he was not to have thought about her previous life. Damn. He was learning more about himself every minute and he didn't like the person who was emerging.

"It doesn't matter," he heard her saying.

"The hell it doesn't," came instantly out of his mouth.

"Ian. I can cope with all of this if you'll only give me a little time to get used to my feelings."

"Babe," he breathed leaning over her so he was talking into her ear. "You shouldn't have to cope. Heather shouldn't have a husband who's unfaithful and I shouldn't have you. But it doesn't solve anything." He stood and walked around to kneel in front of her. "For God's sake, Maggie, for once in your life, let go. Please talk to me. I mean really talk." He rested his hand on her arm and she moved away from him as if his touch burned her. He was getting angry again. "What do you want to hear from me, Maggie?" he asked, his voice escalating. "Do you want me to say I'm misunderstood? That Heather and I haven't slept together for years? Come on. You know none of that's true."

"I told you, Ian. Give me a little time. I'll be fine. I can handle this. Things will soon be as they were before. Please leave now. Go away."

She seemed way too calm to Ian, too deadpan.

"Not on your life, sweetheart. You're going to talk to me. Not our regular little chit-chat either.

You're going to sit here and tell me what the hell you're all about."

He downed his drink and poured himself another. There was no more he could say, odd for an attorney, but he hated confrontations. He avoided them at all costs, which was, in part, why he was in the situation he was in now. But he was here and he intended to see it out. Falling into the green overstuffed chair behind him and away from her, he waited. For the first time he also realized something important to her revelation. He was in love with her too.

Maggie sat on the couch with her eyes closed. When she finally began to speak, he had to lean in to hear her.

She spoke, "Before I moved here I lived in South Bend. I grew up there in a pretty normal family. I did all of the things normal kids do. I'll skip most of that part and get to the crux of the story. I married my high school sweetheart when I was eighteen. Only we didn't live happily ever after like in the fairy tales.

"His name was David. David Fox. He was every girl's dream. Tall, athletic build, dark wavy hair, a little boy charm. The most popular boy in school. What I liked most about him was how he treated me. He put me on a pedestal and treated me like a queen. We were best friends. We went everywhere together. David was the star of the football team. He played and I cheered. When the diplomas were handed out, we got married and the cheering stopped. David changed. He was just another young man with a wife, trying to go to college, hold down a job and play football."

Maggie's lips looked dry and her throat sounded raspy. Ian held up his hand to stop her for a moment and went into the kitchen to get her some water. He was going to make tea but he was afraid if he took too long she would withdraw and stop talking. He grabbed a glass, turned on the tap and filled it half full of water and handed it to her. She seemed to be in a trance linked to the past.

"David got so he had two favorite pastimes," she continued after taking several sips of water. "He liked pushing me around and dating every girl who would go out with him. I tried to stick it out and make it work, but it isn't something I could do alone. I was tired of being bounced off walls and of girls calling day and night."

Ian could tell she was seeing it all again in her mind's eye. "I always believed marriage was forever. Forever ended when David got one of his many girlfriends pregnant. He was thrilled. It boosted his manhood. We'd tried for two years and I still wasn't pregnant. I do believe he was out to prove to the world the problem was mine, not his."

Maggie took another sip of the tepid water and looked at Ian for the first time. Her eyes were dry and her face resolved. "The entire marriage lasted three years. They were very long years. I left him and moved back to my parents. I started taking classes at the community college and working as a waitress at an upscale restaurant in the downtown area, but David couldn't let me alone. He always managed to be around. He made it a point to seek me out every day or two."

Ian remained attentive at she went on with her story. "One day I was sitting on a bench on campus and he came up behind me. He told me I shouldn't have any hard feelings and asked me to go to bed with him. That day I left South Bend. I've never been back. I came here, finished college, and you know the rest."

She took a deep breath and let it out slowly. "I swore I'd never get involved again. Time convinced me I needed some sort of attachment. I like sex. I thought you would be perfect for me. Honestly, I never thought beyond physical need."

She was talking fast now, but he wasn't about to stop her. He sat in amazement at the story unfolding before him. "You were stable, and had a good marriage. You didn't need me or want me. I thought I could take what I needed from you and neither of us would be a loser. I swear I never meant to cause you any pain or to let the relationship grow into anything. I realize now how foolish and naive my thinking was. Had you approached me, this never would have happened. I would've been afraid and pushed you away. It was your lack of need, your independence that I challenged."

Ian was numb at this point. He thought maybe he should say something, but what was there to say. He had been a pawn for years and didn't even know it. He sat watching her with only the twitch in his clinched jaw to betray him.

"I thought of you only as my lover, yet I never considered myself your mistress. It just never occurred to me to turn it around. The other night while I was dressing you called Heather. I heard you telling her you loved her. I'd heard you say it a hundred times before and it didn't bother me. But, Ian, it wasn't five minutes after we made love. The realization hit me, I had been fooling myself. I can't have sex without feeling. I never could. My body and mind are not detached like I wanted them to be."

"What it all boils down to is, I need for you to tell me you love me. I feel dirty and low. Don't you understand? I have become no better than David."

Crying now, she looked at him.

Ian stood up and looked down at her.. He turned abruptly on his heel, without a word, and walked out the door, letting it close behind him.

Ian drove back to the office.

He wandered through it, unhooked the answering machine and listened to the telephone messages. There was still no word from Jim. There wasn't anything to take his mind off Maggie. The liquor he had consumed all day made him tired. He staggered toward the couch in his office and flopped down with his arms behind his head and one foot still on the floor to keep the room from spinning. It was no use. He would never be able to escape his own thoughts.

There was his twenty-five year relationship with Heather. He was surprised how clear his memories of the early years were. All the good times, the bad time, the fun times, they were all there, the long nights sitting up with sick children, romantic vacations, and how close they were then. It was a good marriage. He would have been content with it. The key word was contentment.

Yes, his mind was clear now.

Seeing things for the first time can be so scary. She was probably right; he wouldn't have made the first advance. On the other hand, he didn't push her away. Not for long. He smiled in spite of everything. Imagine him a sex object. Why it began didn't mean much to him. It was a long time ago. What was important to him was now.

Thinking back he remembered her first kiss. It haunted him. Every time he closed his eyes she was standing before him. He might have seemed noble to her during it because he ignored her advance, but he had fought himself over it every minute of every day. There wasn't anything casual or spontaneous at her apartment the first night they shared together. He had lived it over and over again in his mind. Time and time again he dreamed about it before it happened.

What he had with Maggie was good. It was exciting and different from his life with Heather. It was more than the sex they shared. Oh, at first it was physical but now they had so much more. There was their work, music, books, and the quiet pleasure of being together and doing nothing.

Did he love her? Answering would mean he had to put a name on the feeling of emptiness he felt when he left her. Even now, he thought of her in her misery. It would mean he had to label the warm glow radiating through him when their bodies met. It would mean admitting it was Maggie he dressed for each morning.

Oh, yes, he loved her beyond reason.

Could he love two women? Yes, he decided, but

not at the same time for the same reasons.

When he opened his eyes the office was dark. He sat up and rubbed his hands through his hair. The sickening sweet taste of stale liquor made him wince. It was early evening yet he felt as if a day had passed since he lay down. In his mind he had covered many years and many miles in a short time. He went into the bathroom to wash his face and brush his teeth, hoping it would help to make him feel like himself again.

For a long time he watched himself in the mirror. He would have liked to step outside himself to see himself as others did, if only for a few minutes.

He knew he was killing time trying to avoid the inevitable. Taking a towel he mockingly wiped his image from the mirror and went back into the office to call home.

Heather answered.

"Hi, it's me."

"Hi, me," she quipped. "Where are you?"

"I'm at the office. I called to ask a favor."

"Sure, what is it?

"Would you mind if I was to go to dinner with another beautiful woman and come in inexcusably late?"

"Maggie?" There was no jealously or emotion in her voice to betray what she may have been feeling.

"Yes, the hearing's in the morning and it's been a long rough week. We're both a little raw around the edges. I thought it might do her some good. Until Kenny came along, Maggie didn't know her boss was a tyrant." He tried to sound light and cheery.

"No, I don't mind. Is she there?"

"No. That's why I feel it is so important. She left tired and upset with the entire ordeal."

"Then dinner does sound like a good idea. Why not take her to Eau Bistro? I'm sure she would enjoy it and the food is superb."

Ian was so caught up in his own thoughts, this giant lie he was creating, it took him awhile to notice she wasn't talking.

"Heather?"

"Yes?"

"Oh, never mind. Will you be up?"

"Maybe," she added, "I love you." He felt it was an afterthought.

"Yeah, Babe, I know you do."

Ian hung up feeling like a heel, but he reasoned this moment it was necessary. Maggie was his main concern right now. Never having seen her so upset he wasn't sure what she might do. Would she up and leave St. Louis like she did South Bend and he would never see her again?

He didn't want to leave anything to chance. The entire situation was his fault. He was responsible. He was going to straighten this mess out, starting with Maggie.

Lying wasn't something he did often. It wasn't his best subject. He hated it. His job was to find out who was lying in every case he took. He was good at it. Right now he hated himself.

Chapter Eleven

Maggie's apartment was dark and quiet. There was no answer when he rang the bell so he pounded on the door and called her name. Panic rose to his throat when after half an hour he couldn't raise her. He wished to hell he had taken the key she tried so many times to give him. In one final effort he laid his finger on the buzzer and left it there. He was about to use force to open the door when he heard a faint noise. The latch on the door gave way and she stood behind it.

Maggie looked like hell. Her eyes were red and puffy. Mascara was caked on her cheeks where the tears had flowed. Her hair hung limp and tangled around her face.

"Are you all right?" he whispered.

Maggie shook her head indicating she was.

"I'm sorry, Maggie," he spoke, trying to hurry things into a better position. "I never should have left you alone. I needed to sort things out. I swear to you. I never intended to be gone this long."

Maggie stood before him looking small and

tired. He took her into his arms and held her protectively. "Do you want to talk some more?" he asked after a long time.

She shook her head again, this time, no.

"Oh sweet Maggie," he said, reaching to stroke her matted hair. "I need to talk to you." He raised her head by placing one finger under her chin, forcing her eyes to meet his. With his other arm he held her. "I love you. I love your youth, your beauty and your vitality. As I look at you now I wonder if I'm doing the right thing. Ten years from now I will be nearly sixty. You will still be young and beautiful."

Maggie was beginning to stand more on her own now. She buried her face in his chest.

"No, Maggie. I'm not finished. Please listen. I love Heather too. I love her in a different way, but it hasn't been platonic either. The convenient way for me had been to have you both. God, I'm sorry. I didn't take the time to realize what I was doing. I don't know what's going to happen now. I'm going to leave it up to you. I have a wife and three children. I have no right to ask anything of you. Being the coward I am, I'm going to put the entire situation in your hands. What would you have me do?"

"Love me, Ian," she uttered into his chest. "Love me now, one more time. Just let me gain control of myself and I can handle this."

"You're not listening to me." He once again raised her head so he could look into her eyes. He wasn't as gentle this time. "I don't want you to handle anything. I don't want you to cope. I want you to be happy. I want to be happy."

She looked at him in desperation, "You're what makes me happy."

With his lips on hers he picked her up and carried her into the bedroom. There he laid her down and gently untied the belt on her robe. He lingered a moment appreciating her body, then reached down and rubbed a thumb across each breast and smiled as her nipples immediately stood erect. Maggie reached for the top button on his shirt but he restrained her, smiling as he moved his left thumb and replaced it with his tongue so he could hold her arms with his free hand. She began to move eagerly beneath him as he switched from breast to breast, tasting her essence. Finally, he let her go, stood and stepped away from the bed. Maggie followed him and as she did, the robe stayed on the bed. She didn't bother to try to unbutton his shirt this time, but pulled it out of his pants and helped him take it off over his head. Then she quickly unbuckled his belt, pants and zipper and tugged downward until they lay in a rumpled pile on the floor. Ian laughed out loud, because now he was trapped. He wasn't going to be able to finish undressing until he took his shoes off. Using the toes from one shoe on the heel of the other, he kicked them off and stood only in his boxers with his manhood straining tight against them.

Maggie was staring at his crouch as she dropped to her knees in front of him to free him. It was now his turn to squirm. It was easy to move him onto the bed because he wasn't resisting. They took turns then, first her bringing him almost to climax and then stopping to let him do the same to her. When he finally entered her, they were both in a frenzy of desire. Sweat and sweet words mingled as they came together. Ian didn't roll off her. He raised slightly so his body weight didn't crush her and he stayed that way until her breathing calmed down and he felt her relax into a quiet sleep beneath him.

So as not to wake her, he picked up his clothes and dressed in the bathroom. He stood by the side of the bed and watched her sleep. Her beauty stirred him and he had to force himself not to reach down and touch her again. But he knew her well. He knew her pride. As he watched her, he wasn't sure what her decisions would be later when she woke and had time to think. Now that she was no longer shattered and the heat of the moment was over, he left her a simple note on the kitchen counter next to the coffee pot. It gave her a chance to make up her mind once and for all.

Maggie,
If you are not in court in the morning,
I will understand.
Ian

He was to find out, his night wasn't over. Heather was waiting for him when he got home. She was upset and excited; she didn't seem to know what subject to approach first. Before he was completely inside the door she began talking. "Jim called. I tried to call you at Eau Bistro but they said you weren't there. Here is the message he left." She handed him a note printed in her neat round printing.

"Found Kenny's Mother. Sarah Lee Berle. Am waiting to hear from you. She isn't what we expected to find. "

"How long ago did he call?"

"It's been hours, Ian- hours." Adding the repeat of the word hours to her statement spoke volumes. There was no hiding the accusation in her voice or her words. Then came the inevitable question. "Where have you been?"

"With Maggie," he said.

"Why do I have the feeling you mean that literally?" Her voice held no surprise, accusation, or anger. It was flat disgust and disdain.

When he said, "I'm sorry, Heather," he said it all.

"So am I." She was dressed in a pair of black slacks and a sweater in spite of the late hour. She stood rigid before him. Every muscle was strained to its limit. Her hands were rested on her hips. He knew the next several minutes would be the most uncomfortable of their entire marriage and he also knew he deserved it. He widened his stance and took a deep breath. Whatever she said or did was warranted.

What happened next was unexpected. She looked him up and down, clicked her tongue and turned her back on him. She walked away. Reaching the bottom of the staircase, she hesitated and turned to look at him one last time. Then without another word she disappeared up the steps.

Wow. The word popped into his mind. He had had no idea of what would happen between him and Heather, but this wasn't it. Had she cried or slapped him or even been outraged, he could have handled it. The guilt and pain she was passing on to him was a heavy load.

He knew that pain he was causing her was heavier yet.

He wanted to fly up the stairs and tell her he loved her, but it would sound trite and he knew it. He longed to tell her he would cut off his arm if he could take away her pain, and to have her spit in his face would have been too good for him, and he knew it.

God help the three of them. He had created a mess and spent the rest of the night sitting in the den. He couldn't sleep. He couldn't think. All he could do was take the note Heather had handed him and turn it over and over in his hands until the printing on it was so smeared no longer readable.

Morning crept up on him unnoticed. Heather came into the room and pulled open the drapes. The room was flooded with bright sunlight. It was such a shock to Ian's eyes he was forced to cover them.

"You'd better clean up. You've got to be in court in an hour."

"Heather?"

"Not now."

Once again she was gone and he was left alone in the stark glaze of daylight. It took him a few minutes to pull himself out of his stupor. Every muscle in his body ached as he climbed the stairs. In their bedroom he found his suit, tie, shirt and even his underwear lying out on the bed. He didn't know what to think, just that she wanted him out of the house as soon as possible and was helping him along.

He shaved, showered and dressed and walked straight down the stairs and out the front door without a word.

The papers he needed were at the office. He went there and then had to drive all the way back to St. Charles to the courthouse. It was becoming a long day and it had only just begun. He had a disoriented feeling as he went around on auto pilot getting ready for what would present itself next.

Within the last twelve hours he felt he had ruined Heather's life and maybe destroyed Maggie. He didn't know what the day would bring, yet he was pretty sure it could not surpass yesterday.

Chapter Twelve

The courtroom was packed by the time Ian arrived. He knew there was a great deal of interest in the proceedings but he was amazed at the number of people. He didn't need a score card to know who was who. The families of the victims, looking lost, sad and apprehensive, sat to the left of the courtroom. There were five armed guards placed around the room. It was the greatest show of force he'd ever seen at a proceeding. He reminded himself of the mammoth mountain of emotion surrounding the case.

The last two rows of seats on both sides were press people. He'd seen all of the news trucks outside. It was obvious the story had been picked up by the national news. He recognized a couple minor players from "Today" and "Good Morning America" as well as the Fox Stations. What a circus! Ian was surprised Judge Massey was allowing it. The magistrate was a quiet man who seemed to want to get the job done and get out as fast and unscathed as possible.

There were still a few seats available. It was early. One person, however, was conspicuously missing.

Maggie.

As Ian made his way through the crowd and toward the defense table he heard his name being whispered along with comments such as: "That's him." and "He's here."

At almost the same time he was walking toward the center- aisle, Kenny was being escorted through a door to the left of and behind the judge's bench.

In all the time since his arrest, no pictures or descriptions of Kenny had been released. His good looks and clean cut appearance were having the same effect on the spectators as they had had on Ian at their first meeting. People expect ugly people to commit heinous acts. Pretty people are supposed to be the good guys.

Ian stopped at the gate separating the audience from the principles and grasped it. His knuckles were red from his grip, and not knowing what to expect, he hung back trying to see Kenny's face. He had had no word from the jail to say Kenny was any different than he had been when Ian last saw him. If Kenny was in a catatonic state, then for all intents and purposes it might be over. Right here, right now.

As Ian stood for a moment studying Kenny, the boy never looked up. Ian couldn't tell anything. He stumbled against the table as the guard helped him into a chair, but still didn't acknowledge anything or anyone, and he still didn't look up. Ian took a deep breath before joining him at the defense table. It wasn't a refreshing or relaxing deep breath as he had hoped. It was a breath filled with the smells of the musty courtroom and the bodies of a couple of hundred folks with different aftershaves, deodorants, colognes and stale tobacco - it was nauseating.

Someone had cleaned up Kenny as Ian requested. The bruises were still apparent on his face but the cuts were not as noticeable with the blood washed away. Kenny's eyes were alert. Although he didn't move his head from side to side or indicate he was looking around, his eyes were in constant motion. He looked like a madman.

Ian smiled at Kenny for lack of a better way to greet him. Kenny grinned back. It was an unsettling grin. The hair on Ian's neck prickled and bristled. He shook his head as though to clear it. It didn't work.

Kenny's hands were cuffed behind him. A guard was working to redo them so the boy was chained to the massive defense table leg. It gave Kenny little leeway to move and drew the unwavering attention of the crowd. The low murmuring of everyone trying to talk in a whisper was deafening. It was then the lawyer noticed a court artist sitting to the right and one row behind the prosecutor's table. It struck him as odd as it wasn't a closed courtroom. As a matter of fact, it was filling up to a standing-room-only crowd.

It was standard procedure, yet having Kenny's hands cuffed together and also chained to the table by both hands and feet, gave an impression of a killer, not a mentally ill youth as Ian had intended.

Kenny looked like the oppressor, not the oppressed as he had hoped, even if it wasn't true. The game of defending was, indeed, a game.

At ten o'clock the bailiff called for everyone to "Please stand for the Honorable William Massey." Everyone did, and court was in session.

Ian glanced at his watch and then to the door. Maggie had never been late for anything. She must have made her decision. It was something he couldn't think about now. Thank goodness.

Judge Massey went through the formalities and then called the main parties to the bench. A guard unlocked the handcuffs and put Kenny back to his original stance so he could walk to the bench. He stood between Ian and Tom.

Ian asked that Kenny's handcuffs be removed. He went so far as to guarantee his client would be gentlemen, and he added it made his client look menacing. The spectators went wild. Judge Massey rapped his gavel several times before the noise level subsided to a point where they could hear enough to go on with the proceedings. Ian was the only person in the courtroom who thought Kenny would behave himself without being shackled. Looking toward Tom Waters, he noticed his adversary was glaring at him. The animosity in the room was both real and lasting.

Kenny didn't move a muscle during the entire exchange.

Judge Massey looked down at Ian over his half glasses. He then looked at Kenny and back to Ian again. When he spoke, he spoke in a monotone and those at the bench were forced to lean forward to hear him. His words were not audible to the rest of the room.

He asked Kenny to state his full name. Kenny complied in a strong clear voice. He then read the charges to Kenny explaining the State of Missouri was a death penalty state. If he were charged as an adult for the deeds he was supposed to have perpetrated, he would be eligible for the severe sentencing the Judge was laying out.

Ian noted still another dimension of depth in Kenny's personality. The boy said without hesitation he understood everything Judge Massey said. Did he have any questions? No he didn't. They returned to their respective seats, Kenny still in cuffs and chains. The hearing continued.

Thomas D. Waters, Assistant District Attorney, city of St. Charles, State of Missouri, began. Since the judge was the sole authority here, and this was a procedural event, Tom addressed all of his remarks to His Honor sitting above them.

Tom asked for the defendant to be held without bond until the trial. He went through at least ten good points of evidence to substantiate his reasoning. There was false compassion in his voice when he said the State felt the boy should be incarcerated for the charges against him and the danger he would be in if he were allowed to be free on bond.

The boy never moved. He sat ramrod straight. There was one huge difference in Kenny today: his eyes kept moving. They darted left and right and up and down; he was taking in all he could in front of him and what he could see in his peripheral vision.

He gave no indication he was listening or understood or even cared about anything going on around him. Yet, he answered each question as it was asked him by the judge.

Ian's stomach rolled and turned flip flops as the prosecutor recapped the murders with a much unneeded flourish. The room was quiet except for the family of each victim. As the name was announced and the charges read, they cried or screamed in order. It was horrible. Still, Kenny dismissed it all. He sat showing little interest were it not for his moving eyes. Ian felt Kenny was agitated, yet it didn't show to the rest of the room.

It wasn't until Ian stood to address the charges he became aware of separate people in the room, not just a mob. He took a moment to look around. There was a small woman sobbing into her sleeve. Her husband sat with a stoic look on his face trying to comfort his inconsolable lady. The picture was repeated all over the room with sisters, brothers, wives, husbands and parents. For the first time Ian noticed Bob Johnston was sitting in the center of the spectators section. A big-breasted redhead about forty sat next to him. Ian assumed it was Shauna. In the back, perched on a chair next to the door, was Amber.

His presentation was short. He didn't insult the intelligence of anyone in the room by asking that Kenny go free. What the defense did ask for was simple, and delivered in short concise sentences. Ian wanted Kenny moved to a maximum security mental facility. He requested specific and thorough tests be conducted to establish Kenny's mental age, his degree of sanity now and at the time of the crimes he was accused of committing. Ian asked the prosecution to approved Dr. Marie Angerstein head the team who evaluated Kenny.

When he was finished, Judge Massey recessed for thirty minutes to contemplate, consider and make his ruling.

Ian leaned over toward Kenny to ask him if he was following what was happening.

Kenny didn't answer. Instead he quickly turned around in his chair and gave a mean and hateful stare to Shauna, his step-mother. How he knew she was there was a mystery. The entire time he had been in the room he had not moved his head and since they were seated directly behind him and in the middle of the section, it didn't seem possible he could have seen her.

Kenny stood up with such force his chains jerked the table, throwing Ian off balance and everything on the table onto the floor. "Get that bitch out of here!" Kenny screamed lurching toward the railing separating the participants from the observers.

Some people were already out of their chairs, anticipating a small break while the judge contemplated his ruling. With Kenny's outburst, all activities halted. Guards who were seconds before leaning against the various exits or guiding people to the nearest bathroom, now jumped to attention. The two guards who were assigned to Kenny had been standing over by the judge's bench and were watching Kenny. They reacted fast, but not fast enough. One of the officers tackled Kenny as he was about to try to go over the rail to reach for

Shauna. He was going to do this without regard to the pain to himself and the destruction to the table and the rail. His strength seemed superhuman.

Ian took two steps back from Kenny, to give more room to those he hoped were coming to help. It was over. Kenny was subdued with another set of handcuffs and two more guards. He was dragged from the courtroom screaming and cursing and thrashing. He could be heard long after the chamber door closed behind him. Anyone who doubted if the young, good-looking, well-mannered boy seen earlier was capable of horrendous acts of violence and terror no longer questioned it. They had seen the flash of hate and contempt in him as he lashed out at Shauna and everyone was well aware of the rage he would have perpetrated on her had he reached her. All eyes were trained on the woman who was the object of Kenny's outrage. Ian tried not to make eye contact with anyone as he began to gather his belongings from the floor and then took his seat at the now empty defense table. No Kenny. No Maggie.

The talking and speculation among the people got louder and wilder. A dozen St. Charles police officers arrived and cleared the courtroom. During the entire ordeal Tom walked around the room chatting with this one and that one. Ian knew them to be relatives of the victims. The D.A. reminded him more of a funeral director than a prosecutor.

Until then, Ian hadn't considered whether or not he liked Tom Waters. Never in his career had he been in a position where he had to have an opponent other than a soon-to-be ex-husband or wife. As he watched Tom work the room, the emotion welling up inside of him bordered on hate.

Everybody was gone now. Even the D. A. and his staff was in the hall or bathroom or somewhere. He was alone, alone with his thoughts and shaking hands. As he sat at the table he repositioned his briefcase and pen and pencil. He picked up his things and put them back in order, straightened his tie and tried to keep his mind off his personal life. It was impossible. He was so caught up in Maggie and her failure to show up in court, when the bailiff announced the hearing was again in session, he visibly jumped. Tom was back in the room without his cohorts.

Judge Massey began by informing Ian because of his client's earlier behavior he wouldn't be allowed back into the room without more restraints. Furthermore, if Kenny didn't behave he would have to watch the proceedings on TV and testify on camera. Those statements brought another outburst from the crowd who had been let back in to the room. The judge, who had had enough interruptions, ordered the courtroom cleared for the remainder of the day. He added a stern warning letting the people know when this came to trial, he would put up with no monkey business.

As the people were filing out, Ian noticed Bob and Shauna had not come back after the recess. No one spoke again until the big double doors to the corridor were closed. Only Ian, Tom Waters, the bailiff, court reporter and the judge remained.

Maggie's empty chair seemed a hundred times bigger than life as Ian glanced at it.

Judge Massey tapped his gavel several times. The noise reverberated in the empty room. Ian listened.

"It is the decision of this Court, after careful deliberation," he began. "There is indeed sufficient evidence to bind the defendant Kenneth Ray Johnston over for a trial by a jury of his peers for the charges levied against him." Massey stopped again to read his notes. "Before this trial can take place, I order the defendant to be remanded to the Missouri State Mental Facility in Fulton. While in custody he is to undergo a complete mental and physical work-up." He looked over his glasses at Ian. "You may have your doctor look at the defendant, Mr. Michaels, but due to the distance and time involved, I'm requesting the team be headed up by the Chief of Staff at the Fulton facility. Your client will be held in the locked ward of the hospital." He turned his attention back to include everyone.

"I want all of those findings along with the previous tests and records from St. Joseph's Hospital to be brought, upon completion, before this Court for evaluation. It is this Court's opinion that only after such examination can the disposition of the client as to the charges be determined. The prosecutor and the defense council will be notified as to the completion of these tests and a hearing date which will apply. If there are no questions, gentleman, this court is adjourned." He looked Ian in the eye and then Tom. When neither of them spoke, he tapped his gavel one last time and left the room.

Ian was relieved. He was sure the tests would show Kenny to be mentally incapable to stand trial now, and take the death penalty off the table.

Tom looked confident. Kenny was off the street and the pressure to prosecute was off him. He would be a winner either way. Kenny would either be found innocent by reason of insanity and put away forever or sane enough to stand trial. However it went, Kenny would never again walk the streets as a free man.

Ian was exhausted. It was as though someone had let all of the air out of him.

He knew it wasn't over for him. He still needed to know more. His curiosity made it impossible to shut the case away and go on as though it never touched his life.

It would be a long road for him too if he didn't get his life straightened out. Deep in his heart he had felt certain Maggie would be by his side and he cursed himself for being noble enough to give her an out he didn't want her to have.

For now he would proceed with his investigation of Kenny. He would continue with the worst case scenario in mind, the premise Kenny was sane and would be charged as an adult. He would master the world's greatest defense.

It was the only thing he could think to do to keep his mind off Heather and Maggie and his life crumbling around him.

Only one question remained.

Where the hell should he start?

Chapter Thirteen

Ian got in his car and headed toward his house in St. Peters. After driving a couple of miles he realized it wasn't what he wanted to do. There was too much stress already. Taking a huge deep breath he turned around and headed for the Trail Head Brewery in St. Charles' Historical District. The famous Katy Trail began there and went over two hundred miles across the state for avid bicycles, hikers or families out for only a day or a weekend. It had spawned some interesting new businesses along the way. One was the brewery. Most times it would be a place Ian wouldn't go alone. It was a cheery, high octane pub and restaurant at the edge of the river and the trail. He knew it was early enough to get a booth near the back of the place out of the main stream of traffic. The only people there this time of day were those coming off the trail to wet their whistles and grab a bite before going on to their next adventure.

Ian didn't want to be alone, yet he didn't want to be with anyone. It was the perfect answer. To look less out of place, he took off his coat and tie and rolled up his sleeves. He knew the Trail Head served some of the downtown business people, but it was too late for lunch and too early for dinner. He stuck a small notebook in his back pocket and walked over to the river walk about a hundred yards off the parking lot. The river was moving at a fast clip. He picked up a stick and threw it in and watched as it disappeared downstream. It was beginning to snow hard, probably winter's last attempt to hold on. He knew it wouldn't amount to anything. The snowflakes were the size of bottle caps and they melted on the warm ground as soon as they landed. Ian loved the feel of the snow, cool on his hot face; turning his eyes toward the heavens, he let more of the cold wet flakes touch him.

Within a few minutes he could feel his shoulders and neck relax. Turning, he walked back past his car and into the pub. He was always impressed with the place. He looked down toward the sparkling stainless steel brewery vats as he climbed the stairs to the dining room and asked the young college kid who greeted him if he could have the empty booth he saw in the back. The young man smiled at him with a perfect set of ultra-white teeth flashing. On the way back he asked Ian if he could get him a drink. Ian ordered a stout beer they were known for and scooted into the booth. He took out his note pad.

There he sat, notebook open on the table before him and a cold beer in a frosted mug, yet he felt like his best friend had died. Maybe it was a legitimate feeling. He took out his cell phone and turned the ringer back on. He had turned it off in court and hadn't bothered to turn it back on. He called Jim, in Oklahoma City. Jim was a throwback from a different era and refused to carry a cell phone. It was sometimes frustrating to Ian to communicate with messages, but it sure slowed things down and made a person think before he said anything. With a cell phone, Ian always thought there should be a rewind button so all of the things coming without thought could be taken back. With Jim, this didn't happen.

Maybe the thing to do was to go to Oklahoma City and meet up with Jim. He could sure use the distraction and as an added plus he could talk to Kenny's mother himself. But maybe it would give the women in his life a chance to think. The thought brought up a myriad of feelings. He knew a change of scenery would help him. It would give Maggie and Heather a chance to think and him a chance not to.

He held his glass up in the air and caught the waiter's attention, signaling him to bring another beer. So far, within the last two days he had drunk more than he had in the previous ten years.

Putting his phone in his pocket, he waved to his server for the check and took some bills out of his wallet. He had come to a neutral place because he felt he could not go home. He could not go to Maggie's and for some reason he was avoiding his office. The least of the three was the office so he drove there to make his plans. The snow was picking up. He was forced to turn the windshield wipers on to see. He took another look at the roads, still convinced the snow wouldn't stick.

Ian's heart skipped a beat when he saw Maggie's car in its regular spot in the lot.

It was a momentary elation squelched by the memory of the last time he saw her and the realization he had driven her home. He parked his car next to hers and got out, stretching to his full length. Arching his back then touching his toes made him feel much better. Next he turned his body to the left and then to the right like a runner warming up before a race. He looked up at the building, sighed and unlocked the door.

His office was dark and cold.

He was alone.

To add to his already uncomfortable station in life, both women's presence could be felt in the office. Their personalities were intertwined in the decor and in him. There was no separating it. He fought back the tears welling up in his eyes and the emptiness churning in the pit of his stomach.

He wasn't a crier, not at his mother's or father's funerals and not more than five times in his life. Three of those times were when his sons were born. Now he cried all the time. It was his gauge things were falling apart and he with them.

Damn.

At least he should know his own mind. Why? Hell. The decision wasn't his to make. He felt he had lost control of his own destiny. Each woman would search her own mind and heart and he would pay the price of their innermost feelings. Yes, he thought he knew where his heart was, but what good did it do him? He always wanted more. It had always been his nature. Was it a lack carried over from his childhood? Why the constant need for better and more? He knew he didn't deserve more. He had read somewhere about living your life in the light and not hiding in the dark. For the past several years, he'd lived in the shadows. It's funny how things work out.

Enough was enough. He needed to make some forward strides and stop dwelling in self-pity, and to get on with the work at hand.

Not bothering to turn on the main lights, he walked on into his private office and turned on his desk light. Opening the drapes, he stood flat footed before the window and watched it snow. It was a beautiful wet snow and it was beginning to hang onto the cooler things. The branches of trees were turning white as were Maggie's car and the grassy parts of the ground. As he looked up and out further he saw it was covering the swings and slide at the park. It was gorgeous. It covered up all the dirt and smut of life and made everything new again, if only for an hour or two.

Thinking of the streets and roadways brought him back to the office and why he was there. If he were going to Oklahoma City to meet Jim Martin and try to meet Sarah Berle, Kenny's mother, for himself, he had better get with it in case this snow began accumulating. Sometimes freak snow storms and Mother Nature had their own plans and what Ian thought wouldn't enter into it.

Ian again called the number Jim had left with Heather. Again the auditor at the motel told him Mr. Martin wasn't in. He did volunteer the information

Jim was eating at a nearby cafe and he would give him the message when he returned. Ian went on and made his plans. Thursday was not a big travel day and if he worked it right he could get his clothes and be at the airport for the next plane.

Taking a big deep breath, Ian put down his cell phone and called his home from the office telephone. It rang several times before anyone answered it. Finally Heather picked up.

"Hello?" She said in a sing-song, cheery voice.

"Hi, it's me."

The silence was deafening.

"Are you there?" he ventured.

"Yes. What is it?"

"I'm flying to Oklahoma City to meet Jim Martin. My flight leaves in about an hour. Could Rosemary pack me a bag?"

"Are you going alone?" She made no effort to hide the contempt in her voice.

"Yes, of course." He fought to keep his voice neutral lest this conversation go straight downhill. "Heather, please."

"Well, I don't have time to chat. I'll give Rosemary your message."

The dial tone buzzed in his ear before he could utter another word. A dozen clichés about a woman's scorn ran through his mind yet none of them was funny today. He sat for short while with the receiver in his hand. He wanted to call Maggie, yet thought better of it. Her decision was made when she didn't show up in court earlier in the day. Even if she had a good excuse, by now she had had plenty of time to call and make it right. It would be easier for her now, he knew, if he left her alone. He tried not to think of what a life without her would be.

He slapped both hands firmly on his desk, as if to wake himself to the present moment.

Ian had a new-found urgency to get up, get moving and get out of there. The sooner his mind was occupied with other matters, matters he could do something about, the better off he would be.

On such short notice all of the direct flights were booked. He was forced to take a plane going to Chicago, Tulsa, and then Oklahoma City before heading to places further west and ending up in Phoenix. He booked first class in hopes of eating on the plane but was informed no one leg of the trip kept the plane in the air long enough to accomplish serving a meal. Oh, joy.

There was no time in Ian's memory when he was so self-absorbed. Trying to keep his mind in the now was a huge undertaking. Grabbing what he perceived to be an interesting psychology book to read on the flight, he headed home. Angst built up within him with every mile, yet he need not have worried. All of the things he needed for his trip were sitting in a suitcase on the front porch. The house was dark and quiet, by design, he was sure. He picked up the suit case, got into his car and headed to the airport.

Once Ian was on the plane he took a deep breath and thanked the powers that be. The airplane had few passengers. He was the only one sitting in a triple seat. He wondered if coach was full, he dismissed the thought and settled in. He didn't open the book he selected to read on the trip. He looked out the window until his eyes were heavy with strain. Closing them, he fell into a fitful sleep filled with images of a screaming Kenny and dead bodies. When the attendant shook him to let him know to fasten his seat belt for their landing in Oklahoma City, he realized it had to have happened twice before and he was too tired and too upset to notice. When it was his turn to deplane, he stretched as tall as he could and reoriented himself to his surroundings and purpose. He was now more exhausted than before and his stomach was growling from lack of food.

Things got much better when he reached for his suitcase from the luggage carousel only to have Jim reach over and retrieve it for him. The two men were happy to see one another. Ian shook Jim's hand with one hand and patted him on the back with the other. To Ian it was like finding unexpected water in the desert. Jim's casual air put him instantly at ease. His shoulders relaxed and he felt years younger in a mere instant.

They walked to Jim's rental car in an easy silence.

"I got you a room at the motel where I'm staying.," Jim said as they settled in the car.

"It isn't anything fancy but nice. I didn't want to squander all that expense money you pay me," he added with a huge grin.

For the first time in days, Ian laughed. It felt good. "I'm starving. Have you found any good restaurants here?"

"Ah, can you hold on until we get to the motel?

About a block away is the best southern cooking you could hope for, in these here parts," he added in a mock southern drawl.

Ian laughed again. This time he laughed because it felt good. He felt good. Getting out of St. Louis was the best thing he could have done.

The two men chatted as they crossed town. They had been friends for years and could always find a compatible subject. This time it happened to be how no one in Oklahoma City was in a hurry, not like the constant hustle and bustle they were used to. This was a city of meanderers Jim, had decided.

It wasn't until they were settled in Mother's Cafe, an easy block's walk from the motel, they discussed the subject at hand, Kenneth Johnston's birth mother.

Ian could not believe what he was hearing. After Jim filled him in on all of his observations about the lady in question, Ian tried picking Jim's brain. Using every trick he had ever learned in his twenty plus years of law practice, he learned nothing more. After their almost two hour discussion, he surmised Jim must be following the wrong woman. This woman didn't fit the profile of the person Ian pictured or had heard about.

"I assure you, Ian, the Sarah Berle I've have been watching is indeed Kenny's mother.

You know the old saying. People change. They act differently with different people. Maybe she's happy which makes her healthy. I don't pretend to know, but I do know it's her, from the color of her eyes to the mole on her cheek."

It was late by the time they finished eating

chicken fried steak, mashed potatoes and gravy, fresh green beans simmered for hours with bacon and a dessert of apple pie ala mode. Ian couldn't remember when he had eaten so much at one sitting and walking back to the motel helped him get rid of the overfull feeling he had. He only wished it were about a mile further. When they got near the office, each preparing to go a different direction, Jim handed his notes to Ian. He would do it to keep from going over them again and answering the same redundant questions. Had he been a top secret spy with the highest clearance, he would have given away all of his secrets to be done with the subject.

Jim went to his room and Ian to his where he showered and slipped into his favorite gray robe Rosemary was thoughtful enough to pack for him. He should have been tired after his fitful nap on the airplane, his overeating at dinner, and the shear stress of everything else in his life. He wasn't. He was, instead, jazzed. What Jim told him didn't at all fit the profile he had put together of Sarah Berle. Ian tried to tell himself the evils of predetermined ideas about people. Self-talk didn't do a thing to ease his mind.

Ian read Jim's notes one last time as he lay in bed with the bed pillows piled up comfortably behind him. Jim's easy-to-read printing jumped off the page.

Sarah Berle. Age 36. Two children. Boys. Ages 9 and 11.

Monday, March 31: Drove children to school. Went to church. Fixed lunch Senior

Citizens Home, played with husband and

children on front lawn in evening. No activities from the home after seven p.m.

April 1, 2, 3, 4, were carbon copies of the first day. No friends mentioned. No out of the ordinary meetings. A week of mundane tasks related to raising children and having a family. It was a little odd, Ian thought, she went to church every day at The Holy Redeemer Church of the Resurrected Christ.

There wasn't a church service every day at nine when she went, yet Jim's notes said she was there about an hour every morning. When Saturday rolled around, the family had an outing. After a quiet morning, they went bowling in the afternoon and then out to a fast food joint for a late lunch. Jim noted they looked happy and content.

Same old shit.

It was repetitious. This wasn't what Ian had pictured. She seemed to be a pillar of the community. The perfect mother, a volunteer at a local hospital and still she had the time to be President of the Women's Auxiliary at the Holy Redeemer Church.

To say Ian was puzzled was an understatement. There were two possible explanations, either this wasn't Kenny's mother or the innuendos and information he had gathered from people in Missouri about her was false and overstated.

Had Kenny lied about his mother to Dr. Angerstein? Had Amber lied also? Ian felt strange. Was he disappointed? If Jim's notes were accurate, and he was sure they were, it blew his entire theory, not to mention the theories of some two dozen doctors whose work he had read in the last few days.

Piss on it.

He tossed the notebook on the chair and went to bed.

Ian woke up refreshed and disoriented at six. Sitting straight up in bed a rush of panic ran through him until he realized where he was. It was long before sunrise and he felt it was much too early to wake Jim. Although he had showered late the night before, he showered again. He did it because it was routine and because the hot water made him feel better. It always did. Even after taking his time to dress, he felt it was still too early to wake Jim so he set out on foot to find a cup of coffee. The weather was warm and dry. It felt pleasant in contrast to the damp chill in the air further north.

After strolling several blocks he spied a cafe boasting the best coffee in town. The place was bustling. It was called the Roosters Crow, and the windows were decorated with dozens of different kind of chickens and roosters doing human things. They were baking and serving and sitting at tables eating. It was bright and cheery. It was one of those places where everyone who works there looks up and says hi when a new patron walks in the door. The smell itself was enough to make you stay. Bacon was cooking; the smell of sautéed onions and a hundred other pleasant aromas lingered in the air. If you had a favorite, you could pick it out. When he opened the door and walked in, the first person he saw was Jim. He was sitting at the counter with a giant breakfast of eggs, pancakes, sausage, hash brown potatoes, toast, juice and coffee. The food looked delicious to Ian, but he was still full from last night's dinner. He wouldn't be able to face food before noon. "Only coffee, please." He smiled at the waitress who took his order and then shifted his attention to Jim. "How can you eat like that and stay so thin?" Ian asked laughing.

"Oh, I run. I realized a long time ago I couldn't pass up the food. If I ate the food I couldn't run after the bad guys. The only answer I could think of was to run. So I do about five miles a day and eat what I want." On a more interesting note, he added. "What gets you up so early Counselor? Are you ready to slay the lions?"

"My friend, if your notes are accurate, and I'm sure they are, there are no lions to slay. The score would be about Christians three, lions nothing, if my memory serves me. Surely I can't greet Oklahoma City's mother of the year with a good afternoon, did you know you have another son? One who kills people?"

"My, my, you sound bitter. Why are you here?"

"Hell if I know," Ian answered. "I know Kenny killed all of those people, but why? The why is haunting me. He isn't your typical serial killer. They have a type or a certain kind of person they go after. There isn't anything alike about Kenny's victims. They seem so random. Also, serial killers kill people in the same way. They're all hanged or knifed or strangled. Kenny's are again random. Maybe it's the futility of it all, the why. I don't really know. Maybe I'm as nuts as he is."

They sat in silence. Ian drank his coffee. Jim

finished his breakfast. It was a good five minutes before either spoke. Ian broke the silence. "Do you think she's home today?"

"Sure."

"How do you know?"

"Well, she's a creature of habit. She doesn't stray from her normal routine. I figure her for a twice a week laundry lady. Today should be one of her wash days. I'll make you a little bet. I'll bet she hangs everything outside on a clothesline except for her dainty underthings."

"How do you know she wears dainty underthings?"

"Because she's exceptionally good-looking and I'm an exceptionally good detective," he answered with a grin.

It was difficult for Ian to stay inside himself with Jim around. He was tops in his field.

He probably knew if Sarah Berle was right or left handed and if she dried her face or her feet first when she got out of the shower. He would even venture to say Jim knew in what order she put on her dainty underthings. Ian realized how anxious he was to talk to her or at least see her. Jim assured him it would be at least eleven before she had the children deposited at their school and was home from her daily visit to the market for fresh vegetables and her visit to church. He suggested a couple of interesting things they could see while they waited.

He always knew Jim was multifaceted, he proved it every time they worked together. Instead of killing time at the motel or going to a Bass Pro

Shop, Jim wanted to show Ian the National Cowboy Museum. Actually he wanted Ian to see one of the many exhibits of the famous End of the Trail statue by James Earle Fraser. Ian had seen it hundreds of times on post cards and free standing statues. It is a Native American Indian, muscular and forlorn, sitting on a horse, holding a buffalo shield with his head down as if sleeping and barely staying on the horse. Seems Jim had a small replica in his home and was super interested in the history behind it and American artists in general. Ian recognized the work immediately, although he didn't know the why or how of it all. He was once again impressed with his companion. By the time they strolled through the museum with Jim pointing out the pieces he liked the best, it was time to go take a look at Sarah.

Jim didn't think Ian should talk to Sarah alone in case she was ever called to testify at

Kenny's trial. Ian, on the other hand, was as sure now as he ever was. There would be no trial.

Ian thought the two of them together would intimidate her and vetoed the idea. He was going inside alone. He was excited about getting to interview her. They settled it. he would go in and Jim would be within shouting distance, just in case something went awry. Jim let it be known he wasn't pleased with the arrangement.

It was almost lunchtime when Ian walked up to the front door of the Berle home.

Chapter Fourteen

A tall, thin, well- proportioned brunette with big brown eyes opened the door.

Ian forced himself not to stare at her. He looked past her and into the living room. The furniture was old and well used. The room was clean and neat. So far as he could tell the house inside and out was well kept. It was a far cry from the Johnston home.

The woman stood staring at him. He recovered from his curiosity and rudeness and apologized. How foolish he must have looked to her, appraising things like a tax man.

"Excuse me," he began. "I'm Ian Michaels. I'm looking for Sarah Berle."

As they talked, he handed her a business card he had taken from his wallet.

"I'm Sarah Berle. What can I do for you?" she said it with a note of disdain.

"I represent your son in a legal matter in

Missouri. I would like to have a few minutes of your time to discuss it."

Sarah turned white. Ian felt sure she was going to faint so he took her by the arm and led her to the nearest chair.

"I have no family in Missouri, Mr. M..........." She faltered on his name.

"Michaels," he said. "Ian Michaels, and I beg to differ. Perhaps I can jog your memory." He turned over the folder he was holding in his hands so she could see it. On the cover was a picture of Kenny and another of Amber. He refrained from opening it yet. It was a full account of everything Kenny had done in his young life. Ian wasn't sure she was going to stay conscious so he only showed her the pictures of the two children she had given birth to and left so many years ago. "You have a son, Kenny Johnston, and a daughter Amber Johnston. Surely you haven't forgotten them?" Ian didn't mean to come off as curtly as he did.

Sarah Berle got up from her chair and stepped past Ian to go outside and stand in the bright sunshine on the front porch. She looked in both directions. Perhaps she was looking to see if any of her neighbors were watching. Stepping quickly back into the house, she grabbed Ian's arm, pulling him away from the door with her, and then she closed and locked the door. Ian was sure those actions moved Jim closer to the house than he was. Jim would be concerned and curious about what was going on behind the locked door.

"Listen Mr. a a a..."

"Michaels."

"Whatever. I really don't care what your name is. I don't care who you are. I want you to leave now and go straight back to where you came from. Leave me alone." This is more what Ian had pictured in his mind's eye.

"Honestly, Mrs. Berle, I'd like to. The problem is, I need you to answer some questions. There are things I need to know and only you have the answers. Only you can help me."

"I'm warning you, Mr. Michaels. Go away, now or I'll call the police."

"I'm okay with you calling them, Mrs. Berle. I was hoping you wouldn't. I'm trying to keep this as private as possible for you. I've flown all this way to talk to you. I was hoping you could spare a few minutes. But if you insist it would make you feel better, I'll respect your wishes and wait until the police get here before we talk."

Ian was hoping he could bluff her into the interview he felt he needed, hoping if he sat still, as if the suggestion didn't bother him, the police were welcome if they made her feel more secure, she would realize they were unnecessary.

Sarah walked toward the telephone which was sitting on an old-fashioned phone table by the door. He had never seen one like it outside of an antique magazine. One could sit on its dainty seat and use the new fake version of a fifties phone. Beneath the ornate shelf holding the phone there was a place to put a telephone book. Since telephone books were few and far between these days, Ian noticed the space was taken up with a personal address book. Of course, no one need look up 911 anyway.

Covering her face with both hands, Sarah slid into the seat and sat, not moving, for a while.

Ian remained standing where he was. He didn't move and he barely breathed, not wanting to accentuate his own presence. After several minutes she took her hands from her face, took a long deep breath, got up and walked to a settee in front of the window with the most sun and sat down. She didn't sit back, but on the edge like she might have to make a running break for it at any time.

Ian watched her with an interested doom. Had he pushed too far? What in the world was she thinking? "Sit down," she said in a voice he was forced to strain to hear.

Ian sat.

"How'd you find me?"

"Kenny told us your name and the city you moved to. A private investigator did the rest."

"Oh," she acknowledged, as though she had met some fate she was expecting yet hoped would never happen.

"Mrs. Berle, are you aware of what your son has done?"

"Yes, I'm aware, painfully aware. I've been receiving regular reports and clippings of everything Kenny is supposed to have done. They're sent anonymously. I've always suspected they came from his step-mother. If I'm so easy to find, they could've come from anyone. You know Shauna, don't you?"

Ian didn't answer. He didn't want this to become a discussion about family dynamics or the virtues (or lack of) of Shauna Johnston.

Sarah turned her body so her face was in the full sun shining in the window. Her lips moved, yet no words escaped. Ian sat captivated by her good looks and odd behavior. He said nothing. After a long minute, she turned back toward Ian. Crossing her arms under her full breasts, she sat back on the couch and looked Ian in the eye.

"Well, Sir," she said. "Let's get this over with." Then she added. "Actually I haven't got a thing to tell you about Kenny, or Bob, or what kind of life those people live. I've have been forgiven for that part of my life. Part of my forgiveness depends on not thinking about it. No rehashing. No dwelling on the past. It only ruins my future."

"What do you mean by forgiven? Are you speaking, forgiven, in the divine sense?"

"Are you mocking me?" she said, annoyed.

Ian wondered how close the question put him to being asked to leave. He needed to be less straightforward with his questions. He needed to wait and let her answer any question put in his mind by her rhetoric.

"That's exactly what I mean. You know. All my sins have been washed away. I've been reborn into the light of Christ. My life is now dedicated to the service of the Lord and my fellow man."

"If you truly believe what you're saying, Mrs. Berle, then talking to me about Ken could be good. Kenny needs all the help he can get. He's a very sick boy. There's only one way any of us can help him now and it's to try and find out what made him ill. See he gets the medical and mental help he needs instead of rotting in a jail cell for the next sixty or seventy years. I realize Kenny may no longer be an active part of your life, but he isn't only your fellow man, he's your son."

Sitting on her couch she looked straight at Ian. No, not straight at him, he realized. Straight through him to something or someone only she could see. Her eyes were wild. Moving from place to place, she no longer looked only in his direction. Her head never moved. He had seen Kenny do the same thing. Bizarre was the one word in his mind. Ian sat not moving, waiting for what would come next.

The words she spoke next came on the power of a heavy sigh from the depth of Sarah Berle's soul. Ian suddenly had a chill. He was sure the temperature of the room had dropped several degrees yet he knew it wasn't possible.

"I must make you understand," she said as though she were talking to a small child about concepts far above his scope of understanding. "People in my life don't forgive or forget. They relish on your sins. It keeps them going. It puts them on a plane above you. They can blame you for all the things in their lives that are not as they think they should be. It takes them out of the mode of responsibility and shifts it all to outside forces. Very convenient, don't you think?"

Knowing Sarah didn't want or need a response to her rhetorical question, Ian didn't say anything. She was talking now and although Ian wasn't sure she was talking to him, he wasn't going to do anything to break the spell.

Sarah got up. She walked to the window and looked toward the heavens. Again she mouthed some silent words. Maybe she was offering a prayer. He could not tell. After she stood awhile, as if warming her deepest being from the sun, she walked to a chair at the dining room table, she picked it up and put it in front of the window so the sun was beaming on her back and began talking again. This time Ian was sure she wasn't speaking to him. It was chilling.

Sarah's demeanor changed. She sat forward in her chair now, right on the edge. It came over as an act of contrition. Something was about to happen, he didn't know what.

Sarah fixed her stare on a spot above Ian's head and began talking. Lecturing, Ian thought, not like a college lecture, more like someone who is so familiar with the subject, has been over it so many times, it is branded into her mind.

"I met a man when I was thirteen. Lands, we were poor. He'd wait for me after school, just off the road about a mile from my house and a mile from the school. He'd be leaning on his car every day and we'd talk about how small I was to have to walk so far carrying a heavy load of books. After the second week of this he seemed familiar. When he asked to drive me the rest of the way, it didn't seem wrong. The first day he took me right home. The next day we got a bite to eat before he dropped me off at the shack I called home. In a week or so he began asking for favors."

By her posture and demeanor, it was evident she had a clear memory of what she was saying. Ian wanted to get more comfortable in his chair yet was afraid to move. He could only listen.

Sarah, on the other hand, sat as though she was under an interrogation light, one of those single light bulbs swinging over her head.

"He had money in his pocket, a car and a job. I had no idea about men. I didn't realize what he was doing was against the law. I moved in with him. My father had been gone for years and my mother was glad at least one of her children had a bed to sleep in and food to eat. The longer I lived with him, the more I became a slave. I no longer went to school; I cleaned and cooked all day. It wasn't a pleasant situation, but it was better than what I'd come from. Of course I got pregnant. As soon as I began to show, he packed up my belongings, drove me to a town about sixty miles away and dropped me off on a street corner." She shook her head as if to clear the memories out, then she continued.

"I was innocent enough to be ashamed. I stayed with a farm family in Kansas until Amber was born. I worked hard there. In return they gave me room and board. They treated me decently. When Amber was born, they offered to keep her for me until I could go somewhere and get a job and get settled. I had every intention of going back after her at first. But after a week or so of freedom, I told myself she was better off without me and me without her.

She stopped talking and asked Ian for a cigarette. He didn't have one and thought about going out to Jim, who smoked, to get her one. Instead, he sat still, not wanting to take a chance on breaking the momentum and for Sarah to stop talking.

When a reasonable time had passed and Sarah hadn't begun talking again, Ian nudged her. "You thought Amber was better off without you." He repeated her words back to her with the empathy he was feeling in his heart, at the moment.

Sarah took a deep breath and for the first time since she began talking, she relaxed onto the chair so her back was now touching the rungs behind her. She looked more relaxed. Her eyes had become dull now and Ian wasn't sure she knew he was there.

"Bob Johnston came into the diner where I worked. It'd been three years since I left Amber on the farm. We talked and he began to hang around and walk me home after work. His father owned a construction company and I was impressed with it. I swore when I was left on that street corner, no one would ever get the best of me again." Sarah stopped again. If she was having memories now, she wasn't sharing them. Then...

"...I let Bob make love to me. I knew what kind of man he was. I knew if I got pregnant he'd marry me and I was right. Bob was only a way out for me and I knew it. He represented no more dirty dishes with cigarette butts in them. No more disgusting and condescending remarks from vile men. I was going to marry into money.

"Bob's parents didn't see it like I did. They were not happy with me as his choice for a wife and were horribly embarrassed their son was forced to marry a waitress, from a greasy spoon café. They were sure I tricked him into marriage. They weren't off the mark by much.

"Every day Bob worked for his dad. He got up early and came home late. He was dirty, tired and sweaty. They didn't pay him any more than they paid the other men. I was sick all of the time. I began to hate Bob's touch more and more. What's worse, I hated the child growing inside me. Bob insisted I quit my job and stay home. He'd fallen into a pattern of work, shower, eat, watch TV and fall asleep in his chair. He'd want to have sex when the urge arose. It was hell for me and it was driving me crazy."

Ian finally decided Sarah was going to finish her story no matter what, so he interrupted her and asked if he could have a drink of water. Sarah seemed thankful for the break and went into the kitchen. When Ian heard the water in the sink being used to fill a tea pot, he got up and went in there.

Her kitchen was a cheery place. The refrigerator door was filled with drawings the kids had made. A school calendar hung on the wall and was chock full of events and church meetings needing attended. The theme was fresh fruits and vegetables. On the walls were pictures of apples, pears, peaches, bananas, a single artichoke, eggplants and such. They started at the doorway and went all the way around the top of the room. It was a huge eat in kitchen and Ian imagined the family congregated around the massive oak table in the center. Sarah placed two mugs on the table along with sugar and lemon and a variety of tea bags. She pulled out a chair and sat on it. Ian followed suit. Once they were sitting at the table like a couple of old friends, she began her story at the point she left off. "I'd gotten pregnant to trap Bob. I was the one trapped. When Kenny was born, things went from bad to worse. He cried all day and all night for days at a time. The doctor said he had colic. I think he only wanted attention because the so-called colic went away as soon as I picked him up. Bob said my only job was to hold Kenny. I could hardly stand to touch him. Bob, on the other hand, pampered him and carried him around all the time he was home. He even slept with Kenny on his chest." Ian could not tell if it was sadness or disgust causing her face to contort.

"We began to fight over Kenny. I never had time to wash my hair or take a bath or fix my nails. After Bob left for work in the morning, I locked Kenny in his room and turned the radio on as loud as I could so I didn't have to listen to him. It was the only time I felt free. I couldn't make him stop crying anyway. No use both of us being miserable. It was my reasoning back then. I was still only sixteen." Sarah had been talking into her tea cup. Ian felt sure she knew he was there, but perhaps he was wrong. Sometimes, he decided, when someone is trying to bare her soul, the household cat would be as good a listener as a person. She was in a zone, and since she had long since stopped talking to Ian, he made the quick decision to slip out. Sarah was in her own private world now. He was already standing when she spoke again. "Do you know what Kenny did?" Redundant question, Ian realized, so he didn't answer, but he did stand still and not make any more movement toward the door. "After he learned to walk he would toddle around playing. He was extremely quiet. Whenever anyone was around, he would lay around like he was too sick to lift his head. Bob would put him on the floor and his legs would collapse beneath him. The minute it was only he and I, he would grin at me and scamper off, watching me continually with evil eyes."

Suddenly Sarah looked up at Ian. She looked him straight in the eye. "Did I tell you I've been FORGIVEN for Kenny? She bellowed it out like a mad woman. "Kenny was sent to me from the devil to test me, but I WON. Can you see it? I won." Now, she wanted an answer from the stranger. Presuming himself into her world required an answer from him.

"Yes Sarah, I think you may have won," he said.

Kenny had not.

"I began to hate Bob's touch even more. What if I got pregnant again? I began to lock Kenny outside right after Bob went to work and let him in a few minutes before Bob got home. My, how I loved the peace of mind I had when Kenny wasn't in the house watching me with his green sick eyes. I could soak in a hot bath. I could fix my nails and take long leisurely walks. You see, it was the only answer, don't you?" She didn't wait for a reply. "There wasn't anything else I could do. It was much better than having him play in his room. If he got too loud, I didn't set any food out for him. He soon learned to leave me alone. I was out to prove to the devil he had chosen the wrong woman to mother such an evil child. With Kenny out of the way all day, I was finally beginning to enjoy my life, when out of the blue the child welfare folks showed up at Bob's job and told him about Amber. He was furious. They also told him that during their investigation they discovered I was abusing Kenny.

What a crock! I never laid a hand on Kenny." She grinned to herself.

"I had never told Bob about Amber. My goodness, life was bad enough with Kenny. I didn't need another. Besides, I'd left her when she was seven weeks old. I wasn't her mother. I didn't even know her. Bob, on the other hand, went to pick her up. He kept telling me only a crazy lady would leave a child outside all day. He believed every story he heard. When I told him Kenny was the devil's child, he slapped me. The next day I knew something bad was going to happen. They had taken Kenny away and put him in protective custody. After Bob went to work, I got my things together and left. I locked the door behind me and never looked back. As any sane person can see, Mr. Michaels, if I had stayed another day, the devil would have taken me. He would have left Kenny and jumped into my soul. I had a vivid dream about how it would happen. I couldn't let it happen. I knew Kenny was the devil and Amber would be his disciple. I thought about waiting until Kenny came home and Amber was there and burning them up before I left, but I couldn't wait long enough in case the devil was moving faster than I thought.

"Night after night the devil came to me in my dreams. After he left, the Lord would appear. They would hover over my bed and fight over my soul. Finally the three of us made a deal, me, Satan and the Lord. I would give Kenny to the devil. It wasn't difficult for me because he was born of the devil anyway. I, in turn, would spend the rest of my life in service to the Lord. Amber was left out of the deal. She would be who or what she was without undue influence from either side.

And my reward was forgiveness."

Screaming the last sentence so loud brought Jim to the back door. Ian heard him open it and step inside.

Sarah had since fallen to her knees with her arms stretched to the heavens while she yelled. "The devil can't touch me now. The Lord has condemned Kenny to the fiery depths of hell."

"Amen." Ian muttered. His skin was crawling. He needed to leave, NOW.

He felt he had been listening to ghost and horror stories made up by a master writer, because this could not be real. It just could not be. He was afraid to turn around to see what might be behind him. He sincerely hoped it was Jim. Although he was sure he was safe, he took the chance to glance behind him and saw Jim standing there. He was visibly shaken; it wasn't something Ian had seen before.

Ian had a couple more questions he wanted answered. Hoping Sarah wasn't too far into her own world, he ventured forth with them. "Does Amber know she's adopted?"

"I doubt it," she said adding, "Bob isn't the type to tell her."

Sarah was slipping away from him now. He didn't try to ask her anything else. Her thoughts were her own. She no longer wanted to share them with Ian. She was still kneeling on the kitchen floor, now she was muttering prayers with her eyes closed. She rocked on her knees and said words in a language he couldn't understand. As Ian was turning to leave she said to him, much like an afterthought, "I've been forgiven for what I did. The devil still taunts me though. I know he sent you. Kenny writes me letters penned by Lucifer himself. Once the devil even came here, he haunts my dreams. He wants to break our deal." Sarah shook her head at the irony of it all. "Have I not suffered enough? Well, haven't I?" She was screaming out of control now and Ian turned on his heel, caught up with Jim at the door, and they left.

Jumping to her feet, Sarah followed Ian to the door yelling and screaming at him.

"Well man, answer me. Don't just walk out. Answer me."

Stopping, Ian turned to face her. "Sarah, it isn't for me to say. Thank you for your time." With those final words, Ian and Jim got in their rental car and drove away.

They were well out of sight of Sarah standing on the back porch of her house, but they could still hear her persistent cries. "I'm forgiven. For God's sake, man, can you not understand? FORGIVEN. FORGIVEN. FORGIVEN."

Ian didn't relate the conversation to Jim. He doubted he would ever repeat it to anyone. He wasn't sure it was something to be repeated. He told Jim Kenny had been abused as a child and Sarah was a religious fanatic.

As soon as they were back at the motel, Ian went off by himself to write down all he could remember. It was easy. It wasn't a conversation he was ever going to forget. As a matter of fact, he knew he would be lucky if he wasn't haunted by the day's events, for a long time.

Ian was as eager to leave Oklahoma City as he was to get there. Before he could leave, he needed to do one more thing. He was obsessed to see what the Berle children looked like. He didn't know why, but he thought it was important.

He asked Jim to get a picture of the children and bring it with him when he brought his report to the office. Ian could not stand to stay in the city long enough to do it himself.

"I need to get back to some unfinished personal business," he told Jim

"Sure, I'll take care of things here. I'll see you in a couple of days."

Within the hour, Ian was on a flight back to St. Louis.

Chapter Fifteen

Sarah Berle stood at the door and watched Ian Michaels's car drive out of sight. Rooted to the spot, she stared at nothing long after it disappeared. Her trance- like state eventually led her back into the house where she roamed around. She had no sense of time or urgency. She picked up items and keepsakes from her home. Turning them over in her hands to study them as if they were foreign, she set them back where they belonged when she was done. Opening closet doors, she touched the sleeves of her family's clothes and hugged their coats.

There was a horrendous overpowering feeling of terror following her as she moved through the rooms. She knew it was only a matter of time before the terror caught up with her.

Finally in the back hallway she met her fear face to face. It took all of her strength to make her way into the living room where she collapsed into the nearest chair. The sun, such a comfort earlier in the day, was now hurting her eyes and making her feel unsettled so she got up and closed all the drapes and blinds and sat back down, tired, winded and scared. Now she was consumed by the most depressing, defeating, and dejected emotion she had ever experienced. It held her in the chair for a long time like a concrete block on her heart.

Why was she being haunted? She knew little about what she was feeling now. For the second time in her life, she was alone, yet NOT alone. Her other one was there too...

...After Sarah left Bob and the children, she went from city to city. She drifted from job to job and floated from man to man. She drank too much, lied about everything, and accomplished nothing.

At a cafe in a small town in Missouri she met Denise. Denise was a self-professed born again Christian. Denise walked around with a blue bird on her shoulder and a song in her heart. Day after day she talked to Sarah, telling her how she could start over and make a new life for herself.

Denise had bleached blond hair and for some reason chose to shave her eyebrows and draw them back on in a high arch, giving her a clown-like appearance. She wore as much eye make-up as Tammy Faye and bright lipstick to match her outfits. She was loud, and if she noticed anyone was the least bit interested in a conversation she was having, she elevated her voice and became more animated to draw them in. Denise could have been a barker for a circus, yet her goal was to bring everyone back to the church. To Denise, a good healthy dose of the fear of the wrath of God was all anyone needed to go on the straight and narrow and live a good life to get you to the here-after. It should be, she told Sarah, the only goal of your life. To live so you could go to heaven. Always remember, she told Sarah, you are being watched every minute of every day and you shouldn't do anything you wouldn't want God to see. Follow that rule and you would be all right, according to Denise. It sounded good to Sarah. After all, what she had been doing wasn't working.

Denise was the first girlfriend Sarah had ever had. She seemed to want to talk to Sarah for no reason and Sarah didn't have to do anything for her attention and respect. Denise was a good listener without being too critical. For every horror story Sarah told Denise about her life, Denise could tell of a story of redemption equal to Sarah's, but in most cases, worse, making Sarah see the light at the end of the tunnel. Sarah, however, remained skeptical.

Once Denise needed an extra twenty dollars to make ends meet. Lo and behold, as they walked out of the diner to sit at a nearby picnic to smoke, Denise found a twenty dollar bill wadded up in the gutter. Denise insisted. "God provides." All Sarah had to do to wipe out her past and start over with a clean slate was give her life to the Lord. Denise should have been ordained. She had missed her true calling. "Sarah," she said on a daily basis, "time to give in and have the life you deserve."

Sarah listened.

Sarah was a bright child and an intelligent young woman. She began reading all of the literature Denise provided. She was obsessed with

Revelations and all of the happenings taking place at the end of times.

Spring gave way to summer and Sarah attended a giant revival in a tent erected at the old fairgrounds in Ozark, Missouri. Sarah wanted to believe as Denise did. She would go early, find a seat near the front, take a deep breath and relax into the circle of the people who spoke.

For a solid seven days, Sarah learned of sin and the wages of sin. She sat back and listened to what it did to people. Each night at the end of the service she watched as dozens of people went to the front of the tent and were forgiven for their past and renewed. They had come into the tent tired and defeated people and after their trip to the alter she saw them leave lighthearted and smiling.

Sarah was impressed.

"Repent, sinners!" The preacher told of the evils and darkness in the world "Come forward, you children of Satan! Give your soul to the Lord!"

Sarah began to wonder what would happen if she went to the front of the tent with the other sinners. The preacher guaranteed. "All will be forgiven. Your sins will be washed away. Come, Sister. Come, Brother. Let your burden be lifted and your soul be free. The Holy Ghost stands among you."

There was singing and praying and sweating. People knelt in the aisles. Women wept.

People shouted "Amen." Sarah looked around in disbelief. Until then she didn't know what she would do. All of a sudden some powerful magnetic force, a feeling she could not shake off, moved her toward the altar. The same presence with her then was with her now. It was as if she were two people. One person stood outside the other watching what was happening to her, mocking her, and egging her on.

The music inside the tent became more persistent. Hands clapped to the rhythm. More and more people moved forward like a tidal wave of sick humanity washing up to be cured of their afflictions. As they went up, one by one they were forgiven by the masses and multitudes behind them. Body odor and sweat reeked in the heat yet no one seemed to notice, except Sarah, and she was ashamed each night when she became nauseated by the heat and smell. Another sign, she felt, showing she was a true sinner.

Sarah looked upward as the invisible force lay its hand upon her shoulder and pushed her into the sea of sinners and when she reached the front of the tent it pushed her to her knees. She was now among the sinners singing and waving their arms. She cried bitter tears for the wages of sin.

The music stopped.

There seemed to be no end to the number of sinners each night. This was the last night of the revival, yet there seemed to be more than ever, even though they had come up in great numbers all week. Tonight there were about thirty sinners. They poured out their dirty hearts before the congregation. They told all of their sins, big and small. After each confession, no matter how meager or major, the response was the same. "Lord, forgive our Sister. Lord, forgive our Brother."

Some sinners collapsed into sweating heaps on

the floor of the tent when they were drained. Others managed to stay on their knees and sway to and fro muttering "Praise the Lord" to themselves. The preacher moved from sinner to sinner, each in his turn and each in the same manner. The crowd got louder and louder as the ritual continued. Sarah became more dazed and more caught up in the happening.

There she was, on her knees, before hundreds and hundreds of people and it was her turn. Everyone was quiet. They were waiting for her to speak. She didn't want to. She only wished she were not there, in the front with the pulsating masses. She wanted to be somewhere else.

She had to talk. Nothing and no one was going anywhere until she fulfilled her duty and confessed her sins. She knew she had seen in a movie the Catholics shared their misdeeds in the privacy of a little wooden enclosure and only a priest heard their transgressions. At this moment, it seemed like a much better system to Sarah. Maybe she should become a Catholic?

From her position on her knees on the ground of the filthy tent Sarah resigned herself to a simple fact. This meeting was going no further until the crowd got what they wanted. She must tell them what they wanted to hear. When she could put it off no longer, a strange thing happened to her. Another Sarah stepped out of her and stood with her, looking down, a look of disdain on her face and her arms folded over her chest. It was there then and it was with her now. It scared the hell out of her, yet she could not make it go away.

She called it her un-self

Sarah talked. Her un-self watched.

The baby she had and then abandoned.

"Lord forgive her."

How she tricked Bob into marriage.

"Jesus. Cleanse this body before us."

Kenny.

"Oh Lord. She didn't know what she was doing. Take her into your flock."

When she hesitated.

"Go on Sister. Don't hold back. Rid your body of the poisons of transgression. Cast out the Devil. Put him back into the fiery depths of hell where he belongs."

Sarah didn't hold back.

Why should she? They were forgiving her for everything. She told all. She spoke of the men she had, of the money she had taken from others.

None of it mattered now. She was free.

With each new sin she revealed, they reassured her.

"Lord. You have helped this sinner see the light."

When she finished there was silence. It was over. Sarah lay in a worn and wrinkled wet mess at the preacher's feet. She laid breathing with her face in the cool dirt trying to regain enough strength to partake in the mass baptism which was guaranteed to make this new feeling she had remain with her forever.

But it was only after the ceremonies and the baptism her pseudo-self, stopped pushing and jeering and came in again to join her in the person

213

they seemed to share...until now, Sarah had forgotten about her un-self. She had forgotten about the power it reeled the night she was reborn. She always thought it was an aspect of the night. Yet, here she stood again. She was leaning against the wall with a blank expression on her face, her arms crossed under her breasts and regarding Sarah with great interest.

Sarah began pacing.

The big bright eyes of four-year-old Amber were before her now. It was the day the welfare people brought her to the house and Sarah had known with one glance they would always be strangers. She felt no kinship toward the small person and she hated babysitting.

Ah, Kenny.

Kenny had had his fun at the little girl's expense, but Sarah let him go ahead. So long as the little bastard wasn't bothering her, she didn't care what he did.

Why had she had to be forgiven for these things she could now see were her natural choices?

Bob.

Bob wanted to play with those children of Satan. He liked them. Well, he could have them. She wouldn't tolerate them another day.

Suddenly, a horrendous blinding headache.

Sarah groped for something to grab onto before she fell out of the chair. She was only able to see straight ahead of her through a small tunnel of light. It seemed an eternity before she was able to get out of her chair and into the kitchen and the aspirin bottle.

Between her tunnel vision and the tears of pain, she misjudged the bottle. She knocked it and a glass of water she had managed to get onto the floor. It broke into several large pieces. She stood what seemed like miles above it and tried to focus.

"Pick it up," someone said to her.

Sarah didn't move. Horror overtook her.

"Pick it up, Sarah." Now the voice was so familiar and reassuring. The last time she listened she had earned a new life as her reward. She could not bend over and pick it up. God knows she wanted to do the right thing. Later, her friend helped her by reaching down to pick the glass chard up herself and handed it to Sarah. Thoughtfully she handed it to Sarah with the jagged edge away so Sarah wouldn't cut herself.

Sarah took the glass and smiled.

Through her narrowed concept Sarah looked at what might have been. It was standing before her, so much better and so much wiser. She was smiling back at Sarah now. It was a big full- toothed grin of approval. It was all she ever wanted: someone like herself to approve of her.

Grasping the ragged glass, Sarah ran it across her wrist. As her audience applauded her courage she was able to run it across her other wrist. The two of them stood next to one another giggling with delight. They walked around together now, locking doors and dripping a large amount of blood they didn't seem to notice in the euphoria they felt. There was calm and sleepiness. There wasn't anything more to be alarmed about.

The blood running from her arms as they

dangled by her sides was relieving her headache and at last she was able to think. She felt so satisfied and sleepy. Things would be back to normal when she woke up from her nap. There would be no need to mention any of this to Earl or the boys.

EARL AND THE BOYS!

Oh my God. What on earth was she doing? What had she done? She reached toward the phone but she was too weak from loss of blood to make it. She fell to her knees trying to regain some strength. No matter how hard she tried, the feeling of sluggishness overtook her more.

She lay on her back now staring blankly at the ceiling above. Kenny was there now. He was watching her with a small almost imperceptible smile on his face.

Everything came together for her as she closed her eyes and fell into a peaceful sleep. Kenny called her mama from somewhere in the dark behind her eyes.

Chapter Sixteen

Heather sat in Ian's den wondering who it was she was punishing. All of the realities she was facing had been before her for a long time now. She picked up a family picture he kept on his desk. They were happier days for sure. Ian stood tall, his boyish good looks smiling up at her from the polished print.

The boys were kneeling in front of him with grins bigger than a Halloween pumpkin and she was walking into the picture from the left, the object of their elation. She remembered the day well. They were heading to Vale for a skiing vacation. Ian had wanted to have one more family vacation before the boys got so big they didn't want to go along any more. Where had it all gone wrong?

All of the feelings she had now, she had had before, and she passed them off as fantasies. Heather smiled a forlorn smile and sat the picture back where she found it. A woman's fantasies, she realized, usually didn't revolve around her own husband and another woman.

She, however, was a realist. It was bound to happen, this affair with Maggie. She knew Ian well, and although the changes in him over the past years would have been unrecognizable to someone else, they had been big flashing beacons to her, sometimes, manifested in unsettling churnings in the pit of her stomach, when the two of them crossed her mind. She sat here now, alone and in the room where his presence was the strongest, and thought it all through.

Before her husband's indiscretion began, and she was being gracious here, he had never bothered to call home when he was going to be late. They both kept irregular hours, she with her charity work and the boys' activities, and he with his law practice. It was an occupational hazard, and years before they had decided the world of messages and voice mails wasn't for them. He came in the house each evening shouting his arrival much like Jack Nicholson's, Honey I'm home, in The Shining. In those days Ian grinned ear to ear and had the day's news and newsworthy banter to share. It made their lives interesting. He liked to talk about the-sometimes-one-stupid-thing in a marriage causing it to crumble, something small, misunderstood and blown out of proportion reaping havoc and leading to the end of a relationship. He would shake his head and say they needed to keep the lines of communication open and not let small wounds fester so this didn't happen to them.

Once he told about a thirty-year marriage break up because the husband went to Las Vegas, won ten thousand dollars, and didn't tell his wife. He went home, started a savings account with both of their names on it and was going to surprise her the next time they had an emergency. These people didn't have any money and the wife could not get over her husband being able to keep something so important a secret. Over the next few years she doubted everything he said and did. He could not get away from it and finally they were divorced. Ian called it a tragedy. Heather wondered what he was calling their situation.

All of a sudden, Ian changed the rules. She didn't think anything of it at first, then little red warning flags began waving in front of her mind and she knew. He did things in bed they had never done before. Cosmopolitan said it was a sure sign your partner had been with someone else.

Damn, maybe she was stretching with the magazine article, but the signs were there, nonetheless. Ian started calling and checking in because he didn't want any surprises, she knew it now. What a fool she'd been. He began asking questions about her activities and the social obligations she planned for them. He no longer waited for her to volunteer information on where she would be and when she would be home. It had taken Heather awhile to put her finger on the exact problem. Once she put it all together, she knew he was having an affair. The what-was-going-on was difficult, the who was easy. The toll it was taking was devastating.

If anything, throughout this ordeal, Ian was even more attentive and loving than before. He was always a kind man. They didn't argue. Yet, they didn't get deep into each other anymore. At first she thought it was the changing from romantic love to deep caring love, a transition going hand in hand with long, loving relationships. Oh my. How wrong she was. When the answer dawned on her the other night, it was like a small snow ball had been rolling downhill gathering mass and weight and momentum until it had taken on a life and course of its own. The weight of it now sat on her shoulders. She wasn't without blame.

Believing in Ian had been easy. Of course, when you want to believe you can justify anything. Her goal was for their years of trust and intimacy to be out of the reach of the rest of the world. She sat down in his chair, leaned back and smiled a cynical smile.

Now she was going to punish Ian.

Her unwillingness to talk to him or let him come home wasn't working. He was away on business. He had the Johnston case to occupy his mind. On the other hand, here she sat at two in the afternoon, having made no attempt to dress or eat. Her mind continued moving over their lives.

Last night she had watched him from the bedroom window as he drove up to get his suitcase and then leave again. She closed her eyes, as she did then and imagined his familiar gait as he strolled up to the porch, picked up his suitcase and then was off again. He had not tried to ring the doorbell nor did he search the windows to see if anyone was watching him. Odd, she thought.

Was she angry? No. Hurt? No, not after the first shock cleared her system. Numb? Yes.

Numb best described how she felt. Any bad behavior on her part over the years was exonerated. Everything she had ever done wrong in her marriage now paled when compared to Ian's betrayal.

Numbness, Heather reasoned, was the body's way of waiting for the mind to catch up.

The boys worsened her mood. Their demands on her life forced her out of her room and into reality. It was how she ended up in the den. Timothy clomped about the house, the spitting image of his handsome father. He walked like Ian, had the same tenor in his voice and his easy smiling manner.

Enough was enough.

Heather needed to get out of the house. Once back in their bedroom she faced another truth. Even though most of his things were kept here, she didn't feel him as strongly as she did downstairs.

Heather took a shower in Ian's bathroom. She dressed with slow precision. Her every move was dull and mechanical.

Once she was in her car she felt better. It had snowed the night before. It didn't amount to much because the ground was so warm, yet the sun glaring off the white on the ground made it almost impossible to see and warmed her to her core through the windows of her Escalade. Putting both hands on the steering wheel, she took a deep breath and then found her sunglasses before she drove off down the street.

Heather drove around with no destination in mind. She stopped by Panera Bread, but once she parked the SUV, she recognized some of her friend's cars and since she was in no mood to chat, she backed out and kept driving.

Even in her own mind her behavior was bizarre. Still, she had no real plan.

When she did stop, the building she parked in front of was familiar. She parked the car in the spot with 113 painted on the curb in front of it and got out. It was all so easy and natural. It was something she had done a dozen times over the years. Walking toward the door she saw the number 113. It matched the one on the parking space and she pushed the buzzer on the side of the door with her thumb.

It was silent inside. She pushed the button again, this time counting to ten before letting go. It was enough to wake the dead. It was so annoying a little gray haired lady a few doors down opened her door a crack and peeked out to see what was going on. Heather glanced in her direction and gave an it's okay smile before pushing the button again. This time she kept her thumb on the button until it ached. She let go, and gave up. Her shoulders sagged. She turned and headed back toward the elevator. She thought Ian must have lied again. Maybe he had not taken his business trip alone after all. She shook her head in resignation. She had one foot out the door when there was a noise behind her. Down the hall, in the direction she had come from, a door creaked open. She stepped back into the hallway and turned toward the noise, and found herself staring straight into Maggie's eyes.

Neither woman spoke. Heather walked back toward Maggie's apartment as if nothing was amiss. Maggie stood to the side and let her in. There they were, together in the quiet of the place for a long time. Not looking at one another, not speaking to one another. It was Heather who broke the long uneasy silence. "May I sit down?"

"Of course," Maggie answered in a stupor. She sounded drained of all emotion. Heather watched as Maggie pulled her robe closer to her body, as though she didn't trust the robes' belt to do its job.

"Maggie?" Heather was asking. "Are you okay?" There was genuine concern in her voice.

"No. No. I don't think I am," she answered.

Heather closed the distance between them. Embracing her friend, she patted her on the back. She was going to let her have her cry, but Maggie had no more tears.

As if she were struck by a bolt of lightning, Heather knew she was in control. Not only did she have control of herself and the situation but she had control of Maggie. Her numbness was gone. She knew what she would do from this moment on.

"Sit down, Maggie," she demanded in a harsher voice and demeanor than she had used up to now. The difference was so stark to Maggie she looked up out of her stupor and focused on Heather.

"Let's get some food and coffee into you and then we will have a girl-to-girl talk. It has been needed for some time, and now is the perfect time for it."

Maggie didn't resist. She sat on the couch. She was perched on its edge like a baby bird with hallowed eyes and ruffled feathers. Heather took her time in the kitchen. She had a lot of thinking to do. Her muscles were tight like a cat ready to pounce.

Her true feelings about Maggie and Ian were beginning to rise to the surface. She now knew something she didn't know before. This was no casual affair. Maybe it was why when she drove around all of those hours she was drawn to Maggie's apartment. It took only one look at Maggie and the shape she was in, coupled with Ian's actions and looks from the past few days, that brought her to the realization the two of them were in love.

Judging from Maggie's look, her disposition and mental condition, Heather was sure Ian must have told Maggie his marriage would remain intact. Maggie didn't appear to be the happy woman who got her man. It was Heather's plan to proceed on the assumptions she made while whipping up some hot tea and toast.

It was easy to see the girl was in love with Ian. A sexual relationship didn't bring this much pain to bear on anyone.

Hell.

It would all be so easy if it were only sex. She could and would order Maggie out of their lives by threatening her with the indignities of the wounded wife. Now it could not be handled in such a way. It would take finesse and cunning to get this done.

Heather knew she was no longer in love with Ian; but she was entrenched. After twenty years of marriage, an upscale social life, the freedom to come and go as she pleased, and the ability to have a handsome attorney at her side when she needed him, was a fine life and she wasn't going to give it up. She loved Ian, but she was no longer in love with him. This poor tormented girl before her was, in her eyes, a tribute to Ian and a sure sign he still loved her. Her marriage was safe so long as she wanted it and as of now, she wanted it intact. All she had to do was remind Ian of how much he hurt her with this little romp he and Maggie had been having. Once she made he realize how guilty he was, he would be hers again. She smiled in her certainty.

Heather began to view Maggie as a pitiful child. She knew the decisions no longer belonged to Maggie or Ian. They were hers and hers alone. Maggie and Ian were mere puppets now and she would pull their strings. How could they think they would get the best of her.

When the older woman set the tea in front of her husband's mistress, she watched as its warmth seemed to rejuvenate almost immediately. The younger woman fiddled with her toast, turning it over and over in her hands like it was some foreign object she had never seen before. Her body was there, at the table, in her apartment, yet she seemed so far away, as Heather patiently watched, and sat on the other side of the table feeling superior.

Heather saw things so differently now. She was sitting face-to-face with the reality of her husband's indiscretions. She intended to make Maggie pay for what she had done.

It would be a simple matter of telling her what to do and when to do it.

Heather didn't rush conversation. She was amazed at how much she was enjoying this. As Maggie began to relax, Heather baited her with idle chit-chat. Then, when things were running her way.

Wham. Bam. Pow.

"Maggie, we're in a difficult situation. Ian left for Oklahoma City this afternoon, but he won't be there long."

Maggie's eyes darted from her coffee mug to the toast to the door to the window and then settled on Heather. She sipped and said nothing.

Heather continued. "What you did was wrong. I'm sure you're aware of that. It's no longer the important issue, however. The issue now, is what we do, now."

"It has taken care of itself. I'm leaving the area as soon as I can make arrangements," Maggie said flatly.

"I'm not sure that's the answer, my dear," Heather said with authority. "You see, Ian didn't have to tell me about you. He could've let it go on and on. He told me because he felt he had to. He believes himself to be in love with you. The way I see it, if you leave now, he'll sit around missing you. There isn't anything quite as enchanting as a lost love. Especially if you leave to be noble-which is exactly what you'd be doing.

"You're actually suggesting I stay here?" Maggie said with eyebrows arched.

"Unbelievable." she added in disgust.

"Don't misunderstand me, my dear. Any husband's capable of an affair. In spite of it, I want Ian. The quickest way for me to lose him would be for you to leave. His heart would always belong to you. The boys and I'd be mere responsibilities. Believe me. It would only make matters worse."

"What could you possibly want of me?"

"I want you to shower and clean yourself up. Go back to the office. Have things in order and as near normal as possible. Be there when Ian needs you. Stand beside him until he can stand alone. Then if you still want to leave, you can. But, be sure you understand me. You're to break off this affair. Let him see it has run its course. Let him see you as you really are."

Maggie stammered. "He does see who I really am. You are asking something I can't do."

"But you must. You got us all into this and only you can get us out." It was a flat statement of something Heather viewed as fact. But how and why was her thinking as it was? Was she so sure Ian would never have an affair unless prodded? Heather thought maybe Maggie was going to melt into the floor.

"Why?" Maggie asked, being direct

"Because there's no other way, not for any of us. I think you owe this to me for what you've done. And it'll only work if Ian believes it's over for good. He need not know the ending is arranged. I'll see he's kept busy. I'll bring myself back more predominantly into his life. You must make him learn to do without you. I mean what I say. You're to stay away from him. You're to make it clear you no longer want him."

Maggie reached over and put her hand on top of Heather's and began. "I know what I did was wrong. But, you need to be realistic. I'm sorry, truly I am. What you're asking is impossible. I love Ian. I'll go to the office, but only to get my things. Don't you understand? There's really no other way...."

Heather broke into Maggie's words and she was furious. "Now you listen," she said in an authoritative voice as she jerked her hand out from under Maggie's and stood up almost knocking her chair over in the process. "I know Ian. He can't stand for anything to be unfinished. He'd brood and doubt himself forever. You must stay. You WILL stay. You'll prove to him that this thing between the two of you would never have worked. You have to do this for me and because you say you love Ian. I think you owe it to us."

Maggie looked down, seemingly studying the inside of her tea cup. She shook her head. "All right," she acquiesced. "If you're sure it's the answer."

"Trust me," Heather beamed and added feeling superior. "I know Ian."

"I pray you do. You run a great risk playing with love and life and destiny as you are determined to do."

"Now that we have it settled, you had better be getting ready." Before she walked out the front door, she walked over to where Maggie sat and patted her on the back "By the way, we shan't mention our little talk to Ian. Men don't understand these things. Trust me. I know what I'm doing." Her last sentence was lost in the air as she walked out the door and closed it behind her.

***

Maggie sat glued to her chair. She hadn't looked up when Heather left, yet she felt the tension release from the room as the door closed behind her. Ignorance is bliss came first to her mind and she was totally ashamed. But then she didn't think it was ignorance. It was vengeance. Perhaps it was brought on by the hurt and would fade before it destroyed Heather. Maggie couldn't help but dwell on the fact Heather didn't, during their entire conversation, say she loved her husband. It was more like a contest. She had lost and she wanted a rematch.

She sat at the table for a while longer, then she stood, took a deep breath and walked to the front door of her apartment. She turned the deadbolt and tested the door, slipped the safety latch into its slide and tested the door again. After she was sure the door was secure, she walked into the bathroom and shed her robe. Turning the water on in the shower as hot as she could stand it, she stepped in. Water ran over her penetrating all the way to her inner being. It was refreshing. It didn't however, help her. The dirty feeling she had after her conversation with Heather was still with her. All the soap and water in the world would never make her feel clean again, so long as she was a part of this warped plan.

Heaven help them all, because life was difficult enough without trying to rig it.

Chapter Seventeen

Ian was able to get a direct flight to Lambert St. Louis International Airport and arrived a little after eight pm. He usually enjoyed flying. People intrigued him and he liked to watch them and try to decide what they did for a living. This trip held no enjoyment for him in either direction. On the way down to Oklahoma City he was tired and hungry and tied in knots over his personal life. During the return flight, he could not get Sarah Berle out of his mind.

This puzzle he was trying to put together was growing bigger and bigger, yet the pieces seemed to get smaller and harder to match. Did one person's mental illness spawn another's? Ian wished he were smart enough to understand a tiny portion of how the human mind worked. All he had learned in his forty-three years on earth was simple. He knew any person was capable of anything at any time. *How scary is that.*

Getting off the plane, his mood was lighter. At least he was back in familiar territory. Nearly knocking two people over on his way through the concourse to get his luggage caused him to slow down and pay more attention. When he did, he saw Heather coming toward him with a huge smile on her face. It was so genuine; he could not help but smile back. She looked good. Stopping for him to come to her, he had plenty of time to look her over. She had on a bright red suit with a low cut melon colored camisole under the jacket. It accentuated her figure. Her pumps matched her outfit. Her beige spring wrap was folded over her arm. She was garnering looks from most everyone walking by. She had always been a head turner with her almost platinum hair in natural ringlets around her head. Her skin glowed as though she didn't have on make-up, yet Ian knew she spent hours achieving the look.

It occurred to him she looked regal and untouched outside of the world of privilege she enjoyed. He hadn't addressed his personal life while he was gone. Now he was faced with part of it standing before him. This presented him with two solid facts. Maggie wasn't in court and Heather was with him now. What significance this had or what would happen, he didn't know.

Seldom did Ian participate in public displays of affection but he was so relieved to see Heather's smiling and happy face, he kissed her. She was solid and sane and real. He kissed her so hard and with so much feeling she blushed in his arms as he held her at arm's length.

"It's so good to see you," he chattered. "Have you had dinner?"

"No," she answered, relaxing into his mood. "I got a message from Jim, saying he needs to speak to you and he told me what time your plane would arrive."

"Oh, did Jim say what he wanted?"

"No, he only said to call him when you get in."

"Hum?" Ian muttered.

"I was hoping we could have dinner together. Timothy's home with the boys and Rosemary fixed their dinner. "She didn't want to get lost in a conversation about work or Kenny or anything not social so she pressed on.

"Heather?" he turned her name into a question.

For days she didn't want to talk to him or see him and now she wanted dinner together. He didn't know what changed. Maybe it was only time to think. He wanted to pursue it.

She put her finger up to his lips as a "Shhh," and went back toward lightning the mood to where it was a second before. She rested her hand on his chest as she continued. "Ian," she said much too softly for the hustle and bustle going on about them.

"I've done a lot of thinking since we last talked. I've decided the less said about Maggie the better."

"Don't you want an explanation?" He couldn't keep the surprise out of his voice.

"No. No, I don't. I feel the more you're forced to explain, the more details I know, the bigger the gap between us will be. The more I'll have to forgive and forget. It would become a vicious circle. Trust me, darling. It's better this way."

"Are you sure?" He was sure he wasn't hearing her correctly.

"Yes, Ian, I'm very sure. I know I want you and I believe you love me. That's all I need to know.

We'll rebuild what we had on that."

Ian remained silent. He put his arm around his wife's waist and escorted her through the airport and to her car. He should have been on top of the world. His wife was willing to let everything go and take him back. Why then did he feel so rotten? One reason he could put his finger on was her phraseology. She didn't say she loved him. She said wanted. He was almost certain she meant possess.

Also, he didn't know what he wanted. He hadn't had much time to think about it until this very moment, yet he was sure he didn't want to go back to the way things were. This realization hit him when he was offered his life handed back to him intact and it made him sick at his stomach.

Damn.

Maybe he was a fool. Maybe he was crazy, but he was sure he couldn't do it. He knew he must see Maggie again. Right now as he talked to Heather, he wanted to see Maggie. He needed to see her, hold her, see what was wrong with her, and see what she needed him to do.

Heather seemed to be trying to smother him out of thinking for himself. He needed time alone. There was no way he could stay with Heather. He knew it now. The decisions he needed to make could not be made while trying to carry on as if life were normal and happy between them. After having been in the courtroom thousands of times, handling divorce cases, he knew Heather was either very smart or more devoted than he had thought. He wasn't sure which. He hoped it was a little of both.

Ian gave her credit for knowing him well enough

to have realized if he went home with her now, on her terms, it would be over between him and Maggie forever. Right now, with Heather beside him, he felt like a rat for having strayed away from their marriage. She had him pegged. She knew he had integrity. She was trying to force him into a choice he knew she didn't believe he would make. She was so sure; she was going to stake her marriage on it.

It wasn't fair to him or her. He must leave her.

Searching her eyes, he was trying to look past it all and into her real self. He had done it a million times in his office and in court. Get into the heart of the matter. Look in and see what happened to the situation if someone was made to face the truth. The real she had slipped away from him many years ago. Did he want to try to find her again? He had to force himself not to look away. His failure reflected back to him in her eyes. This was the woman who bore his children. Was loyalty enough to rebuild their marriage? He wondered, for the first time, if she wanted him. What he saw in her eyes wasn't love. It was fear. He didn't think she wanted to try a life without him but he knew she needed to.

"Heather. This won't work. It sounds too much like the plot of a dime store romance. Honestly. I would love for it to be as simple as you try to make it sound. The things I did were wrong. They're also unfinished. I know it now." Not once had he blinked as he said his piece. He felt ten years younger.

Heather's knees buckled.

"Let's go somewhere and get a drink." He

thought the airport wasn't the place to finish this conversation. "Where's the car?"

Heather tore her gaze away from Ian's searching eyes and walked away. "I don't want a drink. I don't want to be around people. If what you have to say is so demanding it needs to be said over a drink, just spit it out."

By this time Ian had spotted the car in the passenger's drop off in front of Southwest Airlines check in and was already guiding her to it. He put her in the seat, and walked around, climbed in and started the engine. "I think I should move out of the house," he said resolutely.

"It isn't necessary. The house is big enough for both of us. Move into one of the guest rooms."

"It's necessary, necessary for me. Every day I dislike myself more.

Every day I find out something new about myself. I'm a little old to say what I'm about to say. However, I don't know how else to say it. I need some time alone, time to get to know myself. I need time to figure out what was so wrong in my life causing me to have an affair in the first place."

Ouch.

"Can't you do that at home?"

"It wouldn't be fair to you.

"Ian," she said touching his arm. "Please let me be the judge of what's fair to me."

As he turned toward her, he saw tears streaming down her face. "Darling, I do love you. I..."

"If you love me," she sniffed, "why are you doing this to me?"

Ian put the car back into park and gave her his

full attention. He even reached over and made it a point to take both of her shoulders into his hands so she was unable to turn away from him until he had his say. "Loving someone, and being in love with someone, are not the same thing and you know it. We can't keep living on past memories. Now we sort of co-exist. If we make it through this, it'll make us stronger. Maybe when this is over, we can be together in a way we can both savor and enjoy."

"Has it been so bad?"

"No, quite the contrary. What we had was good. If it's still there, if it's still real, it can stand a separation. If it lasts because it's good and not because we're willing to overlook the bad, then we would have a chance to save our marriage. You deserve much better treatment than you' been getting in the last few years."

"I'm not complaining."

"Only because you didn't know what was going on. Believe me. In my own mind I hope

It'll all work out between us. But I must see Maggie again. She and I have too much left unsaid."

It was quiet. The kind of quiet that makes you want to put your hands over your ears and scream

"Would you still have dinner with me?" Ian broke through.

"What?" She tried to bring herself back to the present.

"Dinner," he repeated. "You've got to eat. Will you go with me?"

"Sure, why not? What difference could it possibly make now?"

While Heather was busy with her thoughts, Ian was lost in his own. He wanted to change the subject and get on neutral ground. He was about to give it his best try. After getting off the highway on Fifth Street in St. Charles, Ian headed to Stone Cellar Fondue. The restaurant was open until eleven and it was after nine.

As they were greeted at the door, the hearth before them was supporting an array of warm and inviting candles. It was an atmosphere promoting calm and they both felt it as they took their seats in the small quaint space. They didn't speak to one another until Ian ordered Classic Swiss fondue and a good bottle of red wine to go with it. They sat quietly as the waiter put Ian through the paces of tasting the wine. They were on their second glass of wine when the Fondue was brought to the table. He hoped they didn't rush him through dinner because the fondue was amazing. The atmosphere was calming and although it was a small space, the tables were cordoned off with a full length curtain giving them the illusion of privacy. It was Emmentaler and Gruyere cheeses blended with a dry white wine, garlic, white pepper and Kirshwasser cherry schnapps. The homemade bread was warm and crusty. He felt things were almost normal between them.

As they ate, he began telling his wife about his bizarre trip. Other than her drinking her wine much too fast, she seemed interested. She listened and participated in the conversation. One thing they both had in common was they could not stay inside themselves. They cared about others and it showed.

He smiled as he talked. She smiled back. It hit him she would be all right no matter how things turned out for them. She was a survivor, so was he.

Heather, being a mother herself, had some insight to Sarah. She said she could not, however, understand not loving your children. She did understand, shaking her head to some of the things they did, wondering what was driving them. Timothy was the ideal child and she had spent years bending over backward trying not to bring him up to the other two when they had some unorthodox behavior. She said she had always shrugged it off as the first child, middle child, and youngest child thing. But to abandon your firstborn and view your second as the devil's spawn was way out of Heather's realm of understanding. Most of her comments about Sarah consisted of No kidding and Oh, my goodness.

Ian still held out the one thing nagging at his mind. What did the Berle kids look like?

The pictures Jim was bringing back, the ones of the Berle children, would confirm or lay his suspicions to rest for good. It reminded him again he needed to call Jim. It was getting late and he decided to let it wait until morning.

By the time they finished dinner Heather was more herself. "When are you moving out of the house?" He was helping her into the car.

"There's no use prolonging it." Oh, my, he didn't want to do this again.

"Then what?" she pushed.

"Let's take things as they come." He reached over and touched her lips with his hand to stop whatever else she was about to say. And then he reached over to pull her closer to him as they drove home. Heather didn't resist. She sighed as she lay her head on his shoulder.

It was well after midnight when they arrived home, yet Timothy was in the den. There were books strewn everywhere. They stood next to one another in the doorway and surveyed the mess.

"What's up, Tim?" Ian asked his son who he now had to look up to.

"Big test tomorrow." He looked around. "Sorry," he added. "I'll pick it up. If I don't ace it, I won't be running this year."

"It is after midnight, Tim." his mother pointed out. "You won't be able to pass if you sleep through it."

"I think I've got it down pat." He began picking up his books and stacking them on a table near the door. "Dad. How's Ken Johnston?"

"As well as can be expected, I guess. He's having a mental evaluation and no one can see him. Why the interest?" Ian asked.

"Oh, the kids at school ask me about him all the time. He's sort of a legend around school."

"What kind of legend? Hopefully he isn't a role model for anyone."

"Not, hardly. He was a weird kid and everything he did always created a stir."

The vagueness of teenage conversation had always frustrated Ian, but he took a deep breath and tried not to let it get to him.

"Like what, Tim? Give me an example."

Timothy perched his lanky frame on the edge of

the leather sofa. "Well, he was always late for class. One day he was running as fast as he could, trying to beat the bell and he didn't make it. The final bell rang as he slid around the corner and into Mr. Duncan, the science teacher. The two stood staring at one another for a little while because over the years people were leery of confronting Ken, you never knew what he'd do." Timothy stopped.

"Go on." His father prompted.

"Well, Duncan made Kenny go to the office and get a hall pass before he could go on. Kenny went into a raging blue funk. He started beating a locker with his fists. When he couldn't beat it any longer with his hands, he lay down and kicked it in until it was totally destroyed.

The police came. No one could believe one skinny kid did all that damage. They tried to keep us out of the halls while it was all going down, but they couldn't. Anyway, Kenny settled down and swore in front of everybody that he didn't do it. I would have believed him too, if I hadn't seen it with my own eyes."

"That's some story, Tim. Anything else?"

"Oh, yeah, plenty. He was always into something."

"Well, go on." He wanted to hear more.

Heather, who had been sitting in an overstuffed chair by the door, with her coat still on, stood and said, "Stop cross- examining him. Timothy. Go to bed."

Tim gathered his books and bag and strolled out of the room in a typical sixteen-year-old fashion.

"By the way, Timothy," his father added. "Your

car's leaking oil on the driveway. Get it fixed and clean up your spill." Tim didn't answer his dad and Heather glanced over at him with a disgusted look. She stood in the doorway waiting for him to acknowledge her. When, after several minutes, he failed to do so, she went up to their bedroom and closed the door.

Ian sat in the den for several hours. He was too keyed up to sleep. He was absorbed with thoughts of Kenny and the case. Only when fatigue overtook him did he slip off his shoes and jacket, unloosen his tie and lay down on the couch. Sleep was such a pleasant thing.

When Ian woke, he went upstairs. Heather wasn't there. The room was dark. The shades were drawn, the bed unmade and the bedside clock was flashing ten fifteen. He walked over and opened the drapes. Sunlight flooded the room. The sun was well up in the sky. He sprinted downstairs.

The smell of bacon greeted him as he rounded the corner toward the kitchen. Rosemary was cooking and humming some familiar tune he couldn't put a name to.

"How do you want your eggs?" He could swear she said it in the same tune she was humming.

"Over easy. Where is the Mrs.?"

"She had an early meeting. She left orders this house was to be quiet until ten. Then I was supposed to cook breakfast. I'm to see you eat a proper breakfast before you go running off.

Will you eat in here or the dining room?"

"What kind of a meeting?" he asked, ignoring everything else said.

"She didn't say. She was outta here at the crack of dawn." Since Ian didn't answer her as to where he would eat, she fixed his plate and sat it in front of him on the island he was leaning on.

He didn't resist. He moved over to the nearest stool and ate the lavish breakfast of bacon, eggs, homemade biscuits, warm apple butter, fresh fruit and Rosemary's always-perfect coffee.

The sleep had done wonders for him. The food eased his stomach. He need not hurry off to the office either. Other than waiting for Jim, whom he had failed to call back, there wasn't anything for him to do. He made a mental note to himself to get his divorce practice back up and running. This thing with Kenny could go on indefinitely. The group of court appointed doctors who were evaluating him were not going to hurry and publicity had settled down. The press had moved on to their next big story and would only give Kenny's case a mention now and then until the tests came back. Ian had a chance to take a deep breath and he thought he had better take it.

His next immediate problem, he thought, was approaching Maggie. He had no idea how to go about it. His emotional threshold was low and he felt like a school boy. He wanted to see her and talk to her but right now, it was too great of an effort.

Maybe tomorrow.

Rosemary pulled a piece of paper out of her apron pocket and handed it to him. It was another message from Jim. It was written in Heather's hand and let him know Jim would meet him at the office at noon. Don't bother to call. The message somewhat eased Ian's mind. One more cup of coffee in Rosemary's cheerful presence, and a nice hot shower and the drive would put him at the office right on time. He wasn't looking forward to being in the office alone.

Chapter Eighteen

Maggie and Jim were both waiting at the law office for Ian. They were easy friends and passed the time talking about the Cardinals and the Mets series taking place a few miles down the road at Bush Stadium. Maggie was perched on the edge of Ian's desk while Jim was lounging on a couch singing the praises of this year's team. The banter immediately stopped when Ian walked through the door, the mood instantly somber.

Jim spoke first. "I think we might have a problem in Oklahoma City." He handed Ian a newspaper he was clutching.

Ian walked around and sat at his desk. Maggie had never taken her eyes off him. She was waiting for some indication as to how it was going to be between them, but it was too late. The moment had passed without a word. Now they would slip into their normal work routine and it would have to wait. She had no idea what would happen. Her heart had been pounding in her chest and her palms damp since he came in. Whatever the effect she had had on him was lost in the matter at hand.

Ian now stood with the Oklahoman in his hand. Jim had folded it so the front page story he would want to read was right in front of his eyes. It read:

Mayfair Woman Found Dead

Sarah Lee Berle, age 36, was found dead in her Mayfair home yesterday evening by her husband Earl. Authorities say suicide is suspected although an investigation is underway after neighbors reported seeing two men at the Berle home only hours before the body was discovered. Mrs. Berle was active in many local, civic and church affairs. Those closest to her refuse to believe she would take her own life. (Obituary 26a)

Ian quickly found the obituary page and read on:

Sarah Lee Berle, nee: Atkins, age 36. Survived by her husband Earl and two sons, David and Matthew, both of the home. Friends may call after two pm on Thursday at the Smith and Kernke Funeral Home in Mayfair. Internment: Resurrection Memorial Cemetery.

Ian laid the newspaper on his desk. He took great pains to straighten the edges of each page so it coincided with the page before it, Maggie could see how upset he was. His words seemed to be catching in his throat.

"How'd you get this?"

"I drove by the house on my way to the school to get your pictures. There were police everywhere. I parked a couple of blocks away and walked back to stand with the crowd. They were talking about a body that was found in the house. I caught bits and pieces of the conversations as I mingled. People were talking about the two men who were at the house earlier in the day.

"They did describe my rental car and how I sat in it outside while the other man was inside for over an hour. I thought I'd best get out of there before someone pointed me out as one of the mystery men. I couldn't get a flight out until this morning. This was the headline in the morning paper."

"Damn. What should we do?"

"Well, after what you told me about her bizarre behavior, I'm certain it was suicide. And under ordinary circumstances I'd suggest you fly back out there and discuss it with the local law. But, she had a different life and I'd hate to see what the truth of her past would do to those boys."

"You're right. Do you know anyone out there well enough to explain what's going on here? Maybe those kids and their father could keep their self-respect. I'd hate for someone to dig deep enough to find out who she really was. If it makes the national news, life as they know it will be gone forever."

"I think I can handle it. What do you think happened?"

"I think her demons caught up with her. They were pretty close while I was still there.

I feel responsible. I wish I'd have left it alone. Damn."

"Don't blame yourself. From what you told me it was only a matter of time before she lost control. She sounded like a time bomb waiting to go off."

"Maybe you're right. It doesn't make me feel any better or ease my mind. And, it adds another victim to this mess."

Jim shook his head. "I followed Sarah for days. I liked her and her family. When she moved it was like watching a thick liquid change shape. Her seemingly gratifying life being cut short makes my stomach churn. On my flight back from Oklahoma City I actually grieved for her and those she left behind." With his other hand he took a notebook from his jacket pocket and opened it. "May I use this phone?"

"Sure."

Meanwhile Maggie had gone and come back with three steaming cups of coffee. She sat one before each of them. She took hers and strolled to the other side of the room to sit on one of the couches, where she sipped it, looking relaxed.

Jim spoke at length to someone on the phone. After a long while Maggie turned her attention to Ian. He was tapping his fingers on the desk and looking toward Jim. To someone who didn't know him it would appear he was intent on Jim's conversation. Maggie knew better, the faraway look in his eyes, the sad and depressed look on his face were giveaways. She knew he sat trying to justify his visit to Sarah. Was it the cause of her wasted death, or would it all have caught up with her anyway?

Jim's voice cut into each of their private thoughts. It seemed the authorities had found out a lot since Jim had left the city. Talks with close friends and her husband revealed Sarah often had bouts with depression. It had been a long time concern she might harm herself during one of her episodes. The detective, Jim called, said so far as he could tell, no one was aware of her decadent past, or of her other children, Amber and Kenny. Even her husband had no clear picture of her early years.

After much discussion with the Oklahoma City authorities, it was decided they would close the case and not destroy her husband and children by dragging them into something they had nothing to do with. The general consensus was to let Sarah be at peace for, perhaps, the first time. It was the unanimous decision.

After all else was settled, Jim handed the pictures of the Berle children over to Ian.

"Is this what you wanted?"

Ian studied them. "Yes. Yes, this'll do nicely. Maggie, I need to see the Johnstons.

Call them. Tell them we're coming. Give them some legal jargon. Make them think they have to see us. Use words like guardianship and parental duty."

Maggie nodded and left the room. Jim stayed. She could hear their subdued voices. They huddled together and were speaking in low tones. For a split second she became paranoid and was unable to work or think. Her stomach flip-flopped several times.

It was only after she heard Jim leave by the side door she was able to make the call to the Johnston home.

It took Maggie the better part of an hour to convince Shauna Johnston of the importance of the visit. It would have been easier had she been aware of its importance herself. She was about to admit total defeat when Shauna gave in with an "Okay, let's get this over with." The meeting was set for eight o'clock the same evening. Maggie made three false starts into Ian's office to tell him about the appointment. This would be their first time alone together since the note. She was scattered and unable to face him at this moment. She used the intercom instead. She said no more than she had to say. "Shauna Johnston has agreed to meet with you at eight this evening."

Maggie felt so transparent. She was shaky and drained from the high-keyed emotion of the past few days. If she didn't get out of the office, she was either going to faint or rush to him.

Why had she agreed to Heather's foolish demands were still beyond her. She did realize now, after seeing him, she could not continue the facade and was going to leave the city as soon as she could make the necessary arrangements.

If the office were the bustling place it had been before Kenny, she could have stayed. Someone was always coming and going. It would have eased the pressure. The reality was different now. She and Ian, Ian and she, much too much pressure, she felt.

One of the telephone lights went on signaling Ian was making a call from his office. She had no control over the feeling starting in her toes and skyrocketing to her head. She could no longer sit and wonder what he was thinking or try to imagine what would happen between them. She felt silly sitting there with nothing to do but wait for his next move.

Maggie became mesmerized by the light. It no

longer represented a busy phone line to her. It became a beacon. It lit up a picture of Ian talking to Heather, laughing and sharing private jokes. The light went out and with it the last of her patience. She got up, put on her coat and walked out.

No.

It wouldn't do, much too dramatic. It would only add to the tension and distance already piled up between them. Her hand was still on the doorknob when she turned around and went back to her desk. Again she used the intercom. Her heart was racing as her own voice sang back to her. "Ian." She wasn't cold, yet not warm. She classified her tone as noncommittal. "I'm finished with everything. I'm leaving for the day." She didn't wait for a reply. As fast as she possibly could, she disappeared out the door.

Maggie, oh, Maggie, what will happen to you? What is happening to you? Questions she couldn't answer.

She went into her apartment by the back door so as not to encounter anyone. Once inside she took off her coat, dress, slip and underwear and tossed them on the couch. From there she went straight into the bathroom and ran a steamy bath. While the tub was filling she pattered naked and barefoot into the kitchen to pour herself a glass of wine. The longer she soaked her long legs and aching back, the better she felt. The wine didn't hurt either. She was thinking more clearly now.

In the morning she would begin making her plans to leave, to hell with Heather Michaels and her bright ideas. Right now she needed more rest and rejuvenation. Grabbing a huge towel from the linen closet she wrapped herself and picked up the wine glass which she refilled as she passed through the kitchen on her way to her room. She felt better than she had in days. She cleared her mind of anything not warm and restful. As her body began to cool down after her hot bath, she became lethargic.

Next to her bed was a night table. As she picked up the newest copy of O and prepared to snuggle in, the doorbell rang.

Shit. Now what?

Whoever or whatever it was, she wasn't interested. All the way to the door she cussed under her breath. On the other side of the security hole she could see Ian's distorted face. When she recognized in her now-relaxed, wine-foggy brain who it was, she thought about getting a robe. As she turned back toward her room, the buzzer sounded again. She turned back and looked at it as though it were a living thing. Before she opened the door, she slipped on the safety chain.

Who was she protecting, him or her? She could only shake her head.

"Hi," he said through the crack in the door. He had a childish grin on his face. "You left without telling me what time to pick you up. How do you feel? You look wonderful." He was talking so fast it was like shorthand.

She was a total blank. "Pick me up for what?"

"Meeting with the Johnston's at eight." he continued.

"Ian, you don't need me to go along."

"Oh yes I do." He was emphatic. "May I come in? This is awkward."

"Actually Ian, I'm tired. I'd rather stay in tonight. I was thinking about going to bed early." Being rude to him wasn't in her DNA.

"I can see that." He laughed looking her up and down. "Honestly. Must we talk through this door?"

She flushed all the way to her toes and hoped he didn't notice.

"Please, let me come in."

"Ian, please."

"Maggie?" his voice caressed her.

They stood looking at one another until she closed the door and removed the chain. He stepped quickly inside lest she change her mind. Never once did he take his eyes off her. She was still blushing. She doubted his attentions were because she made a sexy image standing there. The towel she still wore turban style around her head was vivid green. Her body was covered with a gigantic hunter orange beach towel. With one hand she was holding the orange one. A wine glass dangled between the fingers.

She laughed at the thought of herself and the coldness between them melted. "You drive a hard bargain, Ian Michaels."

"I didn't say a word."

"I know," she smirked. "Make yourself at home. I'll go pull myself together."

Maggie disappeared through the silent swinging double doors separating the living room from the bedroom of the apartment.

"Fix yourself a drink," she called. "I'll be right

out."

He drank two. Still, no sounds of life came from the next room.

Maggie was sitting on the bed following her ritual of putting lotion on her legs when she sensed she was no longer alone.

"Need some help?" He didn't wait for an answer. Walking up to her, he took the tube of cream from her lap and squeezed some on his hands. Warming it between his hands first, he then began rubbing it gently up and down her legs, each time going a little further up her leg and under her towel. She didn't take her eyes off him, nor did she try to stop him. He soon seemed tired of holding back and stood up pushing her back onto the bed. At the same time, she began unbuttoning his shirt. They began to make love soft and easily. When they were through, they lay quietly holding one another. Neither of them dared spoil the rapture of the moment with personal thoughts or words. They lay side by side in their silence.

Chapter Nineteen

Ian stopped his car in front of the Johnston home a few minutes before eight as scheduled. Maggie was with him. She was resting her hand on his thigh as they drove. When they arrived and she removed it, the sensation left him feeling cold.

The only visible change they noted at the house was the flat tire on the car in the driveway had been repaired.

Shauna met them at the door and introduced herself. She was as Ian expected her. He had had a pretty good look at her in court. The atmosphere wasn't, however, what he expected. She was light-hearted and seemed eager to please. Ian wanted to observe her. It was difficult for him to push all of his preconceived opinions to the back of his mind as he watched her.

Shauna Johnston had charm. It oozed forth in her eagerness. It wasn't beauty. She stood no more than five feet three. Her hair was an extraordinary shade of red, more a bright maroon. Her legs were too thick at the ankle and her breasts were much too large for her small frame.

She led them into the dining room where she seated them as a hostess would. On one end were little sandwiches of egg salad and tuna salad with the crust cut off. She offered ice tea, coffee or lemonade. It felt more like a party or an open house rather than a visit with the parents of a mass murderer. Ian felt a cold chill run down his spine. He wanted to look at Maggie to see her reaction. He was afraid Shauna might observe the exchange so he didn't chance it. He smiled and accepted a sandwich and a drink. So did Maggie. Had he misjudged Shauna?

Bob slipped in the back door and took a seat at the end of the table. Shauna took three sandwiches, put them on a plate and sat them in front of him. He glanced up and gave her a shy smile.

Ian knew what was so appealing about Shauna. It was her body language. It hit him so hard he almost snapped his fingers and said, "That's it." Everyone used the term, yet now he knew what it meant. It was moving in front of him now, leaning toward each person as she served, smiling and acting as if that person were the only one in the room, tilting her head with interest as she asked about drink preference. Ian called it the lean. People do it all the time to make you feel important. Hell, he did it. The minute someone opens his mouth, you lean in and give him your full attention. It radiated trust and understanding between strangers. She accentuated it by wearing slacks which were much too tight and a sweater much too low-cut for the occasion.

She acted unaware. When she bent over to serve him he could see her full bosom heaving before him, yet the seductive tone wasn't in her voice nor was the look in her eye.

The old saying "beauty is as beauty does" came to mind as he watched her. She seemed beautiful in her own eyes, and she pulled it off magnificently. She didn't appear to be egotistical or conceited about it. For her it seemed a simple fact. Her clothes might not have been appropriate for this meeting but it didn't seem to matter to her.

When the amenities were over and they had chatted about nothing in particular over refreshments and were sipping on ice tea in an awkward silence, Shauna's demeanor changed. She seemed ready to get on with the business at hand. She wanted to talk.

Shauna said, "I have no allusions about Kenny. I knew one day I'd be asked to tell my story. We're above guilt. No one who ever mothered a child would be able to say that I, Shauna Johnston, didn't do my part: the best I could do. If only they realized I did everything for an ungrateful little bastard who didn't belong to me in the first place.

"I have some truths to tell you about your client. Truths no one else knows." As she talked, she spit a spray across the room. Ian thought it was probably venom. "He's no better than an animal, why couldn't anyone but me see that? In my mind, when we got him it would have been better to euthanize him while he was still too small to do the harm he's done."

As Ian listened, not being able to get a word in, it occurred to him that the things Kenny did were probably not as bad as they could have been.

"I knew something was going to happen." Shauna continued. "I thought he'd do something. When he was younger I'd lie awake at night thinking he'd murder us in our beds. It might have been better than this humiliation. God knows I tried to make a good home for him. He'd never listen."

"When Bob and I were first married we could never get any sleep. Kenny would bang his head against the headboard of his bed for hour after hour. After suffering a week of no sleep I took him to the doctor. After the doctor looked at him, he said 'the young fellow suffers from tension and stress.'

Have you ever heard such nonsense in your life? A six-year-old boy with tension and stress. By god. I put a stop to that quick. One night after everyone was in bed he started his banging.

"That particular night it was deafening. I went in there and grabbed that kid by the hair. I said 'you little son-of-a-bitch', you do that again and I'll give you something to be tense about.' Well, he never did. Tension my foot. It was pure unadulterated meanness. That doctor was way off base. I could tell the difference between mean and sick and I didn't go to some fancy medical school."

"The little bastard," Shauna had continued, "has stolen and lied since day one. When our baby was first born I'd send Kenny to the store for cigarettes. He never came back with any change. It didn't matter if I gave him five dollars or ten. He'd say he lost it. I knew damn good and well the little fucker bought candy with it. He said no. Finally I went down to that store and I ask the old man who ran it if Kenny bought candy. He said no. I was sure then the old man kept some of the money and gave Kenny candy for the rest. The old bastard.

"That sister of Kenny's isn't better, you know? She is just quieter about things.

"Once, a few years ago, I was teaching tole painting downstairs. It seemed like there were always flies in the house. They were especially bad downstairs where my classes met. I couldn't tell where they were coming from. After the students left one day I scouted around. There was a terrible smell coming from underneath the staircase where I kept the winter clothes. When Bob came home I had him pull everything out of there. I found the flies all right. You wouldn't have believed it. Bob's hunting boots had pee in them. Kenny had peed in those boots. I know it was him because he stuffed some of my things in the boots first. There were also mason jars with piss in them. Each one of those jars had my clothes in them too.

"Kenny said my boy Charlie and he did it and it was only a childish prank. They didn't mean any harm. Can you believe it? Well, I got Charlie down there and I asked him point blank if he pissed in those jars and he said no. My kids have always known better than to lie to me I said

'Charlie, I'm only gonna ask you one more time. Did you do this?' Charlie didn't. Kenny did. I knew it to begin with but I didn't want anyone saying I wasn't fair to the little bastard."

Ian glanced toward Bob. He was sitting stone

still with his head down, almost resting on his chest, and a tear rolling silently down his cheek.

"Right there and then I told Bob he'd better do something. I'd really had enough. I went upstairs and got a board from the garage. I gave it to Bob, and he used it. It didn't do a damn bit of good. It wasn't a week later until the kid had 'stress' again and wet his pants. I fixed that little habit of his also. I made that kid wear those wet underwear on his head for the rest of the day. I told him I didn't give a damn what people said. I was going to break him of his filthy habits and I did. And I can tell you. From then on, that kid always went to the bathroom in the proper place."

Once Shauna had begun, it was like a sermon. Both Ian and Maggie had commented later how well she knew her material. It was because, they thought, she had given the same sermon over the years to anyone who would listen.

"About a week later I was downstairs." She had the floor and was obviously relishing in Kenny's horrible deeds. She let it be known, everything she had done, was done in Kenny's best interest. "He came at me with a knife. That time I must admit, I got mad. I told Bob either he goes or I go. Bob packed him up and took him to the child welfare people. They put him in some half way house where he lasted a few weeks before he showed his evil little ass for what he was and they threw him out."

At this point, Shauna had begun to laugh, apparently at what she was saying next.

"Once, when he wouldn't go to school, we had to go to a counselor. Do you know what they came up with? They thought we should reward him. Turn our backs on all the meanness inside him and pay him for behaving. Give him money every time he goes a week without getting into trouble. If he steals from the other children, don't mention it but give him a quarter if he takes out the garbage without an argument. Do you believe that bullshit? If he went to school every day for a week I was supposed to give him another dollar.

"It was the single most ridiculous thing anyone ever asked me to do. They said as soon as he quit getting attention for bad behavior and only got attention when he was good, his bad behavior would stop. Well, well. If I'd done it their way I'd have had all five of them lying and cheating within a week just to get the money. I swear, doctors don't live in the real world.

"One day I thought I had the kid for sure. He stole candy from a church near us and three men came to the house to get the money for it. Hell, I told them they should have him arrested. I told them it was the only way he would ever change. But, they wouldn't do it. They said it was against their principles. I told them, principles or no principles, if they wanted their money they would have to get it from Kenny. I tell you. It has been one damned thing after another since day one."

Shauna was preparing to draw another big breath to continue.

Maggie had glanced up from her notes to steal a look at Ian. He had clearly heard all he cared to hear. Bob still sat silently in his chair. Twice during her dissertation she had badgered Bob into backing up one of her disgusting points she was trying to make. He had only shook his head.

Maggie put down the pen and tipped her chair back on two legs, she looked over at Ian.

He had to call an abrupt halt to the interview. He had learned much much more than he wanted or needed to know from Shauna. All the stories he had heard about people putting their cigarettes out on their children's foreheads, or locking them in closets without food were now real to him.

Immediately. At the precise moment he was sitting at the table with Shauna, Bob and Maggie he decided to start up his regular practice again. It could be months, maybe even a year before the tests and evaluations on Kenny were finished. After his talk with Shauna, Ian knew he had spent enough time on the seedy and perverted side of life. It was all sick. Under the best circumstances it wasn't the type of case he wanted to build his career on. He had a deranged teenage murderer with a dozen witnesses wanting to see him hanged in the public square. He had six random victims, three of them children whose murders were carried out in ways the ordinary imagination could not conceive. There was a religiously fanatic of a mother who committed suicide rather than face reality. Then there was Shauna. What label could he pin on Shauna. Evil step-mother came to mind. She thought she abused Kenny with justification in the name of parenthood. Ian thought it was a shame with all of the medical advances in recent years, they could not develop a pill of compassion and understanding to be given to people like Shauna.

Ian's original goal was to find out why someone would do what Kenny did. He could not speak for the other mass murderers of the world, but he was ninety-eight percent sure he knew why Kenny was: well, Kenny.

He would see it through. The best outcome for Kenny, Ian believed, was life somewhere he could do no more harm. He would handle the final details of the case as they came in.

He would go to trial when the time came, but it was time for life before Kenny once again.

But in his heart, he knew there would never again be a time before Kenny. What he had witnessed and heard in the past weeks would forever cloud the way he looked at things. He would always know there was a deeper story to be sought out.

Kenny had been mishandled since his first day on earth. It is embedded in all of us somewhere, if our parents don't love us then we feel we have no worth. Parents are supposed to be creatures who love you because you are you.

Ian was weary. He didn't want to have to think about it anymore today.

Chapter Twenty

Within two weeks Ian's practice was booming again. The publicity from handling Kenny's case had been astounding. As soon as word got around he was active again, the phone rang all the time. He was now handling real estate, probates, and misdemeanors along with his divorce and corporate load. His old accounts were drifting back as they needed an update or if a problem arose.

Ian found it easier to handle all the cases not in his field before rather than argue with people trying to justify why he didn't want their business. He found the variety to be nice and he wondered why he had chosen to limit himself before. The load on Maggie was evident. Ian asked her on several occasions if she wanted or needed help. She always answered the same way. "I like it here just the way it is."

The one thing they did agree on, however, was the need for law students to do some of the grunt work. It was working out great.

Two or three times Ian had taken the Kenny

Johnston case out and looked at it. Twice to answer administrative orders from the judge and once because even though he told himself early on he would never forget a detail, he wanted to make sure he didn't. He read it all over. It was as bone chilling as ever. Ian also put the pictures of Kenny's mother's other children next to the murder victims and marveled at what he considered a most extraordinary thing no one else seemed to notice.

The first murdered woman, Mary Ann Rogers, could have been mistaken for Shauna Johnston in any lineup. Likewise another dead woman, and Sarah Berle were a matched pair. Thomas Adams and Charlie Johnston: it was the same down the line. It only brought up more questions. How would Kenny know what Sarah Berle's children looked like? Ian felt his mood plummet. He could not find a match for Matthew or Andrea. If they were doubles for someone, they were outside of Ian's sphere of knowledge about Kenny. They could have been random. The image of the last little girl, Andrea, haunted him. She was the cute little blond pixie Kenny had raped and murdered. Ian's feelings of confinement and the need to run overtook him for the first time since he had seen Kenny in jail. He put the file back into its proper place and vowed to let those who did such things for a living handle it.

Damn.

Ian's love life was in limbo. Heather had gone to her mysterious meeting the morning after their discussion. He had gone home after work the next night, again to find her gone. Rosemary told him he was to go upstairs to pick up a message Heather had left him. There was an envelope leaning against his dresser caddy. Although nothing was written on the outside he was sure it was what he was looking for. The message inside was curt, cold, and to the point.

Ian,

I'm beginning to see your point about not being able to think with me around. I'm finding you are having the same effect on me. I will be out for the rest of the evening.

Please pack your things and be gone before I return.

I do love you. I most likely will love you forever. This morning when I woke and went downstairs, I watched you sleep for a very long time. The realization I didn't want to hear your voice or see the look in your eye, surprised even me.

As Always,

Heather.

He had put the note in his pocket, his clothes in a suitcase and left as soon as he could. He checked into the Chase Park Plaza hotel in downtown St. Louis. He paid for two weeks. He didn't know what he was going to do, but he knew he needed to feel settled right now.

It was now sixteen days since the note. He was still in his room at the hotel. He had sent a crew over to the house to clean out his den and have his papers and files moved to the store room in the basement of his office building.

Still, no communication from Heather. She hadn't called him. He hadn't called her. He considered it a shame. It didn't take a genius to see they were drifting apart perhaps forever. Ian knew he loved Maggie. He no longer tried to deny it to himself. He even admitted to a slight obsession. Yet a part of him died every day in what he was losing in the closeness with his family. It was something he would never have again.

At first he hadn't called for fear he would upset her. He then decided to give her time to sort out her feelings. After a while, the reasons he had had for calling her seemed trivial when he thought back on them. The longer there was no conversation between them, the easier it became to let another day go by. He was sure if she needed him, really needed him for something, she would call.

Ian had gotten the boys and taken them for pizza once and a baseball game the second time. They were polite, smiling and generic. It was written on their faces: they were not going to tolerate one word, good or bad, about their mother.

Maggie was another story. He hadn't been with her since the night they visited the Johnston home. There had always been long periods of physical separation in their relationship. They had been brought on by his marriage. Since it was no longer an issue, it was now driving him crazy.

Maggie didn't seem to be avoiding him, yet it was the way things were going. The office was a mad house all of the time. Someone was coming or going, law students were camped out in the conference room most of the time. It made it impossible for a moment alone. Maggie seemed to be basking in it. He did admit it was a pleasant change from the tedious weeks of silence they suffered during the Johnston case. She was busy and happy and more radiant than ever.

There was always someone flirting with her. Sometimes it took all of his control to remain as his desk while it went on. Whenever he heard her laugh with someone over the telephone, he had the urge to pick up the extension and listen in. He wanted to know what made her laugh so he could be the one who made her respond. Whenever she talked with someone in the office, he wanted to jump up and run into the room. He wanted to be the witty and charming person who made her giggle and smile.

When he thought about it rationally, which was late at night in his hotel room, when he should be sleeping, he knew he was being foolish. He was a grown man. He had almost-grown children. He needed to confront her with his feelings. He had had no trouble a thousand times before. Damn. "Who are you and what have you done with Ian?" he said to himself. He had set the rules himself, long ago. He had made the advances except one time on his birthday. Why couldn't he bring himself to do it now?

After all, she did love him. She had made it clear more than once, she wanted to be with him. He wondered if her old fear of being hurt was looming around. Maggie didn't have the safety of Heather in the background to save her from ever having to make a commitment.

It didn't help he was feeling a little guilty himself. He was unable to stop thinking about the years he was satisfied with Heather before Maggie came along. All of it was standing between them now.

Night after night he tried to straighten it out in his mind until he tangled himself up so much he couldn't breathe without sitting up. He found he studied himself more closely in the mirror. Perhaps there was something he could change to make her want him more. Maybe he looked old from lack of sleep. He knew she was looking younger and more beautiful to him each day.

Several times he got himself worked up to the point that when they were alone together, he brooded the entire time. After the moment passed, he would spend the rest of the day kicking his own backside for his stupidity.

It was at those times he almost called Heather. But he knew he would have been calling for his own personal comfort and not because he wanted to be with her. For those reasons, he didn't call.

Damn. What a mess.

He felt like a boy with his first crush, trying to get up enough nerve to ask the girl of his dreams out on a date. What would he do if she turned him down? He was losing reason again, borrowing trouble. Why was he unable to face the facts? Nothing had changed except in his own mind. Things were the same as always. Oh, there was one difference. He felt like an asshole to point it out to himself. Before, he had Heather to fill the voids.

"Ian."

"What? I mean, what is it?" She had caught him off guard, in the middle of his thoughts. Now he was having trouble rediscovering reality.

"Ian, are you all right? You look pale. Can I get you something?"

"No. No, I'm fine. I was thinking about the real estate settlement we have in the morning. I keep thinking I'm forgetting something." he lied.

"Oh, it's all in order. You'll get used to it. I like it myself. I'd forgotten law could be so exciting." As Maggie talked, she moved around behind him and began massaging the back of his neck. It was the first time in a long time. He took in a quick breath.

"Law isn't the most exciting thing in this office," he ventured as he turned to face her.

"And I thought you were too busy to notice."

"Listen. Do you hear that?" He made a gesture to the outer office.

"I don't hear anything."

"That's what I mean. It's finally quiet in here. What do you say we get out of here and have dinner somewhere before someone realizes we're not busy?"

"Oh, Ian. I would love too. But I can't."

There it was. He was losing control again. He had a sudden urge to grab her and shake her until she saw only him. What if she had a date? He swallowed all of his anxieties and waited for her explanation. She didn't offer one.

Damn. Damn. Damn.

"Maggie." He stood up now, looking down at her. Taking both of her hands into his, he looked into her vivid green eyes. "I love you."

Gently she leaned into him and kissed him. "My dear Ian." He could feel each one of her words as her breath caressed his ear. He began to relax at last.

Anything about to develop out of the moment was lost when the telephone began to ring. Maggie glanced toward his desk. In only the short time they were standing now, three lines were flashing. She leaned on him as she reached over to answer one of the lines. As her body pushed against him, he ran his hands down her back to her waist. The call was for him. It turned out to be long and involved. Once more she kissed him. This time it was a light peck on the forehead as she left him to tend to his business.

When Ian finished his call and hung up, he heard the recorder click on. The same old feeling engulfed him. He loosened his tie and in his haste to open his collar, pulled off the button. He got up and walked to the waiting room to substantiate his belief. Sure enough. She was gone. Why couldn't he be reasonable about it? It was after seven pm. She had every reason and right to leave. Why did it get to him so?

He walked across the room and sat down at Maggie's desk. He was about to open one of the drawers when someone began pounding on the door. He went to open it.

"Office hours are over," he said, having opened the door only a crack. He couldn't even see who was talking on the other side. He only knew it was a male voice.

"I'm looking for Ian Michaels."

"Come back in the morning," Ian snapped.

"No. Wait. You don't understand. I'm a messenger from Brown and Hart."

Ian recognized the names immediately. It was Heather's brother's law firm back East.

"All right," Ian opened the door. "What is it?"

"I must give this to Mr. Michaels personally," he persisted.

"Damn it boy. I'm Ian Michaels." Extending his arm, he almost ripped the envelope out of the kid's hand.

The young man held on tight. "You will have to sign for it, sir." Ian threw the door open all the way and reached for the pen in the boy's pocket. The kid flinched as though he thought Ian was going to hit him. In one rapid movement, he signed his name, took the envelope and closed the door.

Now what?

Turning the envelope over in his hands, Ian went back to Maggie's desk again and sat down. A funny chill ran through him and he hesitated, opening the package. He knew what it was and he was shocked. He turned the large legal-sized overnight envelope in his hands. He looked at the front, the back and the front again. He felt he could read the papers inside by osmosis. He had served enough of them himself. He picked up the letter opener off the desk, only to put it down again. Instead, he turned the envelope on end and tapped it hard on the desk to move all of its contents to one end. He tore off about a half inch of the part closest to him, shook the contents out on the desk and let them fall into a pile before him.

Yep. It was what he thought. They were for him all right. Heather had gone to her brother and filed against him for divorce. For some reason he was shocked. Sometimes his own asinine attitude was even too much for him. Why didn't it dawn on him she would file for divorce? Because, he had to admit, he thought he was the one in charge here. He wasn't in charge with Maggie and now he realized, he wasn't in charge with Heather.

By the time he drove to St. Peters to the house he once called home, he was no longer

angry with anyone. He was timid and confused. He stuck his key into the front door lock, thought better of it and rang the doorbell. Heather answered. When she saw it was he she opened the door a crack, walked away from it and let him come in on his own.

"Do we need to talk?" he asked.

"About what?" So innocent.

"These." He held up the papers he carried in with him.

"How did you get those?"

"Heather. Don't play games. How do you think I got them? I was served this evening at the office."

"I'm sorry about that, truly sorry. I asked them not to serve you until after tomorrow."

"Why wait?"

"I didn't want to ruin your birthday."

Ian was at a loss for words. He plopped into the nearest chair. His birthday! Great.

All this bull and another year older. It also didn't answer his question.

"You still haven't answered my question."

"Why don't I ask you a question?" Her mood was deteriorating. "How's Maggie?"

"Let's leave her out of it."

"Can we really? Do you think I'm pleased with this affair you've been having?"

"No. Certainly not. But one day you tell me to

stay. The next day you say to go away so you can think and then three weeks later you sue for divorce. Don't you think a conversation might have been in order? Don't you think you are moving rather fast? This is a very final thing you've done."

"Can you sit there and tell me you are ready to come home and have things be the way they were, before Maggie? I think your visit here tonight is ego driven."

"No. I don't want to come home. And maybe you are right. I guess I thought we would talk before it got to this." Putting his chin into his hands, he stared at the carpet in front of him.

"I really see no reason to continue this discussion. My mind's made up. I know this is your house as much as it is mine. But I'm asking you to leave. Please." Her voice was cold and bitter. He knew it was his fault and he felt terrible about it. Not wanting to leave until things were better between them, he tried again to talk to her. "I did love you, Heather. For the sake of twenty years of marriage, and our three boys, let's try to have some sort of relationship." She need not hate him, he thought. Looking up at her, he smiled a half smile. She was still standing near the door she hadn't bothered to close.

"Maybe someday. for the sake of the boys and all the years we shared. But not now. Now I need to hate you or at least know you for the cheating bastard you are."

"I guess it's really over now."

"Ian, it has been over for a long time. I just didn't know it. I wandered around here in a daze." She

275

gave a nervous laugh. "I went to see Maggie. I tried to ignore the love for you I saw in her eyes. I told her how well I knew you. I insisted she stand by you until this Johnston thing is over. I told her you'd come to your senses. In other words, I made a total fool of myself. I realize now how silly I was. Truth is, I don't care if you ever come to your senses. I need to get back to my life and regain my self-respect. I can't do that married to you. She will always be between us. It is something I'll never be able to forgive and forget. When I think of the times you left her bed to come home to mine, I want to throw up."

". Most of what you and I had was good. Leave room for it."

"My god, Ian. Had it been good, there would've been no need for Maggie."

"Heather."

"Enough, Ian. Read the papers. They're fair. They're proof that all I want from you is out."

Well, it was over. He should have felt relieved. He didn't. The pain in her eyes was mirrored in his. He would give her everything she wanted. It was a tough situation for her. She would have to face family and friends. They were such an important part of her life. He wouldn't have to face those things. He had been around people only if he had to be. He always felt he was forced to do enough socializing in his work.

He felt like dirt.

"Heather," he said, more softly this time.

"Yes?" It was obvious she didn't want to talk anymore. She was crying now, having abandoned the shield of anger surrounding her when he first arrived.

"I'm sorry. Truly sorry."

"So am I." With those final words she walked away and left him standing alone.

He put his head in his hands and sat for several minutes. After some of the initial numbness of their mutual loss wore off, he got up and walked into his den. He loved the room. All of his things were gone. It was empty and gaunt. There was a picture of him and Heather standing together in happier times. He picked it up and took a closer look, setting it back where it was. He turned and walked out of the house, closing the door behind him.

Since it was his decision also, he was shocked at how rotten he felt. It was like walking away from the funeral of a dear friend.

He couldn't face going to his elegantly furnished yet impersonal hotel room. He drove to Maggie's. Outside of her apartment building sat her car. He parked and got out. He lost his nerve. She had said she couldn't see him tonight, and after his final break with Heather it was a horrible thing to do for the three of them. Also, if he found her with someone else it would have been more than he could bear.

Chapter Twenty-One

Maggie was frantic. It was noon and Ian was still not in the office. At ten she had called his hotel. The clerk assured her no one had picked up the key all night. She forced herself to wait another hour before she called Heather.

A court clerk called saying they wouldn't delay court for him any longer and his morning appointments were gone.

At two o'clock, she took a deep breath and dialed his home phone number. Rosemary answered and said she had not seen Mr. Ian in days, but he could indeed be there, somewhere. She would ask Mrs. Michaels.

Heather didn't hesitate to come to the phone. She spoke candidly about their meeting the night before. She didn't ask to be notified when Ian showed up. It was a colder and harder side of Heather she had never seen before. But it was also an emotional response she could relate to because of her own past experiences. She knew it was the only way someone as proud as Heather could cope with what was happening in her life.

Maggie called as many of the late afternoon appointments as she could reach and told them Ian was tied up in court. She rescheduled them juggling around people's personal lives, trying to please everyone. Because it was Friday, most people were willing to cancel and get an early start on their weekends. Soothing ruffled feathers, she smiled at those who made the trip to the office, pointing out what a warm and sunny day it was and maybe they should stroll through the park since they were this close. No one seemed to notice her hands were shaking and her voice quivered ever so slightly as she spoke.

Why had she told him she couldn't see him last night? She prayed nothing had happened to him because of a stupid sentimental birthday surprise she'd been planning.

The office was quiet, too quiet. She stayed until seven. She had already made up her mind not to report him missing until morning. Because of new privacy guidelines, she was getting no information from any emergency room or hospital. God bless the government.

As she was closing up and turning off the coffee and lights, the phone rang. It sliced the quiet like a knife. It was a wrong number. Tears were streaming down her face. She felt caged and helpless. Before she left she wrote several notes on post- its. One she stuck on her desk, one on his desk, one on the side door and another on the mirror in his bathroom.

Tension inside her was so great she was about to explode with emotion. It kept leaking down her cheeks.

Home was no better. She was afraid to use the phone for fear he was trying to call.

Bathing or showering she vetoed because she might not be able to hear if he came to the door or called. Resting was out of the question. She was much too nervous to relax.

Maggie divided her time between looking at her watch and peering out the security hole mumbling "God let him be all right," and checking to make sure her cell phone had a signal.

In the wee hours of the morning, she fell asleep on the couch. She was awakened by a noise outside her door. She rushed to the door, didn't think one second about her safety, and threw it open.

There he stood.

Well, he wasn't exactly standing. He was leaning on the door and when she opened it he nearly fell inside. She began to cry. This time it was tears of relief. He was hurt, but he was alive and standing in front of her. His clothes, what was left of them, were torn, dirty and wrinkled. His eyes were bloodshot and he was unshaven. He had no coat or shoes and appeared to be about to fall on his face.

"Ian," she whispered through her sobs. "Where've you been? I've been frantic."

"It's a long story. Are you alone?"

"Of course I'm alone. It's," she glanced over to the clock on the wall, "three thirty in the morning. Come in."

He again stumbled. This time he landed half on

and half off the couch. She steadied him until he was sitting somewhat upright. "What happened to you? Did you have an accident?"

"Heather is divorcing me."

"I know."

"You do?"

"Yes, I spoke to her this afternoon. But it's not important now. Where on earth have you been? You look hurt."

"After my visit with Heather, I felt lost. I couldn't stand the thought of going back to the hotel. I drove around until I was so sleepy I had to pull over." He shook his head and a nervous unfunny laugh escaped him before he continued. "I pulled over to rest, but I must've fallen asleep. The next thing I knew there was a fist in my face. I was dragged out of the car. I was beaten and kicked and robbed. Appears I picked the wrong place to take a nap. I don't know how many.

I think three, but it felt like twelve. There wasn't a thing I could do. Big brave me rolled up into a ball and laid there trying not to die while they tore up the car and took everything I had on me. Oh, yes, then they took the car." He stopped. She could tell he was in pain. Talking was wearing him out. Reliving it wasn't helping him much either. "It was hours before I could get anywhere to call the police. My cell phone was smashed by someone's boots and pay phones are a thing of the past. Then there were police, reports, doctors, stitches and all of that. Finally, the policeman who stayed with me asked if he could call someone or drop me somewhere. I asked him to bring me here."

"Why didn't you come here after your visit with Heather last night?"

He felt consumed with self-pity as it was, so he didn't tell her. He went on as if she hadn't asked. "You'll be glad to know the doctor at Barnes said I'll live. I might pee some blood for a few days and I need to take these antibiotics because of the scratches and the people they came from. The stitches will dissolve on their own." He touched a sewn gash above his eye. "The only thing broken is my pride. Of course, I might die of exhaustion. I feel like they used a bat instead of feet and fists."

"Why don't you go to bed?"

"I thought you'd never ask." He managed a smile.

They went into the bedroom. He sat on the edge of the bed while she tried to help him take off what was left of his clothes, the slightest movement made him wince with pain. His chest was battered and had an eerie maroon color from the massive trauma it suffered. His knees were cut, his calves bruised and battered. It was a wonder he could move at all. Within minutes of lying back on the bed, she heard his even breathing. He was asleep.

Maggie sat, as if on guard, for about an hour before she felt comfortable enough to lie down next to him without waking him.

It felt so natural to have him asleep beside her. It was the first time they had been in bed together without making love.

Thank goodness there were no office hours on Saturday. She hoped he would sleep the day away. She knew now how much she loved him. When she

283

saw how Heather's decision was affecting him, she wasn't jealous. All she felt was his pain, pain for his loss and suffering after losing something meaning so much to him for so many years.

They slept the morning away. When he woke he turned toward her and stroked her back. She turned and cuddled into the cradle of his arm. There was no need for words. They were content and fell back to sleep. The second time they woke up, Ian headed for the shower. He hoped hot water would soothe his battered body.

Maggie went into the kitchen in search of something to cook. Neither of them had eaten the day before. Maggie was setting Spanish omelets on the table next to freshly brewed coffee when Ian came into the room. He didn't look much better after his shower. He was still unshaven and had put on the same clothes. He stood barefoot in the doorway, wiggling his toes for effect. It was impossible for him to sit up straight because of the pain. He looked down at himself and tried to laugh. "I guess I'm quite a sight."

"You look fine," she lied.

They sat down to eat. Both of them were much too hungry to talk. They ate and were on their second cups of coffee before any real conversation took place.

Ian felt content and relaxed for the first time in weeks. He hated to change one thing, but he knew he must. He needed to go back to his hotel and change clothes, and he thought shoes were important. Maggie had given him a pair of hot pink flip flops. They were much too small. But they would have to do for now. Also, while standing in Maggie's shower letting the hot water soothe his beaten body, he had decided he wanted a place of his own. Right now he felt he needed something permanent in his life. The coldness of coming home to a hotel room, no matter how nice, made him feel unstable. It was no longer the life for him.

It was decided they would meet back at her apartment in two hours. It would give him time to shave, change his clothes and talk to one of his clients who was a real estate agent. It would give Maggie time to take a much-needed shower and buy some groceries.

"This is a really good plan." He touched the tip of her nose playfully with his finger. "I only see one problem with it."

"What's that?"

"I don't have a car. Well, I do but it is difficult to tell where it might be at this moment. It may be a dozen cars by now or it might be bright purple. I assure you most of the finer options it had would be gone."

"Take mine," Maggie said, reaching for her keys from the table near the front door.

"Do you mind? How will you run your errands?"

"It wasn't earth shattering. Worst case scenario, we have take-out."

"Oh, my. I ate so much, I think food isn't going to be an issue for a long while.

Thanks, you're a doll." He kissed her on the forehead and was gone.

Maggie had no trouble busying herself for a few hours. She spent the time cleaning the apartment and herself. The night before she hadn't bothered to remove her makeup and she felt grungy. She showered and washed her hair. Brushing it out, she let it fall straight down toward her waist. Slipping on her favorite pair of faded jeans, and a soft violet v- neck tee shirt, she went in to tackle the mess she had left in the kitchen. She was about to sit down on the couch when he rang the buzzer. He too had on comfy jeans and a tee shirt. He looked happier and more relaxed but she was worried about him. He was still doubled over with pain.

Chapter Twenty-Two

There were three apartments the agent was going to show them. Maggie tried to talk Ian out of going because he was so stiff and sore. He insisted it would make him feel better. The agent drove, giving Ian a chance to lie back a little. They walked through the first apartment but Ian showed little interest. There were small children in the apartment above the one they were looking through. The banging and thudding would drive him crazy. They didn't go into the second one because Ian didn't like the looks of the building. The agent didn't bother with the third saying he had a house and it was "just the ticket." "Just what they were looking for." Neither one of them bothered to correct the man's misjudgment of the situation. Ian insisted he neither wanted nor needed a house. He was only interested, he emphasized, in a place to call his own.

Maggie laughed, when she saw him look at the tiny two story buff brick building with the huge chimney and ginger bread trim: this was it. It was also only two blocks from the Central West End business district. He could walk there anytime and even walk down to the office if he was feeling frisky.

Ian was hooked when he stepped into the front hallway. On the first floor there was a large living room. It had a bay window overlooking what would have been a busy sidewalk were it not for some magnificent landscaping outside the front window making it look like it opened to a bird sanctuary. There was a smaller room straight back from the living room. It had windows on two sides. One entire wall was a stone fireplace and the kitchen on the fourth. There was a tiny half bath, as an afterthought. Ian figured it was the pantry at one time. It was well decorated and served its purpose. Off the kitchen was a staircase winding up to the second floor. The stairs were wide for the age of the house. At the top of the stairs was one huge room. It had windows all the way around it except for the wall where there was a closet and the bathroom. Ian smiled when he opened the door to the closet and it too had a window as did the bathroom. It was, he thought, the biggest bathroom he had ever been in. They looked out all of the windows to orientate themselves to where they were and what they could see from the second floor. They were like little kids on an observation platform. When they had had their fill of looking out, they walked back downstairs.

Maggie pointed out a shelf about two feet down from the ceiling in the kitchen. It ran all the way around the room. When they stepped out the back door, it was into a small courtyard with a privacy fence surrounding it and a small hot tub tucked under a wooden canopy on the far side of the space. It was wonderful. From the dark stained hardwood floors to the cheery yellow kitchen, it was the greatest place they had ever seen.

Ian had two questions. Could he buy it and when could he move in? Yes and any time.

It was part of an estate and wasn't on the market as yet but the family didn't want it to sit empty.

Ian wrote a check for a deposit and took the key from the agent's outstretched hand.

He felt as if he had purchased a dream. In college he had lived in the dorm and then slept in his office. Next he had a house with Heather and now he had His house. He couldn't have been happier. He smiled so big his face hurt.

"Let's go shopping." he said. "I know exactly what I want."

Maggie giggled at his eagerness but she said, "Why don't we wait until tomorrow? You'll have had a good night's sleep. Maybe you won't grimace when you walk."

"I feel great," he said, swinging her around by both hands.

They practically had to put he out of the last store at closing time. Maggie quit keeping track of the money he'd spent after the third store. He bought a brass bed with cannon ball posts, a dresser, a chest of drawers, a valet chair and a love seat for the upstairs bedroom.

He picked out towels, sheets, blankets and for the kitchen he got dishes, pots, pans, a toaster, coffee pot, silverware, glasses, mugs and a popcorn popper.

The small downstairs room was going to be a den. He bought a small oak desk and a cushy chair and a television. For the living room he selected a couch, love seat and two chairs, all with wooden arms contrasting with the floors. Oh, yes, and an oval braided rug in bright colors for the living room. He also bought several smaller throw rugs for the rest of the house. They put those in the car and took them home with them.

Maggie was surprised by Ian's sense of color, style and design. He didn't ask her for any help. Once in a while he would say this is perfect, isn't it? She didn't know how he did it, but he managed to pick out everything himself, yet make her feel a part of the entire process.

They drove back to the house and dropped off the rugs and several smaller items they had carried. Ian didn't want to leave. He walked the three short blocks to Culpepper's and returned with soup and burgers. They ate in front of a small fire he built from the wood pile stacked in the far corner of the back yard. They made love on one of the new rugs where they fell asleep. They woke up tired, stiff and happy on Sunday morning.

By the next weekend, everything had been delivered and was in its proper place. The real estate agent called with the price the estate wanted for the house and Ian said yes. He felt he had found his dream home. He couldn't believe it was less than fifteen hundred square feet.

Ian and Maggie were still together and had been since he showed up beaten and battered on her door step. From the office they went to the house and from the house they went to the office. Maggie had gone to her apartment during the day to get clothes and necessary items. Ian had talked to his insurance agent and was going to pick out a new car on the weekend. Meanwhile he had a rental.

It was the most glorious week of Maggie's life she told him, for the first time since David.

Ian's week wasn't as good. Once he made arrangements with Heather to go and get more of his belongings. It was a less than cordial meeting. Another time Timothy came to the office to have his say. He felt he was now man of the house and wanted his father to know how he felt about all he perceived had happened to the family. Although Ian never discussed either incident with Maggie, the pain was apparent in his eyes.

Nearly a month past before Maggie gave the surprise she'd bought Ian on the night he had been assaulted. One night after dinner while they were sitting in front of the fireplace listening to music, she finally presented him with another tie tack. It was supposed to be for his birthday and in remembrance of the first one she gave him. He told her of all of his insecurities during those weeks. Smiling he told her how much he truly loved her and needed her. "Move in with me." he insisted.

"I hardly go home now."

"I know, but let's make it official. My divorce is final. Let's begin a new life. Together."

Maggie turned away from him. She folded her arms across her chest as if she were chilled. "Things have been going so well. Don't complicate it. Let things stay as they are."

Putting both hands on her shoulders he turned her around to face him. "Maggie," He whispered. "I'm not David. I love you. I want you. I need you. We're good together. I want to marry you."

The look of fear and confusion flashing in her emerald eyes made them appear black. It was real. When he held her in his arms, she quivered.

It was tense between them for several weeks. She began spending more time at her apartment without him. He decided to step back for a while, to give her some space. He made it a point to reassure her at every turn.

The next time he asked her to marry him, he didn't intend for her to say no.

Chapter Twenty-Three

Days turned into weeks which turned into months. Ian and Heather were on speaking terms. The boys were thriving. Timothy visited alone and sometimes hung out at the little Central West End house. The other two boys were there every other weekend. Maggie didn't have much of a presence when they were around, thinking it was family time with their father. When she did agree to visit while the boys were there, it was relaxed and the laughter flowed. Ian told her he felt like an advertisement for peace, happiness and success.

Maggie had made it a point to spend more time at her own place. She didn't want a permanent commitment with Ian this soon, maybe never. She was in love with him, yet needed more time to be sure he was who she thought he was. There was never a time in her life she had been so happy.

Almost one year to the day the whole Kenny Johnston mess began, the phone rang.

It was Judge Massey's clerk wanting to meet with Tom Waters and Ian about bringing Kenny to justice. The tests were completed. A team of physicians and physiologists and psychiatrists had finished all of the examinations on the boy. They had been read, studied and compiled. The results were recorded and it was time to decide what to do with him. The judge was being considerate to the prosecutor and the defense. He could have called with a date and come hell or high water, every one needed to be there. Instead, he wanted a twenty minute meeting the next week in his chambers early enough so as not to ruin anyone's schedule for the day.

The meeting was short and sweet. Massey was giving them one month to look over the findings, and bring any and all arguments to court on the twelfth of April. He then handed Tom and

Ian a bound packet about the size of War and Peace, said "Happy reading, see you in court." and left his chamber.

Ian and Tom were left sitting alone together facing the judge's desk. Tom gave him a nod. "That was quick."

"Yes, very," Ian agreed.

"Well, I don't really know what to say. If this says our killer is insane, it will be a quick trial. If he isn't, then this could take a while."

"He didn't give us much time to prepare witnesses or put a case together."

"Maybe there's is no need," Tom said, flipping through the huge findings.

"Well, we'll know soon enough." Ian was still perplexed.

"Hold on to your hat, Ian," Tom said. "The

tornadoes will start to blow as soon as this becomes public. The findings here are going to be worth a fortune to some reporter very soon. I'll be glad when it's over."

"So will I. Well, guess I have some reading to do. I don't quite know what to make of this. I thought he would say either, we're going to trial or he needs to be committed."

"Maybe he'll still say it. Could he just want us to read it because of all of the work, money and time?"

"I don't know. Have you ever had anything like this happen?"

"No. Actually, insanity defense is rare, except on TV, that is. In thirty-one years as a prosecutor, this is my first one."

Ian chuckled out loud. "Well, in my twenty plus years as an attorney, this was my first criminal case. Guess we're in this together."

Ian went to the last chapter of the thick packet and read to himself. He made a clicking sound at what he read. After seeing Ian's reaction, Tom also flipped to the back and began reading. "This is bizarre," Tom said

As if on cue, both men stood up.

"Well, I now know what I'm going to do," Ian remarked.

"Me too." Tom acknowledged in much the same tone. "Guess I'll see you in court."

"Guess so."

The two men shook hands and walked out of the building together. They were still side by side through the parking lot and as they got into their cars, which were parked beside one another. They didn't speak again or look at one another, or say goodbye.

Chapter Twenty-Four

It didn't take long for the Johnston case to be on everyone's lips again. When Ian got back to the office, he and Maggie took care of the rest of the morning clients, then instead of going out for lunch, they locked the office doors and began pouring over the reports. The way they did it was probably unorthodox. Ian took each section of the summary, which in itself was a small novel. He would read a section out loud to Maggie. Any part of the summary they didn't understand, they looked up under the section number and read how the examiner came to such a conclusion. They worked on the report all during lunch for an entire week before they felt they understood and were familiar with what the doctors had agreed to so far as Kenny was concerned. It was numbing, frightening, enlightening, and scary.

Each day brought more publicity. The murders were recapped in the newspapers in all of their gory detail. Pictures of each victim appeared with a biography of his or her life and a listing of parents, siblings, and what had changed in the world in the past year and on and on.

Ian's divorce was highlighted. Heather took the boys back east for spring break to escape the constant harassment and questions. Maggie went to her own apartment most every night lest someone followed her, then her life with Ian would become front page news. Ian left his car parked at the office most nights and took a cab within a few blocks of his house. He walked the rest of the way, making stops for dinner, trying to stay out of the limelight and keep his new address a secret.

The month dragged on.

Ian went to see Kenny once. It was a mind-altering experience.

The Johnston family also didn't escape publicity this go around. There was a lengthy interview with Shauna in the paper and another on the local television news. She had her own spin on all of it in what she called 'reflection.' Ian had to turn it off.

The next day, he wished he had watched the entire thing. All hell had broken loose after the interview. The response of the community was overwhelming. Every night there were letters to the editor and to reader's forums. Social media massacred her with candid remarks as to Shauna's fitness to raise children. There were cartoons and sayings and song lyrics. She was severely chastised everywhere for her behavior and attitudes. Ian thought in another era she would have been tarred and feathered.

Bob Johnston was forced to quit his job. He got pushed around every time he left his house. Most of it was because of what Shawna blurted out in her fifteen minutes of fame. All the same, people judged him for standing by and letting it happen. A few days later a story appeared saying the Johnston's had moved from their home, in the middle of the night. No one knew where they were and everyone was glad they were gone. Ian knew someone would move heaven and earth to be the first person to find them. He also knew they were summoned to be in court.

Someone had tracked down Sarah Berle. A story about her suicide was front and center one morning. At least it wasn't on television and Ian hoped none of the details made the Oklahoma City news. The problem was always the same. We live in a small world and people travel.

Running the office without constant comments from their clients on the 'big event' coming up, was difficult. Ian was horrible at it. Maggie, as always, had a knack for pointing out the importance of clients keeping their minds on their own legal problems without managing to alienate anyone.

Daily Ian found himself sinking into the same old funk he was in the first time and wanted it over. He tried to keep foremost in his mind his first duty was to make sure Kenny got the best possible defense. He did what he could to prepare himself and become familiar with the material he had. He tried his best not to dwell on the murder victims. Actually, he tried not to think about it at all. It was a tall order. The closer they got to trial, the more fervor there was. It was overwhelming.

Ian made no public statements. He learned little from everything he read, and he read it all. He was sure; however, every day would bring a new story, a new interview, or a new theory. He blessed the families each morning. He wasn't a religious man, but if it was affecting him as negatively as it was, he could not imagine the horror the people grieving the victims had to feel.

***

The night before the hearing was a long one. Ian tossed and turned lying first on his left side and then on his right. Maggie was there. She had come late in the evening under the cover of darkness. Now she lay beside him, breathing slowly and evenly. He lay on his side facing her for a long time. Propping himself up on one elbow, he fought the urge to touch her. Beads of perspiration stood out on her forehead and neck. It was too cool outside for air conditioning and too warm for heat. The windows were open yet no breeze relieved the stagnant air. It only made the situation more unbearable.

Reaching for her, Ian was going to wipe the sweat from her brow. He thought better of it. He knew the only reason was so she would wake up. Letting a big sigh escape him as he turned over, he tried again to sleep.

The office was closed for the day and court began promptly at nine. Long before the alarm went off, Ian was up and showered. He dressed with extra care and still had time to fry some eggs, hash browns and make toast and coffee before Maggie ambled into the kitchen.

They ate a tense breakfast. Ian got all of the

papers he thought he would need for the day while Maggie showered and dressed.

When she came back down the stairs, she was dressed in white. She had an angel-like glow and Ian couldn't keep his hands off her. Funny, he thought. Something distracted him as they were about to walk out the door. They drove Maggie's car past the office and Ian got out and drove his own car. He did so in case he got caught up at the courthouse, she wouldn't have to sit and twiddle her thumbs. He felt cold and alone as he got out and walked around to the driver's side to give her a kiss before they went the same way, separately. Again he was struck by how beautiful she looked in her white linen suit, with blue piping around the lapels and outlining the pockets. She wore simple blue earrings in the shape of butterflies, and blue high heels. Her hair was in a bun on the back of her head secured by a big blue barrette. It was a picture he would always hold in his mind. A chill ran down his back. He was more uneasy than he had ever been. He stood so long looking at her, she finally said "Ian, if we don't go, we'll be late. It would be a terrible way to start the day."

Ian didn't say anything to her. He put the tips of his fingers to his lips and then to hers. In spite of his nervousness, he gave her his best smile and got into his car.

Maggie followed him to the government center.

Usually, a defendant is allowed a few minutes with his attorney before trial starts. It wasn't the case this morning. Ian was told to take his place out front and Kenny would be brought in the side door as he was in the preliminary hearing. True to their word, about five minutes before the proceeding was to begin, the door opened and two guards escorted Kenny through the door.

Kenny was dressed in a pair of new brown khaki slacks, a plaid shirt, and shined or new shoes. His red hair was cropped close to his head. The curls were gone. Instead of making him look older, the haircut did the opposite. It made him look smaller and younger than his now-seventeen years.

The courtroom was dead silent. Ian looked around. It was full. Every seat was taken. There were chairs added in front of the back wall. Guards were at every entrance. There was no jury, of course. Every eye in the place was on Kenny. He looked young, rested, happy and unaware of the situation he was in. It was enough to bring a single tear to Ian's eye. Could this have all been avoided had Kenny had some help a few years ago? He shook his head and tried not to think about it. It was too late now. People were dead, lives were ruined, and Kenny was sitting before his accusers to answer for the crimes.

Kenny stuck his handcuffed hands up to Ian to shake his hand. Ian, not knowing what else to do, shook his hand. The guard then put a loose chain around Kenny's leg and through the table leg. He left him enough room to get up and down, but little else.

In the couple of minutes before the judge made an entrance, Ian tried to explain to Kenny when he would need to stand. Otherwise, he counseled him to sit quietly no matter what happened or what was said about him. Kenny only grinned. All of his attention was focused on Maggie. She had never met him. She furnished him with a piece of paper and a pencil, much like trying to keep a small child busy in church or at any adult function. Again, Kenny smiled up at her, docile and happy. He gave no indication he had any idea why he was there. If he did know, he didn't appear to care.

Kenny immediately began chatting with Maggie about the Garden at the hospital and how he had learned to grow things. He excitedly, yet in a low whisper, explained germination to her. He talked about his room, his roommate, the food, and how much he wanted to go back after his 'outing'.

Ian sat mesmerized by the conversation to his left. Kenny sat between him and Maggie. He listened to Kenny's speech patterns and thought it was the conversation of a boy much younger than Kenny. Maggie had nothing to compare him to but words on paper. She found him both personable and delightful.

How many Kennys was this he had met over the past year? Shaking his head, Ian gave his attention to the door as everyone stood. Judge Massey entered through his chamber and took his seat behind the bench.

There was an undue amount of murmuring and chatter among the gallery visitors. Massey struck his gavel hard on the desk, three times, the courtroom became quiet. The judge then gave a little spiel as to how, if there were any interruptions, comments, or unnecessary outbursts, he would clear the courtroom and close the trial to the public. He didn't mince words. Complete silence followed.

Everyone was seated except for Ian, Maggie, and Kenny standing behind the defense table, and Tom, his assistant Danny Davis, and Sherry McCormick, a paralegal standing at the prosecution table.

Judge Massey read all of the charges against Kenny. It was a long and painful ordeal. At the end of his dissertation, he asked how Kenny pleaded. Kenny didn't say a word or even act like he knew where he was. Ian leaned over and whispered into his ear, and in a few seconds, Kenny looked up at the judge, then panned the courtroom with his youthful sparkling eyes. He looked back toward the front of the room and said "Not guilty," in a booming theatrical stage voice.

Judge Massey signaled for everyone to be seated. He hesitated before he began. It was as though he wanted to say more or do more than he was about to but didn't know how to go about it. His voice was grave. "As you are all aware, because of the nature of the crimes and the actions of the defendant in the months and even years before his alleged attacks and murders with which he is charged, the court felt it necessary to delve into his mental state and capacity. Mr. Johnston was examined for several months by a highly regarded group of the best doctors in both the medical and mental arena. The findings were compiled and reviewed by the examining physicians as well as sent to some of the leading minds in the country.

"Last month, the findings were given to both the prosecution and the defense. They had one month to discuss and question any findings in the report.

Everyone involved in this endeavor has come to the same conclusion.

"Kenneth Ray Johnston has been ruled criminally insane. It has been deemed, he isn't now or will he ever be able to understand what he did. It is the opinion of this court, the defendant is guilty of all the charges against him. He has admitted, in the course of the last year of his confinement, to the horrendous deeds for which he is charged." There was dissent in the courtroom. Voices were beginning to rise and chaos was erupting. Judge Massey stopped and surveyed the crowd before him. He banged his gavel on the bench several times. The look on his face reflected his sympathy for the observers. He could not imagine sitting there knowing your loved one was taken from you by some kid. Your life ruined for eternity by some random act, and now the kid seemingly wouldn't have to pay for it.

The job he had to do as keeper of the order of the court ruled over his outward emotion. He hit the gavel on the wood three more times in a no-nonsense way. The courtroom was again silent. The judge sat quietly. He put his hand up and took off his glasses. He took a tissue from somewhere on the desk and wiped them. He put them back on his face. He began again.

"Any more outbursts and I will clear this courtroom. Believe me. I have the utmost sympathy for all of the families and loved ones of those touched by the terrible deeds perpetrated here. I'm sure each and every one of you has an idea of what you would like to see done here. Let us get on with the ruling."

Everyone again settled down. It was different this time. The tension and apprehension hung like a dense fog over the courtroom. Although no one was talking or moving, it was easy to feel the mood in the courtroom and it wasn't pleasant.

"Will the defendant please stand." Ian and Kenny and Maggie stood up in unison.

"Please approach the bench." Ian had to wait until the guard standing to the right of Kenny came over and unlocked the chain around the table leg. Kenny got up, with Ian guiding him as to what he was supposed to do. "Kenneth Ray Johnston. It is the finding of the Criminal Court of the County of St. Charles in the State of Missouri that you are guilty of all of the charges leveled against you. It is further the finding of this court the defendant has diminished mental clarity to the point he cannot be tried in a court of law for those charges.

"Kenneth Ray Johnston. You are hereby reprimanded to a maximum security mental facility for the rest of your natural life with no possibility for parole. Court is adjourned."

It was unnervingly quiet in the room.

The Judge gathered papers together, but didn't look up.

Tom and his crew sat and spoke in muted tones among themselves. Kenny and Ian walked back to the defense table and sat down. Maggie looked at Ian, an unreadable look on his face.

Then it happened.

A giant of a man stood up and yelled, "This is bullshit! There was no justice here today!"

Guards from every point in the room came rushing toward him. Kenny turned around to watch the commotion as did everyone else in the room. Even the people who were exiting, talking among themselves, stopped to look at the man. Reporters and news people who had bounded from the room to file their stories, stopped.

Kenny's body lifted from the chair. It was a delayed noise that followed. The chair seemed to explode under him. Like a rag doll he was thrown upward out of the chair. One leg landed on the judge's bench and as Massey rolled his chair out of the way of it, the judge fell and hit his head hard on the step behind him, rendering him unconscious.

Ian instinctively moved away from the body. There was a burning in his left arm. He reached to touch it fearing it was no longer attached. It was. He felt blood running down his face from where a piece of the chair Kenny was sitting in had splintered from the blast and hit him just above his left ear. He had no pain. He felt he was watching everything in slow motion.

People were dropping to the floor. Nothing else happened. Only one blast blowing Kenny into a dozen pieces. It destroyed the defense table and injured Ian, and several others he could see. He could not, however, see Maggie. There were people everywhere. After some time passed and it was apparent nothing else was about to happen, Ian tried to stand.

It was then he saw her. His beloved Maggie was lying face down about ten feet from where she was sitting before the blast. She was in an unnatural pose. Ian stood up to go to her. He fell from the pain in his arm and head. The last thing he remembered in the courtroom was wanting to help Maggie and not being able to move. He passed out.

There was a large piece of the table protruding from Maggie's right leg. She had been there, sitting at the table, and then she wasn't. Her white suit was crimson with her own blood. Tom Waters stood over her. He was trying to comfort her and was telling her help was on the way.

Then she closed her eyes and gave in to her fatigue.

Chapter Twenty-Five

Ian opened his eyes. He heard a steady beeping noise. The room was dark and barren. He tried to think about where he was and why he was there. He turned his head. It was a hospital. He was hooked to IV's and a heart monitor. Trying to sit up, he grabbed his arm which burned and hurt through his fog. Someone was trying to speak to him. "Ian. Good to have you back, old friend." It was Jim Martin. Jim was trying to smile and be friendly and light. It wasn't working. There was pain in his eyes.

"What happened?" Ian ventured.

"Well, I wasn't there, but I sure heard a hundred variations so I will put some of them together for you and try to explain. First, my friend. How do you feel?"

"I'm not sure. My arm burns. What happened to it? Also I feel like I was hit with a Mack truck in the back of the head."

"Well, I will give you the condensed version and we can fill in details later. Seems Jacob Payne,

Andrea Payne's father, was prepared for what he considered an unjust verdict. He planted a small plastic explosive under Kenny's seat. I guess he wasn't going to detonate it except if there was what he called an 'unacceptable outcome.'"

"How's Maggie?" Ian asked. "I remember trying to go to her, but I passed out."

"She's still in intensive care.

"Oh, my god. Jim. Take me there," Ian pleaded and tried to get out of bed. Almost passing out, he was forced to lie back down.

"Hold on there, partner," Jim said holding on to his friend and forcing him to lay back against the pillow.

"You aren't ready to get up, and Maggie's in good hands."

"Will she be okay?" Ian was beside himself with pain and worry.

"She's still listed as critical, as is Judge Massey with a head injury and Tom's paralegal with her right arm severed by a piece of metal from a chair leg. There were a lot of body parts that day.

But it could have been a lot worse. The guy had six charges set but when he saw Kenny flying piece by piece around the room, he didn't set anymore off."

"How on earth did he manage to get them in there in the first place?" Ian's voice was weak. The monitor showed his heart was pounding from the news about Maggie and the automatic blood pressure monitor measured high enough to set off an alarm and send two nurses running into the room.

"Well," smiled the first nurse. "Doris," she said to the lady behind her. "Look who decided to wake up!" They both seemed pleased.

Ian only stared at them and asked over their heads to Jim. "How long have I been lying here?"

"Three days."

"Three days? How can that be? Am I hurt that badly?" This time he directed his questions to the nurses who were hovering around him, checking IV's and adjusting and resetting the alarms on the monitors.

"Well, Mr. Michaels, Dr. Creighton will be in here shortly to discuss things with you.

I can tell you, with what we heard and saw, it's a wonder there were not more deaths and serious injuries that day. You're one lucky fellow, considering how close you were to the bomb."

As if on cue, a young, strong-jawed and tired - looking doctor came through the door.

"Well, Mr. Michaels, good to see you awake. I'm Eric Creighton, your doctor and surgeon."

"Good to be awake, I think," Ian said. "Listen, Doctor. I hear my secretary is critically injured and still in intensive care. I must see her. "

"Maybe tomorrow." he answered.

"I must see her now," Ian insisted. "I must."

"Let's check you over," the young man insisted, totally ignoring Ian's last request.

Glancing up at Jim, Ian gave him a mournful look and nodded. Jim understood and walked out of the room heading to ICU to check on Maggie and come back with a report.

After the doctor left, Ian felt enlightened. He

found out Jacob Payne was a young veteran. In the military he was a demolitions expert. After his only daughter, Andrea, was murdered and raped by Kenny, his life fell apart. He was allowed to come home from Iraq. By the time he arrived, his wife Kim, of nine years was on the verge of a mental breakdown. He was allowed to stay home and stay with her. Even though he didn't leave her side, she regressed into someone he no longer knew. Young Jacob became obsessed with his hatred of Kenny. He followed every word written about him. He would sit for hours in his car in the parking lot of St Joseph's hoping for a glance of Kenny as he went with others and armed guards outside for recreation. He watched with binoculars through the windows of the psych ward hoping to catch Kenny as he ate. He told authorities it seemed as though Kenny had a great life. Three square meals a day, a nice room, no responsibilities. Andrea, on the other hand, was lying in a cold dark grave. She would never have another dance lesson. Her laughter would never be heard again in the sad house he shared with his ever-dwindling wife.

One day while watching Kenny, he got an idea. He was dying himself sitting daily sipping coffee and being afraid to leave his wife more than a few minutes because she could not function without him. He decided to take a part-time job at the courthouse as a janitor. Not one associated his name with one of the victims of the young mass murderer Kenny Johnston. It had been seven months and not a word had been printed about Kenny. Jacob didn't answer a lot of the questions on the application for employment, the ones asking if you were part of a trial or a judgment or were engaged in any legal proceedings. He answered NO. And he felt he wasn't. All he did was wake up every day and grieve with his failing wife and wait some more.

When the papers began to print the stories about Andrea and the others, he came up with a plan. If Kenny was convicted of murder and sentenced to death, he would do nothing. Anything short of the verdict he wanted and thought fair, he was going to have justice for him and his wife and everyone else whose life was ruined because of the little bastard. First, he found out in what room the hearing would take place. Then he familiarized himself with the seating of the attorneys and their defendant. Next, he made sure he was on the cleaning crew who serviced the courtroom daily. The night before, he made sure again he knew where everyone would sit. It was pretty easy because the court clerk had come in at the end of the day and put materials about the case on the tables before the room was locked for the night. Jacob planted six charges. One was directly under the chair where Kenny sat. One was under Maggie's chair, one under Ian's. He was taking no chances he wouldn't get his target. For good measure he put one under the lip of the bench in case Kenny was standing there when the verdict was read. There was a huge bomb under the window sill of the window nearest the defense table. And the sixth bomb was in Jacobs's pocket. Thank god he only exploded one of them.

The damage he had done with one explosive was horrific.

Judge Massey might not make it. He was eighty-one and when the chair rolled off the back of the platform it sat on, his head hit the floor in an odd manner causing a lump on the back of his head and brain swelling. They had drilled holes in his head to relieve the pressure. All hope wasn't lost.

Sherry McCormick, the paralegal, was holding her own. They reattached her arm and with therapy she would be fine, though she wouldn't, ever have full use of her arm. She did, however, have an arm.

Tom Waters and nineteen other people were treated and released from the hospital the same day for cuts, lacerations requiring stitches, shrapnel removed from hands, arms and legs and on and on. They were a lucky bunch, the doctor related. The plastic explosive used was situated to do damage only to Kenny. It hit its mark. There wasn't much of Kenny left whole. It was a sad ending to an even sadder reign of terror.

Dr. Creighton told him about his own injuries. He had a severe concussion and it had taken over one hundred stitches to close the wound above his ear. His arm was cut and cut deeply into the muscle. It would take a long while to heal. The doctor said it was a use-it-or-lose-it sort of injury. He would have to do the exercises and therapy. Because of the muscle injury, it was a serious deal.

Creighton told him he slept so long because of the sort of trauma suffered. Anytime the body is hit as hard as they were all hit with the parts of the tables and chairs flying around, it does serious damage. The damage cannot always be seen, but it is there and the body shuts itself down to a sleeping and protective mode to try to give its parts time to heal.

Dr. Creighton seemed ready to talk about Maggie. Finally. "The only reason I'm able to tell you about her is because everyone agrees you are her next of kin, even your ex-wife and your buddy Jim, who has been sitting vigil since you got out of surgery.

"Your friend, Miss Dane, lost a lot of blood. A piece of metal from the leg of the chair Kenny was sitting in, hit her in the leg, severing an artery. There's really no good reason why she's still unconscious. We've run cat scans, MRI's and blood work. As of yesterday, the graft of her artery is considered a success. Her blood volume is normal. There's no reason, we can ascertain, why she has not regained consciousness. We've done all we can do. We're now playing a waiting game. We're keeping her well-nourished, well hydrated, and warm and what we think is comfortable. It's up to her now if she wants to fight the horrible trauma and pain or if she gives up.

Ian felt he was going to pass out. He needed to get to her. NOW.

He was sure he could make a difference in her outcome. He said nothing to the doctor about his feelings. Not going to Maggie's bedside wasn't an option. He wouldn't be told no, so he didn't ask.

Dr. Creighton left and Ian lay back on his pillow waiting for Jim to return. Crocodile tears streamed from his eyes.

Losing track of time, Ian fell in and out of a fitful sleep waiting for Jim to come back from ICU.

He must have slipped in because one of the times Ian opened his eyes, Jim was sitting in a chair watching him.

"What did you find out?" Ian asked in a hoarse whisper.

"Not much. You're the only one listed on the visitor list. That doctor came up while I was there and added you. With all the new rules, I don't know a thing. I didn't even get past the nurses' station so I could get a peek at her."

The room was dark. It smelled of medicine and stale air. Ian wanted to open the blinds and get some light in the room. It was a difficult job, but he managed it. When he did, he saw Maggie. Her hair was twirled up around her head. Someone had tried to brush it and get it out of the way. It was dirty and matted. She lay on her back with numerous tubes and monitors. There were no flowers or cards, no music or sounds of any kind. It was more than Ian could bear.

She looked thin and frail. Her mouth was open slightly. Her breath was even and quiet.

He had to suppress the urge to get up, if he could, and shake her awake. Instead he wheeled himself over as close to the bed as he could and picked up her hand. It was cool and damp. He rubbed it between his palms trying to rub some feeling into it; perhaps she would feel him in the room.

When he could stand it no longer, he muscled himself out of the chair into a standing position.

Sweat ran down his face and the back of his neck. He sat on the side of the bed, lest he fall on the floor. He sat there for hours, ignoring the pleas of the nurses to go back to his room and rest. During his time in her room, she didn't move or change positions unless the nurses came in and did it for her. They did, every two hours.

Dr. Creighton entered and ordered Ian back to his room and to bed.

He assured him word would be sent down if there was any change in Maggie's condition. If he didn't go NOW, his name would be taken off the visitors list. Ian took the threat seriously and left. But not before he whispered in her ear how much he loved her and he would be back as soon as he could.

Ian spent his next day much like the one before. When he awoke, Jim, wheeled him up to ICU where he stayed, whispering to Maggie and telling her how much he missed her and all of the things he wanted to do when she was well.

Nothing changed. The next day Ian was discharged from the hospital. Before he left, he visited with Judge Massey who was now out of ICU and talking. He told Ian he knew nothing good was going to come out of the ordeal with Kenny. He said he didn't know what he would have done if his family had been torn apart by the little bastard. His wife was with him. She grasped his hand and gave him a loving smile. She told Ian the judge was retiring. They all smiled.

Sherry McCormick was doing well. Her arm was better than anyone expected.

Ian smiled at her when she said she thought she

would go into another line of work.

After Ian's discharge, he went home. The house seemed off-color after the stark white of the hospital for all of those days. The hollow sound of his footsteps on the wooden floors seemed to echo his need for Maggie to wake up. He kept seeing shadows where there weren't any. Jumping at each one, he would turn hoping it was Maggie. He realized how empty the house seemed without the prospect of her now being there. He chastised himself for having such a thought.

He went upstairs and took a hot shower, letting the water run over him until it was cool. Putting on a pair of worn jeans, a tee shirt and his favorite ball cap, he walked back downstairs, out the door and toward Kingshighway. He walked until he could flag down a taxi to take him to the government center in St. Charles so he could retrieve his car. From there, he went back to the hospital to sit vigil with Maggie.

His arm throbbed, from hanging it down while he was in the shower he wasn't supposed to take. He didn't give a damn.

Pulling a chair close to her bed, he again lifted her limp hand into his and prayed.

"Please, God. Let her wake up. Let her live. Don't let Kenny do any more damage. Please let it be done."

In his desperation, he hoped and prayed if he held her hand long enough and tight enough he would transfer his life force to her and will her to wake up.

Hour after hour he sat guarding her from death.

He stroked her limp arm and assured her time and time again he loved her and would never leave her.

Once in a while fatigue would overtake him and his head would bob up and down eventually touching his chest where it would rest until he got a few minutes of much-needed sleep so he could continue on.

When he first felt her move, he thought it was a dream. He sat still, but it didn't happen again for an hour or so. Then he felt it again. It was a slight stretch against his hand.

Standing up, Ian searched her eyes for movement. He was rewarded. Faintly, ever so faintly, her eye twitched. She tried to speak, yet her mouth was much too dry and she was much too weak.

Afraid to give her anything or cause anything to happen, he scampered out the door and called to the first nurse he saw. "She is awake. Can you come?" Not only did she come, but so did every other person not involved in the care of another patient at the time. It was a quiet and reserved celebration of life in the room, and all Ian could do was grin, a stupid grin. He didn't care how silly he looked, he could not stop grinning.

Now Maggie's eyes were open and she looked into Ian's. "I'm here," he said. "I'm here and I'm never leaving. The worst is over now. Everything will be fine."

Although she was too weak to speak, he detected a smile in her eyes and he relaxed for the first time in a long time.

***

The next day, Maggie was moved out of ICU and into a regular room on the surgical floor. Three weeks later she was moved to a rehab facility attached to Barnes Hospital. Barnes was within walking distance of Ian's house. It was great.

Twelve weeks in all. Ian made it his personal duty to tend to her every need. He filled her room with flowers of every color, and cards making her laugh through the pain.

As she was awake longer, he read to her. He bought her a cassette player so she could listen to her favorite music when she was too tired to do anything else.

Each morning he would stand by the window and describe the day to her. He always began with the sky and worked his way to the ground including the smallest of details.

When she was allowed up in a wheelchair, he pushed her everywhere, bribing nurses so they could have picnics on the lawn.

Her leg was a source of constant pain. She had a series of skin grafts but didn't complain. The doctors began talking about her going home and continuing her therapy as an outpatient. Ian and Maggie were thrilled.

Ian begged her to come home with him. He had long since had her furniture put in storage and her personal belongings brought to the little house they both loved. She hadn't even complained at his bold move.

"Well," she said in a playful voice, "they want to

kick me out of here in the morning, and thanks to you I'm homeless."

"Hardly homeless," he said putting both hands on his hips in mock frustration. "The house is ready. We're ready for you to come home."

"Is that right?"

"Yes, you already said you would marry me. So it only makes sense to me."

"I said I would marry you when I could walk down the aisle without the aid of this cane. There is a difference." She winked at him.

"Besides", she added looking out the hospital window, "What do you want with me? I'm scarred and beaten and battered and I come with tons of baggage."

"We're all scarred. We always will be. We're survivors, Maggie. There has been enough horror and destruction. Let's add happy ending to this saga."

"Well, Ian, when you put it like that, how could a girl refuse?

A NOTE FROM THE AUTHOR

I live in the beautiful Ozarks on a small farm with my nine dogs, six cats, two mules, four donkeys and five horses. I also have sheep, cattle, an apple and a pear orchard. I love my farm, but my true passion is writing. However, I have to do it in my spare time.

Born in California, and raised in Illinois, I spent the first 20 years of my career in the medical profession. Later I went into sales, and sales training before coming to live on my farm.

I've been writing since I was big enough to hold a pencil and have had articles published dozens of times in newspapers. I'm a Fellow in the American Society of Poets, but don't write much poetry now days.

Diggitty is one of my nine dogs and will have her own series of children's books. The first in this series is *The Adventures of Diggitty the Dog,* out currently, is meant to help kids learn in a fun environment. The idea was born when I took apples and pears to the local Farmer's Market and began giving them to the youngsters, only to find out they didn't know what real apples and pears looked like.

I believe if kids know and understand about food, they'll be more likely to make better eating choices. Diggitty is just the mischievous and happy character to help with the task. The next books in the series will feature dairy cows, chicken and ducks, vegetable gardens. Who knows what trouble we might get into on the farm?

Tattered Wings is my first psychological thriller. I hope you enjoyed reading it as much as I did writing it. However, now I'm working on a series of mysteries based on true crime, featuring Cole Dobbs, the sheriff of a small Midwestern county. Look for book one soon.

Thank you and happy reading,

Susan